BADGER BOY

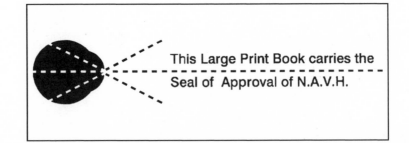

This Large Print Book carries the
Seal of Approval of N.A.V.H.

BADGER BOY

ELMER KELTON

THORNDIKE PRESS

An imprint of Thomson Gale, a part of The Thomson Corporation

Detroit • New York • San Francisco • New Haven, Conn. • Waterville, Maine • London

LIBRARY OF CONGRESS CATALOGING-IN-PUBLICATION DATA

Kelton, Elmer.
　Badger boy / by Elmer Kelton.
　　p. cm. — (Thorndike Press large print western)
　　ISBN 0-7862-9144-3 (lg. print : alk. paper) 1. Comanche Indians — Wars — Fiction. 2. Indian captivities — Fiction. 3. Large type books. 4. Texas — Fiction. I. Title.
　PS3561.E3975B33 2006
　813'.54—dc22   2006028854

U.S. Hardcover:
ISBN 13: 978-0-7862-9144-1
ISBN 10: 0-7862-9144-3

Published in 2006 by arrangement with St. Martin's Press, LLC.

Printed in the United States of America on permanent paper
10 9 8 7 6 5 4 3 2 1

This book is dedicated to two school friends from long-ago days in Crane, Texas: Ted Hogan and Joe Pearce.

CHAPTER 1

The Texas frontier, spring, 1865.

Rusty Shannon saw brown smoke rising beyond the hill and knew the rangers had arrived too late. The Indians had already struck, and by now they were probably gone.

He had expected trouble, but his pulse quickened as if the smoke were a surprise. He signaled his five fellow patrol members and spurred his black horse, Alamo, into a run. He did not have to look back. The men would follow him; they always did though he had no official rank. He was a private like the rest, but they had fallen into the habit of looking to him for leadership. Nor was he noticeably older than the others. Orphaned early, he could only guess he was about twenty-five, give or take a little. A harsh outdoor life had made him look more than that. He had accepted the responsibility of leadership by default, for no one else had offered to take it.

Back East, the strong nicker of the war horse was fading to a faint and painful whinny as the tired and tattered Confederacy kept struggling to its feet for one more battle and one more loss. To Rusty's independent, red-haired manner of thinking, it was high time the Richmond government conceded defeat and let the guns fall silent. Even from his faraway vantage point at the edge of Comanche-Kiowa country he saw clearly and with pain that the war had bled both sides much too long.

The Texas frontier had a war of its own to contend with, and it was far from over.

Rusty Shannon was tall and rangy, some would say perpetually hungry-looking. Meals were a sometime thing when frontier rangers scouted for Indians. Often the men were too pressed to stop, and at other times they simply had nothing to eat.

He considered himself a soldier of sorts, though he owned no uniform. Texas had not even provided him a badge as a symbol of ranger authority. The cuffs were raveled on his grimy homespun cotton shirt, the sleeves mended and mended again. His frayed gray trousers seemed as much patch as original woolen fabric, for the long war had made new clothing scarce and money scarcer.

Red hair bristled over his ears and brushed his collar. Forced to be frugal, rangers cut each other's hair. It was often a rough job of butchery, but appearances were of little concern. Staying alive and helping others stay alive were what counted on the frontier.

Riding their assigned north-south line past the western fringe of settlement, the patrol had come upon tracks of fifteen to twenty horses at dusk yesterday. By order of Texas's Confederate government in Austin, the rangers were duty-bound to locate and take into custody any deserters or conscription dodgers who might be idling out the war in the wild country beyond the settlements.

Rusty knew the approximate whereabouts of fifty or sixty such men banded together for mutual security, but they were of little interest to him. If the Confederacy wanted them captured it should send Confederate Army troops to do the job. Five or six rangers were no match for so many brush men even if they invested a full heart in the duty, and he had no heart for that kind of business.

He had regarded secession from the Union four years ago as a grave mistake though fellow Texans had voted in its favor. He saw the war as folly on both sides, North and South. If a man did not want to take part in it, the authorities should leave him the hell alone. Officialdom did not share his view, of course. Remaining with the rangers on the frontier kept him out of the military's sight.

Freckle-faced Len Tanner had swung a long and lanky leg across the cantle, dismounting to study the tracks. "Conscript dodgers, you think?"

That was a possibility, but instinct told Rusty the trail had been made by Comanches or possibly Kiowas. Perhaps both, for they often joined forces to venture south from their prairie and mountain strongholds. The Indians were well aware that white men of the North had been at war with white men of the South for most of four years. They did not understand the reasons, or care. What mattered was that the fighting's heavy drain upon manpower left the frontier vulnerable. In places it had withdrawn eastward fifty to a hundred miles, leaving homes abandoned, strayed livestock running wild. Settlers who dared remain lived in jeopardy.

After sending one man back to company headquarters near Fort Belknap to report to Captain Oran Whitfield, Rusty had set out to follow the trail. Len Tanner rode beside him. Rusty had never decided whether Tanner's legs were too long or his horse too short, for his stirrups dangled halfway between the mount's belly and the ground. Eyes eager, Tanner said, "Tracks are freshenin'. We ought to catch up with them pretty soon."

"Catchin' them is what we're paid for."

"Who's been paid?"

The Texas state government was notorious for being perpetually broke, unable to meet obligations. Wages for its employees were near the bottom of the priority list, especially for those men in homespun cloth and buckskin who rode the frontier picket line far away from those who wrote the laws and appropriated the money.

Darkness had forced Rusty to halt the patrol and wait for daylight lest they lose the trail. He had slept little, frustrated that the raiders might be gaining time. Night had been no hindrance to the Indians if they chose to keep traveling.

Now he saw a half-burned cabin, a man and two boys carrying water in buckets from a nearby creek and throwing it on the smoking walls. He remembered the place. It belonged to a farmer named Haines. Hearing the horses, the man grabbed a rifle. He lowered it when he saw that the riders were not Indians. He focused a resentful attention on Rusty.

"Minutemen, ain't you?"

Ranger was not an official term. The public often referred to the rangers as minutemen, among other things.

Looking upon two blanket-covered forms on the ground, Rusty felt a chill. The blankets were charred along the edges. "Yes sir, Mr. Haines."

"How come you always show up when it's too late?"

Rusty could have told him there were not enough rangers to be everywhere and protect everybody. The war back east had drawn away too many of the state's fighting-age men. The ranger desertion rate had risen to alarming levels, partly out of fear of being conscripted into Confederate service and partly because the state treasury was as bare as Mother Hubbard's cupboard. Even on those rare occasions when a paymaster visited the frontier companies, he never brought enough money to pay the men all that was due them.

It was futile to try to explain that to a man who had just lost so much. "We'll bury your dead," Rusty said, "then I'll send a couple of men to escort you and your boys to Fort Belknap."

The farmer set his jaw firmly. "We've got nobody at Belknap. Everybody we have is here, and here we're stayin'."

"You've got no roof over your head."

"We saved part of the cabin. We can rebuild it. You just stay on them red devils' trail."

Rusty saw only the man and the two boys. Fearing he already knew, he asked, "What about your womenfolks?"

The farmer cleared his throat, but his voice fell to little more than a whisper. "They're here." He knelt beside one of the covered forms and lifted the scorched blanket enough for Rusty to see a woman's bloodied face. The scalp had been ripped from her head. "My wife. Other one is our little girl. The Comanches butchered them like they was cattle."

"How come they didn't get the rest of you?"

The farmer looked at the two boys. They still carried water to throw on the cabin though the fire appeared to be out. "Me and my sons was workin' in the field. The heathens came upon the cabin so quick they was probably inside before Annalee even saw them. I hit one with my first shot, and they drawed away. All we could do for Annalee and the baby was to drag them outside before they burned." He looked at the ground as if ashamed he had been unable to do more.

Rusty was undecided whether settlers like Haines who remained on the exposed western frontier were brave or merely foolhardy. Either way, he would concede that they were tenacious.

Ruefully the farmer turned his attention back to his wife and daughter. "Conscript officers decided to pass me by on account of my age and my family." He cleared his throat again. "I wish they'd taken me. My family would've moved back to East Texas and been safe." He gave Rusty a close scrutiny. "You're a fit-lookin' specimen. Why ain't you in the Confederate Army?"

"I figured I was needed more in the rangin' service."

The Texas legislature had fought and won a grudging concession from the Richmond government to defer men serving in the frontier companies. But the agreement was often ignored by conscription officers who raided the outlying companies and took rangers whether or not they were willing to go. Those drafts had increased as the Confederacy's fortunes soured and its military ranks were decimated by battlefield casualties. So far Rusty had avoided the call, though he had a nagging hunch that time was closing in.

The farmer rubbed an ash-darkened sleeve across his face. His voice became contrite. "Sorry I jumped all over you. I know it's not your doin' that there ain't enough rangers. It's the Richmond government's fault, takin' off so many men to fight a stupid war a thousand miles away. And the Texas government for lettin' them get away with it. Damn them all, and double damn Jeff Davis."

There had been a time when such words could put a man in mortal danger from rope-wielding zealots determined to rid Texas of dissidents. Rusty had helped cut down the bodies of his friend Lon Monahan and Lon's son Billy from the limb of a tree in the wake of the hangmen. Now and then in the dark of night the memory brought him awake, clammy with cold sweat and fighting his blanket. He had long harbored the same opinions as Haines but spoke them aloud only to friends he could trust. He had witnessed too much grief brought on by night-riding vigilantes like Colonel Caleb Dawkins who did not go to war themselves yet demanded that others do so or die.

The farmer cautioned, "There was sixteen,

eighteen Indians. I don't see but six of you."

"We're lucky we've got six." The five who accompanied him, like Len Tanner, were men Rusty felt would stay with him if they skirted along the rim of hell. He looked again toward the bodies. He shuddered, for he had seen too many like them. "If we come across a minister, we'll send him. You'll want proper services for your folks."

"Much obliged, but I can read from the Bible same as any preacher."

The older of the two boys appeared to be around twelve, the other perhaps ten. Rusty felt sorrow for them. They would have to finish growing up without their mother. But at least they still had their father. Unlike Rusty, they had not lost all their family. Surely the war back East would sputter out before they were old enough to become soldiers.

The war here was another matter. He could see no end to it.

The farmer pointed. "I'm fearful for August Faust, my neighbor. I hope him and his family saw the smoke and forted up."

"We'll go see," Rusty promised. He signaled the patrol and set off in the southeasterly direction the Indians had taken. The tracks were plain enough to follow in a lope.

He expected more smoke ahead, but he

heard sporadic firing instead. Someone was still fighting at the Faust place. When the picket cabin came into full view, Rusty rough-counted eleven Indians. Most were afoot and taking cover wherever they could. It stood to reason that a few others were behind the cabin, out of his sight. Fifty or sixty yards away, two warriors held a number of horses.

It was not normally Comanche or Kiowa custom to make a frontal assault on a well-defended position. They preferred to catch their quarry by surprise with a quick, clean strike, pulling back if resistance proved stronger than expected. Evidently that had been the case here. Almost every time an Indian raised his head, fire and smoke blossomed from the doorway or a glassless window. Someone was firing from the back as well. The raiders had the cabin surrounded, but they were a long way from taking it.

Tanner grinned. "They only got us outnumbered by three to one. We ought to crack this nut pretty easy."

The befreckled young ranger would willingly go hungry for three days to get into a good fight. He had, several times.

"Then let's be at them." Rusty drew his pistol and loaded the chamber he customarily kept empty for safety. He preferred the rifle, but it was difficult to use from a running horse.

The rangers were two hundred yards from the cabin when the Indians discovered them and ran for their mounts. In the excitement three horses jerked loose and loped away, wringing their tails. Two Indians set afoot swung up behind others. A third mounted a spare animal whose owner no longer needed him. Rusty saw an Indian lying beside a tall woodpile but did not take time to determine if he was dead.

A man with an old-fashioned long rifle stepped out of the cabin and took a parting shot. An Indian slumped forward but grabbed his horse's mane and remained astride. The man shouted, "Go get them!"

Rusty called, "Everybody all right?"

"Nobody killed." He waved the rangers on. "Get my work horses back if you can."

Horses and mules were almost as important as life, for without them a farmer had no way to plow his fields, no way to travel except to walk. The war had pulled most horses out of this region except wild bands ranging free beyond the settlements. Few farmers were equipped to catch those, much less to break and train them. And should they manage to do so, chances were that either the Indians would steal them or a government horse-buying team would come along and take them away. It would leave Confederate scrip or worthless promissory notes, which Rusty regarded as legalized theft.

The Indians cut immediately to the creek. Timber there was heavy enough to give them partial cover for their escape, though it would slow them as they dodged through the trees and undergrowth, the entangling briars.

Rusty said, "We'll stay out here in the open and keep up with them." Sooner or later the fugitives would have to quit the timber and ride into the clear.

Tanner turned in the saddle. "Look back, Rusty."

Two raiders had broken out behind the rangers and were racing toward the cabin. Startled, Rusty reined the black horse around. His first thought was that they intended another try at Faust or one of the other settlers who had come out of the cabin and gathered in the yard. He spurred in pursuit, intending to keep the warriors too busy.

The pair slowed their mounts and leaned down, grabbing the fallen man by the arms and lifting him up between them. Men in the yard fired a couple of futile shots.

It was a point of honor among plains warriors not to ride away from the battlefield and leave a wounded or dead comrade behind to be killed or mutilated if rescue was at all possible. By white men's standards the Comanches were savages. Though Rusty deplored their propensity for random killing, he respected their bravery. He wondered if he could muster the courage to do the same thing.

The main body of warriors crossed the creek and emerged on the other side, beyond the protective timber. They retreated northward, pursued by three rangers who were no match for them in numbers should they decide to turn and counterattack. Rusty reined up, knowing he was unlikely to catch the fugitives. He was not sure he even wanted to. They seemed to be retreating back toward the reservation, taking with them a dozen stolen horses. Even in the unlikely event that the patrol caught up and killed them all, it would make little difference in terms of the larger war between white men and red. There would still be enough to keep the fight going . . . Comanche, Kiowa, sometimes Cheyenne and others.

The black horse's hide glistened with

sweat. Rusty slowed him, then brought him to a stop. The three rangers who had pursued the main group abandoned the chase and turned back. Two more Comanches left the creek and circled around them, striking out northwestward across the prairie in the wake of the others. Rusty stopped and drew his rifle but knew his shot would be wasted. A snowball in hell stood a better chance.

A single rider crossed the creek and took after the pair. Rusty recognized Tanner's lean form. He waved his hat and shouted, "Len, get the hell back here!"

He feared the Indians would lead the reckless Tanner off by himself, then turn and kill him. Fortunately the wind was in the right direction to carry his voice. The ranger drew rein and reluctantly returned.

"Damn it, Rusty, they'll keep splittin' off in little bunches, and first thing you know we'll be wonderin' where they went."

Rusty was aware of that. He had seen similar escapes in the four years he had served a frontier company. It was a familiar Comanche tactic to divide up, knowing the pursuers were seldom able to follow them all. The last small bunch, though closely trailed, would somehow manage to disappear like a puff of smoke.

Shortly he looked back over his shoulder

and saw three more warriors on open ground north of the creek, racing away. They had concealed themselves in the timber until the pursuit had passed.

Tanner argued, "There ain't all that many of them. What say we show them who's the boss?"

Rusty considered his choices. "The odds are too long. We'll just keep trailin' after them so they won't turn and come back. Maybe we can crowd them into settin' the stolen horses loose."

Moving into a stiff trot, he gathered the patrol and half a dozen loose horses the Indians had taken, then abandoned under pressure. Rusty hoped these were the ones stolen from Faust and perhaps the Haines' farm.

He picked out the oldest man, whose thin shoulders were pinched, his face weary. "Mr. Pickett, if you don't mind, I wish you'd take these horses back to the Faust place. The rest of us'll pester the hostiles all the way to the river."

Oscar Pickett seemed relieved. He was too old for such rigorous duty, but he would die before he would admit it aloud. "What do you want me to do afterward?"

Even men twice Rusty's age readily took his directions. He tried to give them in a manner that sounded like friendly suggestions rather than commands. "Stay at the Haines' place a while. Your horse needs a rest. You can come up to Belknap tomorrow." The rider appeared more tired than the horse, but Rusty wanted to spare the older man's pride.

He turned to the rest of his rangers. "What do you say we go aggravate those Comanches?"

Steals the Ponies was his name. He had stolen several this time, only to be forced to abandon some under pressure of the Texan war party that had dogged the raiders so closely. The loss nettled like prickly pear spines digging under his skin. He had contended all along that the white horsemen were too few for real warriors to run from. But Tall Eagle had assembled this raiding party, and it was for Tall Eagle to say whether they fought or retreated. The older warrior had decided at the first cabin that their medicine had gone bad because one of his followers was wounded by the opening shot. The feeling had been reinforced when they failed to take the second cabin by surprise and the *teibo* horsemen interrupted their siege.

Next time, or the time after, it would be

different. The younger, more eager warriors would sooner or later pull away from Tall Eagle, for he was beginning to lose the nerve he needed for leadership. Steals the Ponies would organize his own raiding party as his father, Buffalo Caller, had frequently done before him. Then he would be the one to decide whether to attack or pull away.

His father's forays had not always been successful, but he had never turned and run like a frightened dog. Buffalo Caller had eventually died in a raid on a white settlement. His was a fitting death for a warrior.

Frustration prompted Steals the Ponies to stop for a show of defiance. Tall Eagle shouted for him to keep up, but Steals the Ponies defied him. He turned back toward the little group of white horsemen who trailed behind. They made no effort to close the distance but acted as an annoyance, like so many heelflies. They must belong to the formidable Texan warrior society known as rangers, he thought. Rangers stuck like cockleburrs.

He doubted that the white men could understand his words, but they would understand his gestures well enough. He crisscrossed his war pony back and forth in front of them, shouting insults, waving his bow over his head.

One of the white men rode a little ahead of the others. His face was dark with several days' whiskers, but he sat erect in the saddle, a young man's way. Steals the Ponies decided on a challenge. He raced toward him, waving the bow, drawing an arrow from his quiver. The other rangers quickly moved up to flank the leader. Steals the Ponies saw that the young Texan had no intention of answering the challenge.

He knew he was within range even of the rangers' pistols, but he had made a display of courage and would not compromise it by turning and running away. He was close enough to see that the rider's whiskers and shaggy hair were red.

That shook him a little. More than once, his father had told him of a troubling vision about a red-haired man. The day Buffalo Caller was killed, he had been in a close fight with a ranger whose hair was the color of rusted metal. Though someone else fired the fatal bullet, Steals the Ponies had always felt that the redhead's strong medicine was somehow responsible for his father's death.

This might not be the same man. Then again, it might. Steals the Ponies shuddered, but pride would not allow him to run. He turned slowly away from the white men, letting them know he was not afraid though they could easily kill him. For a time he held his pony to an easy pace that kept him within range if they should choose to shoot. They did not. He supposed their forbearance was a tribute of sorts to his valor. He stopped again to deliver a loud, defiant whoop, then moved on to rejoin the others.

He hoped Buffalo Caller might be watching from the spirit land to which he had gone. His father would be proud. He wished his foster brother could be here to see this, but Badger Boy was too young to ride on such an expedition. He would hear of it, though, and perhaps he would be inspired to become the greatest fighter of them all.

The warriors gave Steals the Ponies their silent approval, all except Tall Eagle. Tall Eagle rebuked him with a scowl. Steals the Ponies smiled inside, knowing the leader was jealous. The older warrior could have made the same gesture but had not chosen to do so. Perhaps he had not even thought of it. Word of Steals the Ponies's exploits would spread among The People. They would say he was a son worthy of his father and a model for his younger brother to emulate.

He had shown the *teibos* his courage. Perhaps the next white men to see him would remember and be afraid.

CHAPTER 2

Rusty raised his rifle to bring down the Indian who taunted him. He held the bead a moment, then lowered the weapon across the pommel of his badly worn saddle.

Len Tanner drew in closer. "You're the best shot in the outfit. You couldn't miss."

"He's got guts, paradin' himself that way."

"Ain't your fault he's got more guts than good sense. Shoot him."

"Too easy. I'd take no honor in it."

"Honor, hell! There wasn't no honor in them killin' that woman and little girl."

The warrior brought his pony a little closer. Tanner became more agitated. "Looks to me like he's askin' for you to do it."

"He's darin' me to come out and meet him in the middle ground. I'm not a schoolboy. The only dares I pay attention to are the ones I give myself." He knew if he killed the young Comanche the others would turn back and do their damndest to kill *him.* They would stand a good chance of getting it done. The price would be one ranger for one Indian. There were already so many Indians, and so pitifully few rangers.

"We bloodied them some and spoiled their party. Won't do any harm to leave them somethin' they can brag about when they get home."

Home might be the broad and mysterious high plains of Texas, the land known as Comanchería, where the wild bands still roamed free. Or it might be a reservation set aside north of the Red River shortly before the war began between the states. It was under Federal jurisdiction, which meant that any Texan who strayed upon it and managed not to be killed by hostile Indians was subject to arrest as a Confederate belligerent unless he could convince the authorities that he was trying to escape Confederate service. In that case they were likely to impress him into the Union Army. Rusty saw no net gain in that. Though he did not want to fire upon the United States flag, he would not like to fire upon fellow Texans either.

He wished the only thing he ever had to shoot at was meat for the table.

Some men with more courage than

scruples periodically invaded the reservation to steal Indian horses. That fanned Indian anger at all Texans and made them more eager than ever to raid south of the Red River. Some of these horse thieves were brush men, fugitives from Confederate conscription. They used aversion to the war as an excuse, but many would have been outlaws whether there had been a war or not. It was in their nature. They seemed indifferent to the misery their forays brought upon fellow citizens.

Rusty's horse stood relaxed in the camp corral, enjoying the brushing his owner gave his black hide. Rusty stood upwind so the breeze would not carry dust and loose hair into his face. Both horse and rider had been granted a rest after days out on patrol. Rusty examined Alamo for sign of scalds or saddle sores, a hazard when a horse was used long and hard. Out here a man took care of his mount before he took care of his own needs. Everything was too far away for walking.

Len Tanner paused in brushing his own horse and gazed to the east. He pointed with the brush. "You don't reckon that'd be a paymaster comin' yonder?"

"I think they've lost the map to this place." Rusty walked to the rail fence for a better look. He wondered if the rider would make it all the way into camp before his mount collapsed of fatigue. The animal was thin. The state provided little money to pay for grain, so horses had to subsist on whatever grass they could find. Only recently had showers begun to fall after two years of drought across most of Texas.

Half of the company had deserted during the winter and early spring. Rusty could not blame the men for saddling their horses in the dark of night and stealing away. They had not been paid in months. Confederate scrip found little favor among the merchants of nearby Fort Belknap town anyway, even those few who still boasted about their continuing enthusiasm for the Southern cause. The last time Rusty had been sent away to buy horses for the outfit, he had felt like a thief. The rangers had authority to take the horses with or without the owners' consent, paying with promissory notes on the state government. The paper was worth more than the promise. People could save it and write letters on the back.

Tanner said, "Maybe we ought to go see what's happenin'."

"Captain Whitfield'll call if he needs us." On patrol, Rusty was nominally in charge. Anything and everything was his business.

In camp, Captain Whitfield was in command, and nothing was Rusty's business unless the captain saw fit to make it so. Whitfield was a large man who carried a navy Colt on his hip, a bottle of whiskey and a Bible in his saddlebag. He was accomplished in the use of all three.

The new arrival dismounted wearily in front of the captain's tent and tied his horse to a post. He leaned against the horse, stamping his feet to improve blood circulation in tired legs. His clothes were as ragged as those of the Fort Belknap rangers. Rusty thought he recognized him as a ranger from another company.

Tanner leaned against the fence, watching. "He don't look like no paymaster. A paymaster would steal at least enough to buy him a decent suit of clothes."

Rusty went back to brushing Alamo. He could feel the ribs without pressing hard. The horse needed a month's rest on grain and green grass, but he was no more likely to get it than Rusty was to receive the pay rightfully due him.

Presently he saw Captain Whitfield walk to the mess tent and ring a bell that was normally sounded at mealtime. It was only the middle of the afternoon. Rusty jerked his head as a signal to Tanner, but Tanner had already dropped his brush in a wooden tack box and was on his way to the corral gate, burning with curiosity.

Reluctantly Rusty laid his brush aside. More Indians, he thought. He had not caught up on sleep since the last skirmish.

The company was down to a fraction of its normal strength because of desertions and a shortage of men willing and able to put up with the privations of frontier service. Of those still in the company, more than half were out on patrol.

Whitfield was middle-aged and broad of hip. He would probably run to belly if ranger rations were not perpetually meager and duty hours long. As it was he probably would not render out two pounds of fat. He tugged at a bushy, unkempt mustache while he watched seven men amble up in no particular hurry and cluster around him. Two squatted on their heels. Army officers had admonished Whitfield several times about his company's lack of military order, but he paid no more attention to them than to the buzzing of flies around the corrals. He considered it absurd to require the men to stand in a straight line or at attention. All that mattered was that they listen to him, whether he was giving orders or reading to them from the Book.

Whitfield had formerly been a sergeant and had taken over the company soon after the outbreak of war. He had inherited the captaincy when the former commanding officer, August Burmeister, had ridden north to join the Union Army. Rusty had never heard Whitfield express favor for either side in the conflict. He suspected that, like himself, Whitfield had chosen frontier service rather than take up arms against the Union. The compromise gave ease to a conscience torn between two loyalties.

Whitfield's eyes were troubled. "Boys, I've been brought some bad news."

Tanner asked, "We've lost the war?"

"Not yet, though it looks like the end is upon us, praise the Lord. Reason I've called you together is to tell you the conscription officers are on their way again."

Rusty saw nothing new in that. Conscription officers had come several times before, trying to persuade younger rangers to resign from frontier duty and join the Confederate Army. They usually left with a recruit or two.

Whitfield said, "The war has taken a bad turn, so they're grabbin' everybody they can get. Frontier service won't keep them from takin' you now if you're halfways young and not too crippled to walk or ride a horse."

His gaze fastened on Rusty. "I know some of you never did have strong feelin's for the Richmond government."

Whitfield had read Rusty's mind a long time ago.

The captain said, "The position I'm in, I can't be givin' you advice. Anybody wants to leave before the conscript officers get here, I ain't stoppin' him. Just don't take any horse that don't belong to you." He stood a moment to let the message soak in, then strode back to his tent.

A tingle ran up Rusty's back. He listened to a rising buzz of conversation around him.

A young ranger said, "If they want me that bad, I reckon I'll go. War ought not to last much longer anyway."

Another responded, "They'll have to chase me plumb to Mexico."

Rusty listened to the two men argue, but they were no help to him in making up his mind. He walked to Whitfield's tent and found the captain sitting at a table, where a Bible lay open. In violation of standing orders, Whitfield was pouring whiskey from a bottle into a streaked glass. He looked up.

"Have a drink, Shannon?"

"No, thank you, Captain. I want to keep my mind clear."

"Mine is too damned clear already. I don't

understand what Richmond is thinkin' of. There's women and children dyin' out here because they ain't left enough fightin' men to protect them. Now they want to take even more for a war they're fixin' to lose anyway."

"Those people back in Richmond never saw a Comanche. They don't realize the problem."

"The Book tells about times of tribulation. Lord help us, we're damned sure livin' in one." Whitfield took the contents of the glass in one swallow.

"Captain, I need to tell you . . ."

"Don't. Don't tell me a thing. What I don't know, I can't answer for. Just do whatever you feel is right and don't allow anybody else to sway your judgment."

Rusty rarely let anyone do that. "If the conscription officers find most of the company gone, they're liable to bear down hard on you."

Whitfield snorted. "What can they do? I'm too old to be sent to the army. They can't fine me because I'm as broke as the rest of you. I doubt they'd shoot me. So what's left except to send me home? I'm ready to shuck it all and go back to the farm anyhow."

"You've been a good officer. I'm proud I got to serve with you."

35

"Get you some grub out of the mess tent. You can't travel far hungry."

"Just a little salt, a little flour. I can probably scare up enough game to keep me in meat."

"I wish I could trade you out of that good black horse, but you'll need him worse than I do." Whitfield extended a large, rough hand.

Rusty went to the tent he shared with Tanner and several others. He rolled his bedding and his few clothes — a woolen coat, an extra shirt no less patched than the one he wore, a pair of trousers with one knee out. His small war bag held his razor and a few incidentals.

When he had first come to Belknap from the Shannon farm down on the Colorado River, he had brought considerably more with him. He had led a pack mule named Chapultepec, which his foster father, Daddy Mike Shannon, had brought home from the Mexican War. The mule was old now, but not too old to suit a deserter named Lancer, who had ridden away on him a couple of months ago.

This was one of the few times Rusty had ever seen Len Tanner looking solemn. "Where do you figure on goin', Rusty?"

"Ain't had time to figure. I just want to

be gone before the conscription outfit shows up." He was reluctant to part with his longtime friend. He had few friends anymore and no family at all. "I'd be right pleased if you went with me."

Tanner considered. "I've thought about lightin' out, but like as not I'd either run into the conscript officers or the Comanches. The army might not be so bad. Maybe they'll feed better, and pay us to boot."

"I wouldn't bet a wore-out pocketknife on that."

"You can't cross the Red River onto the Indian reservation. They'd give you a Comanche haircut before your horse dried off. Some folks have run away to Mexico, but that's a far piece from here."

"I'd be a lost child in Mexico. All the Spanish I know is a few cusswords Daddy Mike brought home from the Mexican War. Reckon I'll just drift west and hope nobody is interested enough to trail me."

"You're liable to come up against some of them brush men hidin' out in the thickets. They'd as soon kill a ranger as look at him. Instead, why don't you slip down to that farm of yours on the Colorado River and marry that Monahan girl?"

Rusty warmed to the thought of Geneva

Monahan. The truth was that he had already considered that possibility, but he chose not to tell Tanner. He did not want to cause his friend a conflicted conscience should the authorities press him with questions. He reached out his hand. "Be careful, Len. Don't let some Comanche lift your hair or some Yankee sharpshooter bring you down."

"Nobody's ever killed me yet."

He built a small fire in the bottom of a dry buffalo wallow, hoping it could not be seen from a distance. He did not need it for warmth but only for broiling a slice of hindquarter from an antelope his rifle had brought down. He made a poor sort of bread dough by mixing a bit of flour with water and a pinch of salt, then curling it around a stick to hold over the coals. He wished for coffee, but the war had made it scarce. Most Texans were substituting parched grain or doing without. He did not even have grain.

Before it was good and dark, when he was through, he would kill the fire. He doubted that conscription officers would be so bold as to prowl about this far from protection. There was always a risk that Comanche eyes might discover the flames, though he had seen no sign of Indians.

While he waited for his simple supper, the full weight of his situation settled upon him like a heavy shroud. He had not felt so achingly alone since he had buried Daddy Mike beside Mother Dora and turned his back on the Colorado River farm where he had spent his growing-up years. The ranger company had been a family of sorts, though its members came and went. Almost the only constants had been Len Tanner and Captain Whitfield.

His thoughts drifted to another family far away, and to the wisp of a girl named Geneva Monahan. Someday, if peace was ever allowed to settle over the land, he intended to marry her just as Tanner had suggested. Then once again he would have a family of his own. From here, and for now, that seemed a long time off.

He had ridden west from camp, intending to confuse anyone bold enough to trail after him. Tomorrow he would find a place where hard ground or thick grass should lose his tracks, then he would turn southward. To travel much farther west would take him to the escarpment marking the eastern edge of the staked plains, still the hunting grounds of free-roaming Comanche and Kiowa bands. To venture onto those broad plains alone was to flirt with death, either to wander lost and succumb to thirst or to be cut down by arrow or lance.

He was on or near what once had been Texas's Indian reserve on the Clear Fork of the Brazos River. The state and federal governments had set it up in the 1850s in hope of curbing Indian raids and encouraging the horseback tribes to become peaceable farmers and stockmen. Many of the less warlike had accepted, realizing they were about to be trampled under by an unstoppable horde of white settlers. But many Comanches and Kiowas had remained unrestrained and unreconstructed, invading and plundering the settlements at will. Rightly or not, frontier settlers blamed reservation Indians for much of the raiding. Their persistent protests eventually forced abandonment of the reserve. Its residents were given a military escort to new reservations north of the Red River shortly before war began between the states.

Rusty had been present at the removal, serving as a volunteer ranger. The haunting memory still lay heavily upon his conscience. He regretted the sad injustice of haste that did not allow the reservation Indians time to harvest their crops or even to gather their scattered livestock. They had tried the white man's road in good faith, only to be dispossessed because of acts committed by other Indians. Rusty understood why many formerly peaceable ones had later taken to raiding south of the river, or at least aiding and abetting those who did. Even so, it had been his job for most of four years to thwart them the best he could.

When he finished eating, he kicked dirt over the fire to smother it. It might have been seen despite his precautions. To sleep here was to court trouble. He rode another mile in the dusk before coming upon a narrow creek. It seemed a likely place to spread his blanket. He staked Alamo where the horse could graze within reach of the water.

He tried in vain to sleep. Heavy in spirit, feeling cut adrift from all he had known, he lay looking up at the stars and thinking of so much forever lost to him. His mind ran back over the long years to Daddy Mike and Mother Dora Shannon, the couple who had taken him in, a lost child orphaned by Indians, and had raised him as their own. He remembered a pleasant boyhood on the Colorado River farm so far from here in both time and distance. It still belonged to him by inheritance although it had been a long while since he was given leave to visit there.

He thought of Geneva Monahan, who had

moved to that farm with what remained of a war-torn family, seeking refuge from the dangers of their own place nearer the frontier. It had been the better part of a year since he had last received a letter and much longer since he had seen her. He pondered his risk in traveling there to visit her and to look again at the farm the Shannons had bequeathed to him.

Finally, he thought about the years he had patroled the frontier. He thought of the comradeship, the shared perils and disappointments and occasional small victories. That it had come to an abrupt and unexpected end left in him a sense of emptiness, of work left hanging, incomplete. He had had no time to formulate plans. The most urgent consideration had been to remove himself from the conscription officers' reach. Where to go from here was the major question. He faced several alternatives, none of them to his liking.

He pulled the blanket around him, hoping morning would bring him an answer. But the question continued to nag him. He could not sleep. He got up, finally, and started toward the creek for a drink of water. Alamo snorted, acknowledging his presence.

The sight of distant firelight stopped him

in mid-stride. He thought first it might be a lantern in some settler's window, but he dismissed that idea. The only cabins he had seen since leaving the ranger camp had been abandoned, their owners electing to move away from the Indian danger. No, this was a campfire. Two possibilities came to mind: brush men or Indians.

The brush men, a combination of outlaws and fugitives from military service, tended to congregate in out-of-the-way places and in numbers that kept them relatively secure against attack by either Indians or civil authorities.

Rusty stared at the distant fire and considered his options. The law be damned; he had never felt any moral obligation to pursue conscription dodgers for benefit of the Confederacy. Now that he was no longer part of the company, brush men were none of his business.

Indians were another matter. This far south of the Red, an Indian campfire almost certainly meant trouble brewing for someone. His safest course would be to saddle up now and be far away by daylight.

He told himself this was none of his business either. He no longer had any ranger obligations, no oath to live up to. If the Indians moved toward the settlements, someone else would probably find their trail. Only by purest chance had he seen this fire in the first place. Had he not been obliged to leave camp he would not have traveled this far west. If he rode away now no one would be worse off than if he had never been here.

He tried to convince himself as he saddled Alamo. He mounted and turned the horse southward. He rode a hundred yards and stopped, looking back toward the fire. He felt a compulsion to know. Were they really Indians? And what could he do about it if they were?

He followed the creek westward, holding Alamo to a walk to lessen the sound of his hooves and to avoid stumbling into deadfall timber that might make a noise. When he was as near the fire as he dared ride, he dismounted and tied the horse to a tree. He moved on afoot, stopping often to listen. He smelled the smoke and meat roasting over glowing coals. He saw figures moving about.

His skin prickled. These were Indians, right enough. He counted at least eight and reasoned that others were beyond the fire-light. For a moment he entertained a wild notion of firing into their camp and giving them a scare that might make them retreat to the reservation. He abandoned that as a bad idea. In all likelihood they would swarm over him like wasps disturbed in their nest. Taking his hair might only increase the warriors' desire for more, because enemy scalps aroused a competitive spirit. Symbolizing manhood and fighting ability, they were trophies sought after and prized.

The Indians had posted no guard. This was a basic flaw in the Comanche approach to war that Rusty had never understood. He did not know if it was a sign of arrogance or simply a false sense of security. They did not normally like to fight at night, and perhaps they felt that no one else did either.

He drew away from the camp and returned to his horse. His skin still tingled with excitement. "Old feller, we wouldn't want to run into those boys in the daylight."

Prudence told him to head south, but he hesitated. The honorable thing — the responsible thing — would be to double back to the ranger camp and sound an alarm. Perhaps enough men remained there to head off this band as they had done the last raiding party, forcing them to retreat north of the Red before they could strike outlying farms or ranches. But he would be riding into the clutches of the conscription officers. It was a foregone conclusion that they would want him for the Southern army.

The image of Daddy Mike flashed into his mind — Daddy Mike and a Union flag proudly draped on the wall of the Shannon cabin. Back in the 1840s, Mike had campaigned to have Texas brought into the Union. He had fought for that flag in Mexico. He had sworn that nothing would ever cause him to fire upon it, though his passionate rhetoric had led to his being declared a traitor to the Confederacy.

Daddy Mike's fierce patriotism had been burned into Rusty from the time he was old enough to grasp the meaning of the flag. He would rather face prison, or worse, than fight against the Union to which his foster father had proudly given full allegiance.

But Rusty thought of the Haines woman and the little girl. Other settlers would likely fall victim should these raiders not be turned back. Innocent blood would stain his hands if he rode away, taking care only of himself. Even before he decided at a conscious level, he turned Alamo eastward, going back the way he had come.

Perhaps the conscription officers had not yet arrived. Perhaps he could deliver his message and steal away before anyone had a chance to stop him. Perhaps . . . But more likely they would grab him like a wolf grabs a lamb.

He gritted his teeth and put Alamo into a long trot.

CHAPTER 3

Rusty judged that it was near noon when the Fort Belknap settlement loomed up ahead. All along he had hoped he might encounter a friend and impart his information, then slip away without actually entering camp. Unfortunately he saw no rangers or anyone else he knew well enough to trust. Some residents of the settlement had no liking for the rangers, who interfered with their chosen work of stealing reservation horses and running liquor to the same Indians they stole from. He would have to take his chances.

Len Tanner's legs always looked too long for the rest of him. Ambling out of the open corral, leading his horse, he spotted Rusty. Surprise yielded to regret. "I thought you'd got clean away."

Rusty sensed the answer before he asked, "The conscript officers here already?"

"Two of them, fixin' to take most of the

company away. Me included." His eyes were solemn. "What in the hell did you come back for?"

"I ran into Comanches. The captain needs to know."

"He won't have enough men left to do much about it. They're just waitin' for the last patrol to report in so they can pick over the rest of the outfit."

Rusty flared. "Strippin' the frontier companies . . . I don't know how they expect the settlers out here to hang on against the Indians."

"That's gov'ment for you . . . talk big about how much they care, then go off and leave you to fight the wolves by yourself." Tanner looked uneasily toward the headquarters tent. "Tell me what you want the captain to know, then fog it out of here before they see you."

Captain Whitfield stepped from his tent, a well-fed middle-aged stranger beside him. The stranger wore a Confederate uniform, nicely tailored though begrimed from travel.

Rusty caught a sharp breath and held it. "Too late. That'd be one of the conscript officers, I suppose."

Two steps behind that officer came another man wearing a badly weathered Confederate coat with sergeant's stripes. The left leg of his civilian trousers was folded and a wooden leg strapped into place at the knee.

Tanner looked as if he had contracted colic. "Head man, walkin' with the captain, calls hisself Lieutenant Billings. Acts like he owns the world. Sergeant's name is Forrest. Been to war and got his leg shot off."

Despite the wooden leg, Forrest's back was straight and unyielding as if he had been a soldier all his life. Rusty summoned up his defenses, for stern military types always made him ill at ease. Like Captain Whitfield, he had never understood or seen good reason for strict military discipline.

He feared he was going to dislike the sergeant.

Captain Whitfield's eyes revealed misgivings as he approached Rusty. "Back from patrol a little early, aren't you?"

Whitfield knew very well that Rusty had left with no intention of returning. Covering up for me, Rusty thought gratefully. "I came across a Comanche war party last night. They camped better than half a day's ride west of here."

"How many?"

"I counted eight, but it was dark. I'm guessin' twelve or fifteen."

Whitfield turned to the army officer,

frowning. "This is what I've been tryin' to tell you, Lieutenant. Time you take most of my men, I won't have enough to face a small war party, much less a real invasion."

"I have my orders. The army doesn't ask for opinions. It says 'jump,' and all we can do is ask 'how high?' "

Bitterly Whitfield said, "I'd like to put that Richmond bunch out here on the picket line and let them fight off Indians for a while. They'd see for themselves that Yankees aren't the worst thing we've got to worry about."

The recruiting officer stared at Rusty, his eyes probing so hard that Rusty felt the man was reading his mind. "You said you saw the Indians more than half a day's ride from here. Isn't that a long way to be scouting by yourself?"

Stiffening, Rusty fished for a good answer. "We're shorthanded." He suspected the officer sensed the truth and was trying to coax an admission of desertion. The day that happened, hell would have six inches of frost on the ground and the fires would be out.

Captain Whitfield put in, "Better one man than no men at all. And that's what it's gettin' down to."

Sergeant Forrest spoke for the first time.

51

"How do we know these are hostile Indians?"

Whitfield replied, "Since they were removed from the Texas reservations, any Indians found inside the state's boundaries are considered hostile."

"They might just be hunting buffalo."

"This time of the year they'd go out onto the plains. They wouldn't come down this way to hunt . . . not for buffalo."

The lieutenant demanded, "When did you say that last patrol is due in?"

"They should've been here already."

"Good. We want to start back toward Austin as soon as possible."

"Can't you wait 'til we see about those Indians?"

"War does not await the convenience of anyone. We have no time for running after a bunch of bow-and-arrow savages."

Rusty felt compelled to retort, "You would if they raided *your* place and killed some of *your* family."

Billings demanded, "What's your name, ranger?"

Rusty drew himself up army-straight. "David Shannon. Folks that know me call me Rusty."

"Well, David Shannon, I don't for a minute believe you were scouting out there by yourself. I believe you were running away to avoid conscription."

Rusty did not meet the lieutenant's eyes. He had never considered himself a convincing liar, though he had known many occasions when a lie acceptably told was far preferable to the truth. "Captain Whitfield knows. He's the only man I report to."

"You'll be reporting to *me* as soon as we start back to Austin. Don't you forget that."

Rusty knew he had been trapped the minute he rode into camp. He unsaddled Alamo and began working off his frustration by vigorously brushing the sweaty black hide where the saddle had been. The lieutenant started back toward the headquarters tent, his stride victorious.

The sergeant called after him, "We're a long ways from Austin and farther yet from Richmond. A day or two oughtn't to make much difference."

Billings faced back around. "Need I remind you, Sergeant, that I am in charge here?"

"I never forget that. I was just thinkin' . . ."

"You are not here to think. You are here to obey orders."

"I don't question your authority. I just meant to remind you . . ." He stopped in the middle of the sentence.

Billings and a reluctant Captain Whitfield returned to the captain's tent. Sergeant Forrest stayed behind. He asked Rusty, "Are you sure you could take us back where you saw the Indians?"

"I could, but they wouldn't be there anymore. I figure they're headin' off yonder" — he pointed to the southeast — "where the settlements are thicker."

"If we angled across, shouldn't we run into them, or at least come upon their tracks?"

"You're forgettin' the lieutenant's orders."

"I never forget orders. But sometimes I ignore them when I see a good reason."

"You don't seem to have much fear for authority."

"It was family connections that won the lieutenant his commission. I got these stripes on the battlefield. And this wooden leg besides. After all that, there's damned little that son of a bitch can do to scare me." He walked toward the tent.

Rusty decided he was going to like the sergeant after all. As for Billings, he remembered that Daddy Mike came home from the Mexican War with a jaundiced view of lieutenants.

Rusty discovered Len Tanner silently

watching him. Tanner said, "Accordin' to the sergeant, Billings has never seen war against the Yankees. Never even been out of Texas." He waited for Rusty to comment, but Rusty had nothing to say. Tanner added, "How come men that never went to war theirselves are so anxious to send other men there?"

The last patrol arrived about noon, bringing the company's strength to eleven men. Captain Whitfield walked among the new arrivals. "Get yourselves some dinner as quick as you can, then saddle fresh horses." He gave Lieutenant Billings a defiant look. "We're goin' after Indians."

Billings stepped in front of him, his right hand dropping to the butt of a pistol. "The hell you are! I am taking these men to Austin."

Whitfield spread his feet apart in a stance that said he would not be moved. Rusty had never seen him more determined. "This is my camp, Lieutenant, and you are a long way from home."

Billings whirled around, seeking the sergeant. "Forrest, put this man under arrest."

Forrest shook his head. "The captain makes good sense. I'd advise you to listen to him."

The lieutenant started to draw the pistol from its holster. Rusty took a long step forward and grabbed his hand. He twisted the pistol from Billings's grasp. The officer stared at him in fury, then turned upon the sergeant. "I'll have you court-martialed for this."

"Do it and be damned. I never intended to make a career out of the army anyway. Tell them anything you want to. Tell them I got drunk and dallied with lewd women, if that's your pleasure."

Looking around as if seeking help, Billings saw only hostile faces. He gave in grudgingly. "I won't forget this. I could have every one of you shot."

Forrest said, "You're a long way from Austin. If you want to get there, you'd better talk less and listen more." He reached for the lieutenant's pistol. Rusty gave it to him. "I know you've never had to face the Yankees. You ever been in an Indian fight?"

Billings calmed a little. "No. I have been denied both pleasures."

"I've done both, and there's damned little pleasure in either one. You can go with us or stay in camp, whichever suits you best."

"I'll go, if only to keep some Indian from killing you before I can have you properly shot."

Forrest handed the pistol back to the lieutenant, who recognized reality and holstered it.

Captain Whitfield said, "This is no time to fight amongst ourselves. If we can turn back a raid, we'll save some settler families a lot of grief. That ought to count for somethin', Lieutenant."

Billings glared at Forrest. "We'll see how it counts in a court-martial."

Whitfield delegated two rangers to remain at camp. One had reported in sick. The other was the aging Oscar Pickett, exhausted by the long patrol in which he had just participated. Rusty had to leave Alamo behind, for the horse was too tired to undertake another trip. He picked a dun confiscated from a thief caught running stolen horses down from the Indian territory. The rangers had chosen to keep most of the mounts because they lacked the manpower to go looking for their rightful owners. That had been Captain Whitfield's stated justification, at least.

The day was more than half gone. Rusty thought they would need the devil's own luck to find the Indians before dark. He did not feel that lucky. Captain Whitfield sent him out in front to scout, though any ranger could have led the way as well. Where they might connect with the Indians was anyone's guess.

Billings came forward and rode beside him awhile. Rusty suspected the lieutenant was watching him to be sure he did not seize an opportunity to slip away and avoid Confederate service. The officer seemed to have banked the coals of his anger, though he would probably fan them back to life when the mission was over.

Rusty said, "This ain't the healthiest place for you to be."

Billings growled, "As long as I am here, I want to get the first shot at the Indians."

"Like as not, *they'll* fire the first shot. And if they hit anybody, it'll be whoever is up front."

Billings contemplated that possibility and dropped back to rejoin the others. Sergeant Forrest caught up to Rusty awhile later. He rode with his peg leg secured by a leather loop tied above the stirrup. "What did you say that threw a booger into the lieutenant?"

"Just told him the man out in front is usually the first one shot."

Forrest looked back with distaste. "I wouldn't mind if he *did* get shot. Just a little bit, not enough to kill him. He would be a better educated man."

"Somebody like him has got no business carryin' authority over anybody. How come he's never gone back east to fight the Yankees, since he seems to hate them so bad?"

"The same family connections that got him his commission. He claims he's more valuable here, hunting down conscription dodgers. I'll have to admit that he's a human ferret."

"Every man to the job he's best at." Rusty stared ahead a minute, searching the horizon for any sign of movement. "Can he really get you court-martialed?"

"I've got connections of my own, and he knows it." Forrest frowned. "But *you'd* best watch him. He's got a special grudge against you. You might not make it all the way to Austin."

"Not if I get a chance to slip away."

"I'll help you if I can. But first we've got this job to see after." Billings shifted his weight. Rusty suspected that riding with the wooden leg presented some problems in balance.

Rusty had never been to Austin. He could only imagine what it was like. He asked, "What's goin' on back yonder in the settled country?"

"Did you ever see an old quilt coming to pieces at the seams, scattering threads and cotton everywhere? That's Texas. The whole Confederacy too, I would suspect. Money's not worth anything. People barter whatever they've got to get whatever they need, if they can find it at all. Local governments are falling apart. There'd be riots in the streets, only there isn't much left to riot for."

Rusty had surmised as much from rumors and from bits and pieces of news that had drifted into camp. "High time the war was over."

"Pretty soon now, I think."

Forrest watched while Rusty dismounted to study a set of tracks. Rusty soon determined that they were made by a shod horse headed west. Probably a fugitive from conscription, not the Indians they sought.

Forrest said, "You haven't spent your whole life trailing Comanches. What did you do before?"

"Seems like a long time ago, but I growed up on a farm. Farmin' is what I was best at, 'til other things got in the way."

"They've gotten in the way for all of us. We're alike in that. But we don't have the same loyalties, do we?"

Rusty knew, but he asked anyway. "What do you mean?"

"I suspect you've stayed in the frontier service to keep from going into the Army of the Confederation."

"I was just a boy, but I remember how hard Texas fought to get *into* the Union. I've never understood why it got so hell-bent to leave it."

"Slavery was part of it."

"I've got no slaves. Neighbor named Isaac York has one he calls Shanty. He's the only one I know."

"Some of the war has to do with rights that Washington tried to take away from us. Those people back East live a different life than we do out here. What gives them the right to tell us what we can and can't do?"

Rusty shrugged. "Richmond has done the same thing. I ought to have the right to stay on the farm and mind my own business, but the Confederate government won't let me. It wants me to go fight in a war that I didn't start and didn't want."

"There are times when duty overrules our individual rights."

"If we're not fightin' for our rights, then what *are* we fightin' for?"

"I can't answer that. I'm only a sergeant. What's left of one, anyway."

"You lost that leg fightin' Yankees?"

"A minié ball. Came close to dying of

blood poisoning."

As Rusty had expected, darkness descended without their seeing any trace of their quarry. They made camp without fresh meat. The captain had forbidden any shooting that might alert the Indians.

In the early-morning sun soon after breaking camp, Rusty saw the Indians three hundred yards ahead, strung out in single and double file. He quickly raised his hand, signaling those behind him to halt. He did not look back, but he heard the horses as Whitfield and Forrest spurred up to join him. Lieutenant Billings seemed to have rethought his ambition to shoot the first Indian. He stayed behind.

Rusty pointed. "They've seen us. They're pullin' into a line."

Whitfield's hand jerked up and down as he counted. "Eighteen. They outnumber us damned near two to one." He looked at Forrest. "Any suggestions?"

"My old commander always said, 'When in doubt, charge.' "

Rusty could not see a good defensive position for either side. Rangers and Indians were all in the open.

Whitfield asked Forrest, "Did your commander always win?"

"He did 'til they killed him."

Whitfield considered. "Indians can count, same as we can. Looks to me like our best chance is to hand them a surprise."

Rusty said, "They've already seen us. How can we surprise them?"

"By doin' what they don't expect." Whitfield turned to Forrest. "You ready to take your old commander's advice?"

"Nothing is better than a good cavalry charge to throw a scare into your adversaries."

Whitfield turned to his rangers. "Check your cinches. You wouldn't want your saddle to turn."

The men dismounted and drew their girths up tight. Rusty glanced toward Billings. The lieutenant appeared to have taken ill.

Forrest noticed it too. His voice dripped with sarcasm. "Pretend they're Yankees."

Billings made no reply. He wiped a sweaty hand on the gray leg of his trousers. Austin must be looking like paradise to him.

Whitfield removed his hat and bowed his head. "Lord, we're fixin' to get ourselves into a right smart of a fight. We hope you're on our side in this, but if you can't be, please don't be helpin' them Indians. A-men."

Forming a line, the rangers and two

conscription officers put their horses into a long trot. After a hundred yards they spurred into a run. The Indians shouted defiance, waving bows and the few rifles they had. Wind roared in Rusty's ears. The Comanche line began to waver as the rangers neared. Rusty sensed the Indians' confusion. Captain Whitfield had called it right; they had not expected a determined charge by an outnumbered enemy.

The rangers were fifty yards away when the Indian line split apart. A few warriors fired rifles or launched arrows wildly, then followed the others in disorganized retreat. The ranger line swept through the opening. Pistols and rifles cracked. The rangers pulled their horses around. Whitfield stood in his stirrups and shouted, "We can whip them. Give them another run, boys!"

This time there was no Indian line. Warriors were scattered, addled by the audacity of the inferior force. Three lay on the ground. A fourth was afoot, chasing his runaway horse.

Whitfield ordered, "Keep them broke up. Don't let them get back together."

The rangers themselves broke up, pursuing small groups of Indians in various directions. From the first, Rusty had concentrated on one warrior he surmised might be the party leader. He brought his horse to a quick stop, stepped to the ground, and squeezed off a shot. Through the smoke he saw the Indian jerk, then tumble from his horse.

Rusty started to reload. Billings spurred past him, shouting, "I'll finish him!"

The Indian was not ready to be finished. He rose up on shaky legs and fired a rifle. Billings's horse plunged headlong to the ground. Billings lay pinned, a leg caught beneath the struggling animal. Pressing one bloody hand against a wound in his side, the Indian limped toward him. He held a knife.

Billings cried out for help.

Rusty finished reloading, then remounted and put the dun horse into a run. The Comanche saw him coming and moved faster. Billings's voice lifted almost to a scream. "For God's sake, somebody!"

Rusty knew a running shot was chancy, but if not stopped the warrior would reach the lieutenant ahead of him. He brought the stock to his shoulder and braced the heavy rifle with his left hand. The recoil almost unseated him. The powdersmoke burned in his nostrils.

The Indian fell, then started crawling. Billings struggled but still could not free himself.

Rusty slid his horse to a stop, dropped the reins, and swung the rifle with both hands. He felt the Indian's skull break under the impact of the heavy barrel. His stomach turned.

Billings's face glistened with sweat, his eyes wide. "Oh God! Are you sure he's dead?"

"Dead enough." Rusty knew the disgust was palpable in his voice, but he did not care. He dismounted, fighting an urge to club Billings as he had clubbed the Indian. "Instead of goin' after one of your own, you came runnin' to try and finish mine when he was already down. I ought to've let him gut you."

A quick look around assured him that no other danger was imminent. The war party had broken up. Warriors were fleeing in several directions, most pursued by rangers.

A single rider approached. Fearing he might be Comanche, Rusty hurried to reload his rifle. He was relieved to recognize Sergeant Forrest.

Billings's fright gave way to impatience. "You just goin' to stand there? Get this horse off of me."

Rusty glared at him. "You brought this on

yourself. I wanted to keep that warrior alive."

"What for? There's still plenty of Indians. I'm ordering you, Shannon, get me out of this fix."

"Order away, damn you. I'm not in the army yet."

He tugged half-heartedly, in no real hurry. The horse's dead weight barely budged.

Billings's voice went shrill again. "Put some muscle into it. You want those savages to come back and catch me helpless?"

Rusty saw merit in that proposition. "That'd suit me, except they'd catch me too. I turned my horse loose to save your ungrateful neck." True, he had let go of the reins, but the dun horse had stopped a hundred feet away. The excitement over, the animal was beginning to graze. Rusty saw no reason to point out that he would be easy to catch. He watched Forrest's approach.

"Maybe me and the sergeant together can get you loose."

Forrest dismounted on the righthand side because of the wooden leg.

Billings complained, "It's about time you got here. I can't get this red-headed peckerwood to be any help."

Forrest frowned. "I saw enough to know that this red-headed peckerwood saved your life, and with some risk to his own." He leaned down to inspect the fallen animal.

Rusty said, "There's still a little life in that horse, Sergeant. You'd best watch out for his hooves if he commences to kick."

Straining together, Rusty and Forrest managed to raise the animal a little. Billings wriggled free just as the sergeant's breath gave out and forced him to turn loose.

Forrest told Billings, "Better be sure that leg's not broke." His voice sounded hopeful.

Billings rubbed the limb and found it intact though skinned and bruised. He rebuked Rusty. "You ought to've shot that Indian good and proper the first time. He wouldn't have killed my horse." Still sitting on the ground, he jerked his head quickly from one side to the other, eyes wide with concern. Looking for Indians, Rusty supposed.

"What'll I do now?" Billings demanded. "I've been set afoot."

And we ought to leave you that way, Rusty thought. It'd do you a world of good, walking back to Belknap. "There's several Indian ponies runnin' loose. I'll try to catch one for you."

"Then don't just stand there talking." Billings arose shakily and limped to where the

Indian lay. He picked up a painted bull-hide shield. With the Comanche's own knife he cut a leather thong from around the warrior's neck and removed a small leather pouch. Rusty knew it would be the Indian's medicine bag, containing sanctified articles supposed to protect him from harm. They had brought him no luck today.

Billings cut two eagle feathers from the warrior's braided hair. "Too bad he wasn't wearing a headdress. That would look good hanging on my wall."

Rusty reflected that Comanches did not often encumber themselves with full headdress on a hasty raid like this one appeared to be. Billings stuck the feathers into his hatband. Rusty hoped they were infested with lice. "I'll see about catchin' you a horse."

Sergeant Forrest said, "I'll go with you."

Billings reacted with fright. "Don't go off and leave me here alone."

Rusty worked up a little saliva and spat dust from his mouth. "If any Indians show up, just lay down and play dead."

Riding away, he told the sergeant, "I almost wish I'd left him and that Comanche to sort things out for theirselves."

"Don't expect gratitude. If anything, he'll resent you more than he already does."

"After I pulled his bacon out of the coals?"

"He's a proud man, though God knows he has little to be proud about. To him you're an inferior, and you've made him beholden to you. That'll itch at him like a case of the mange."

Slowly the rangers gathered. Captain Whitfield was the only casualty. He had taken an arrow in the hip. The wound did not appear deep enough to cripple him permanently, but his ride back to Fort Belknap would be grueling punishment. Blood poisoning was always a possibility.

The captain tried to cover the pain with a forced smile. "At least we've scattered them to hell and gone."

Rusty pointed to the dead warrior. "That was the leader, I think. I was hopin' to take him alive so we could use him to make the others turn back."

Whitfield pressed a bloodied neckerchief against his hip. "We set half of them afoot. Ain't much they can do but give up the game and go back where they came from."

Typically when Comanches split they regrouped at some previously agreed-upon gathering point. Rusty could see three Indians half a mile away, moving north. Two were on horseback, a third walking.

Whitfield said, "Let's back off a ways and

give some of them a chance to come get this one. Then we'll follow them so close they can't do anything except return to the river."

"We?" Rusty asked. "You'll do well just to get back to camp."

Whitfield saw the logic and nodded in reluctant agreement. "I'll take one man with me in case I fall off my horse and can't get back on by myself. I'm leavin' you in charge, Rusty. You and the sergeant." He made a point of leaving the lieutenant out.

Billings was freshly mounted on a horse Rusty had caught. It was skittish, fighting its head. Rusty hoped it would keep the officer so busy staying in the saddle that he could cause no trouble. A brand on its hip indicated it had belonged to some settler before a Comanche had laid claim. Billings objected, "We've already lost a lot of time. This wasn't our responsibility in the first place, chasing somebody else's Indians."

Whitfield said, "You can go with me back to camp. The rest'll come along when they finish the job."

That suggestion was met in the same sour spirit it was given. "I intend to file a protest when we return to Austin. You people will have hell to pay."

Whitfield grimaced at the pain in his hip.

"File and be damned. Take over, Rusty." He turned his horse and started away, giving no indication that he cared whether Billings came along or not.

Sergeant Forrest said, "I'll go with the rangers."

Billings accepted the decision with poor grace. "You make certain you still have all of them when you get back to Belknap."

Forrest's only answer was a grunt that could mean anything or nothing. He glanced at Rusty. "You're holdin' the cards."

Rusty nodded. "We'll do what the captain said . . . back off and give them room. If that's all right with you."

"It's all right with me if we don't see Austin before next Christmas."

They waited afoot, giving their horses a chance to rest. After a time, several warriors who had not lost their mounts returned to retrieve the man who had fallen. They lifted him and placed him belly-down on a black pony. Shortly they caught up to several who were afoot, some of them wounded. The rangers followed at a couple of hundred yards, close enough to be an irritant but not enough to present an immediate threat.

Len Tanner remarked, "To them, we must be like mosquitoes that buzz around your face but don't bite."

Rusty said, "We want them to know we could bite if they was to give us reason."

It did not appear that the Indians were going to give them reason. They trudged northward at a pace slow enough to accommodate those who had to walk.

The sergeant pulled in beside Rusty. "You were unhappy about having to kill that Indian."

"I've killed Indians when I had to. This time, I oughtn't to've had to. If we'd made him a prisoner, I figured the others would give up the raid."

"They gave it up anyway. It's my feeling that you had more reason than that."

Rusty considered before he replied. "If things had taken a different turn a long time ago, I might've been ridin' with them myself."

The sergeant's mouth dropped open. "With the Indians? But you're white."

"You've heard of the big Comanche raid on the Gulf Coast back in 1840? I was there. Just a little tyke, not much more than walkin' good. Best anybody could figure, the Indians killed my folks and carried me off. Intended to raise me for a warrior, I guess. Later on, when volunteers hit the Indians at Plum Creek, Mike Shannon and a preacher named Webb found me on the battleground. Mike and Dora Shannon gave me a home."

"Do you remember anything about your real folks?"

"Just a foggy picture, is all. Never could even remember their names. And nobody ever found out who they were."

"Tough, being left an orphan at that age."

"The worst of it is not knowin' who I am. By raisin', I'm a Shannon. By blood, I have no idea. I see strangers and wonder if they might be kin. I might have kinfolks livin' right down the road from me and I wouldn't know it. Sometimes I wonder if I'm kin to *anybody.* It's like there's a piece of me missin', and I'll never find it."

"Everybody needs family. Without family, a man is like a leaf loose on the wind."

"My real folks couldn't have done better by me than the Shannons did. They treated me like I was their own. But if it hadn't been for the fight at Plum Creek, chances are I'd've been raised Comanche. Or I'd be dead."

"So you feel a kinship to the Indians."

"Don't know as I'd call it kinship, exactly. After all, they must've killed my real folks, and they've killed lots of other good people. But I could've become a Comanche myself if it hadn't been for luck."

"Maybe it wasn't luck. Maybe the Almighty had other plans for you."

"I don't think He planned for me to go back east and shoot at Union soldiers."

"I've suspected all along that you're not much in sympathy with the Confederacy."

"When Daddy Mike came home from the Mexican War, he hung an American flag on the wall where we'd look at it every day. He never wanted to forget what him and others like him went through to get Texas into the Union. Even after Texas seceded, he never backed away from that."

"So now the Shannons are gone and you've got nobody."

"There's a young woman down on the Colorado River. If this war ever gets over with . . ."

"Good for you. When a man spends his life alone it seems like he shrivels up inside. We all need somebody."

Rusty grimaced. "Nobody knows that better than me."

At last the visible remnants of the Comanche raiding party reached the Red River. Rusty was reasonably sure the rest would come along soon, or perhaps had already crossed at some other point. Once the Indians reached the far side, the rangers rode up to the river to water their horses.

Rusty was careful where he let his mount step. The Red was notorious for quicksand. The riverbed was wide, but the river itself looked deceptively narrow. Much of the water seeped along just beneath the wet sands, out of sight.

The sergeant eased up beside him. "You know, don't you, that the other side is Union territory?"

"It's also Indian territory."

"But the Indians we trailed have gone on. If someone from this party were to cross, there's nothing I could legally do to make him come back."

Rusty grasped what the sergeant was trying indirectly to say. His skin began to itch. "I've got no business on the other side. No Texan has."

His mind ran back to the sorrowful time when he had been among a party of volunteer rangers escorting friendly Indians across the Red River against their will, throwing them off a Texas reservation they had been promised would be theirs forever. He had felt ashamed, though he understood the settler anxiety that had led to Indian removal. The intervening years had not lessened his feeling of guilt. To go across the river now would reopen old internal wounds, even if the Indians did not inflict new external ones upon him.

The sergeant said, "If we happened to look the other way, you could slip free and go wherever you want to."

"Where I'd most like to go would be my farm down on the Colorado River."

"Other conscription officers might find you."

"There's a lot of timber down there. I'd make them hunt awful hard."

"Then I'd suggest you hang back when we start east. I'll make it a point not to be watching you."

"You'll be in trouble with Lieutenant Billings."

"A mite more won't make any difference. The day the war is over I'll be leaving the army anyway. It doesn't have much place for a one-legged soldier."

Rusty reached for the sergeant's hand. "Maybe in better times we'll see one another again."

"That'd pleasure me." The sergeant turned to address the other rangers. "Anybody share Shannon's leanings?"

Len Tanner said, "If you can stand my company, I'll string along with you, Rusty."

"Thought you'd decided to go to the army."

"I'm afraid I'd have to kill that Billings

before we ever got to Austin. At least notch his ears and teach him the ranger code of conduct. I expect there's some silly law against that."

"I'd be tickled to have you."

No one else offered to stay behind. With luck, Rusty thought, the war might be over before any of these men reached the battle-fields back east.

Aside from his farm, far away, almost every possession he had was on his back or tied to his saddle. But he had been obliged to leave his black horse behind. To try to retrieve Alamo now was too risky. Return-ing to camp a second time would ask more from good luck than one man was entitled to.

To the sergeant he said, "Please ask Cap-tain Whitfield to watch out for my horse. If the outfit breaks up he can take Alamo home with him. I'll find him when this foolishness is over with."

"I'll tell him."

The sergeant motioned for the men to move out.

Tanner said, "I'm only sorry that we'll miss seein' the big explosion."

"What explosion?"

"The lieutenant when he finds that we slipped out of his hands. He's liable to swell up like a toad and bust wide open."

Rusty watched the departing riders, then cast a glance back over his shoulder toward the river. He felt uncomfortably exposed out here in the open. A prickly feeling ran along his spine.

"I've got a notion somebody's watchin' us. We'd best be travelin' too."

"You lead, and I'll foller."

CHAPTER 4

Len Tanner was unusually quiet. Most of the time the lanky ranger had much more to say than Rusty thought necessary. He would ramble aimlessly, sometimes stopping in the middle of a sentence and jumping to a totally unrelated subject. That he was quiet now indicated he felt as conflicted as Rusty about their sudden leave-taking.

After one of the long silences Rusty asked, "Wonderin' if you did the right thing, comin' with me?"

"I'm *always* wonderin' if I've done the right thing. I've been known once or twice to make a mistake."

"I can't imagine when that was."

"What'll we do when we get to that farm of yours?"

"We'll plow and plant, and keep our eyes peeled for conscript officers."

"You still got the Monahan family livin' on your place?"

"Been a long time since I heard from them, but they're still there as far as I know . . . Mother Clemmie and Geneva, and the two younger girls. And Clemmie's old daddy, Vince Purdy."

"It's a damned shame what Caleb Dawkins done to Lon Monahan and his boy Billy . . . takin' them out and hangin' them like horse thieves, and for no reason except they didn't want Texas to leave the Union. There was lots of people agreed with them."

"And some of them died for it."

The memory was still bitter as quinine. Rusty tried to keep it pushed back into the darkest corner of his mind, but sometimes it intruded, ugly and mean. Farmer Lon Monahan had been too vocal for his own good, persisting in voicing unpopular political opinions at a time when Confederate zealots like Colonel Caleb Dawkins made such expressions potentially lethal. Rusty had helped cut the bodies of Lon and his son Billy from the tree where they had been lynched. An older Monahan son, James, had fled to the West, beyond reach of Dawkins and his night-riding patriots.

Too late to save the Monahans, the extreme fanaticism had diminished as the war's casualty lists had grown and its hardships had spread disillusionment to the outermost reaches of the Confederacy.

Tanner smiled. "That Geneva's a pretty little slip of a girl. If you hadn't already put a claim on her, I'd do it myself. How long since you heard from her?"

"Got a letter a year or so ago. There was probably more that never reached me. No tellin' what went with our mail."

"At least you'll be seein' her pretty soon."

"If she's still on the farm where I left her and her folks." Because he had not heard from her in so long, he could imagine all manner of misfortunes that might have befallen the surviving Monahans.

Tanner said, "Wish I had a girl waitin' for *me.* I never knew how to act around women, or what to say."

"It's hard to picture you not havin' somethin' to say."

"Always seemed like when I opened my mouth the wrong words came out. By the time I knew what I ought to've said, the girl would be gone."

"I was awkward around Geneva 'til we got used to one another. After that, things just seemed to come natural."

Tanner considered awhile, then asked, "Did you and her ever . . ." He left the question unfinished.

Rusty's face warmed. "She ain't that kind."

Tanner looked sheepish. "I was only wonderin' if you ever talked about marryin'."

"Oh. Well, it was understood, sort of. I never felt like I ought to ask her as long as the war was on."

"Maybe you should've. Things can change when you're gone for a long time."

Rusty fell silent, trying not to think about the violent deaths of Lon and Billy. He preferred to recall Geneva, to bring her image alive in his mind. He tried to hear the music of her voice and see her as he had first seen her long ago.

Tanner's edgy tone shook him back to sober reality. "I thought we was all by ourselves."

Rusty jerked to attention. His skin prickled as five horsemen pushed out of a thicket. One cradled a rifle across his left arm.

Tanner pulled on the reins. "At least they ain't Comanches."

"Just the same, they don't look like they've come to bid us welcome." Dismounting, Rusty slipped his rifle from its scabbard. He stood behind his horse to shield himself. Holding the weapon ready across his saddle, he watched the oncoming riders.

Tanner followed his example, eyes tense

but not afraid. Tanner was seldom afraid of anything he could see. "Brush men?"

"I don't know who else would be so far out this way." Rusty did not like the riders' somber expressions. The black-bearded man carrying the rifle pushed a little past the others. He gave first Tanner and then Rusty a hasty appraisal that brought no friendliness into his sharp black eyes. He leaned forward, focusing a fierce suspicion on Rusty.

"Who are you men, and what's your business?"

If these had been Comanches, Rusty would have no doubt about their intentions. The fight would already be underway instead of hanging in the air like electricity before a storm.

"Name's Shannon . . . Rusty Shannon. This here's Len Tanner. We're headed for my farm."

"Ain't no farms out this way."

"Mine is down on the Colorado River."

"You're a long ways from home. How come you so far west?"

The other riders were unshaven, which added to their formidable appearance. None had a beard as black as the leader's, however. Rusty sized them up as probable army deserters, conscription dodgers, or simply fugitives from the law for various and sundry crimes. "We didn't come to cause trouble. We had no idea there was anybody around."

One man spoke hopefully, "They got honest faces, Oldham. They don't look like conscript officers."

"Now, Barlow, you know you can't tell what a conscript officer looks like. They don't wear a uniform, most of them." Oldham cut his sharp gaze back to Rusty. "Maybe you're rangers."

Another rider pulled a paint horse up beside the leader and gave Rusty and Tanner an accusing study. His eyes reminded Rusty of a wolf's. He was a youth of eighteen or nineteen, his uneven whiskers patchy, soft, and light in color. "They *are* rangers, big brother. I seen both of them over at Fort Belknap."

The paint had gotch ears, a sign it had probably belonged to Comanches at one time. Rusty could only guess how this youngster came by it.

Tanner admitted, "We *was* rangers. They was fixin' to drag us into the army, so we taken French leave. Like most of you, I'd judge."

"That don't hold no water with me, Clyde," the youth said to Oldham.

"Me neither, little brother."

The one called Barlow said, "It could be the truth. Lately the army's been grabbin' everybody that ain't missin' an arm or a leg, right down to boys and old men."

Clyde Oldham objected, "Then again, these could be spies, sent to find us and bring the army."

The youngster declared, "Only safe thing is to shoot them." He seemed eager to start.

Barlow pressed, "What if they ain't spies?"

Oldham scowled. "Then we've made a mistake. Too bad, but I never heard nobody claim that war is fair. Half the time it's the wrong people that get killed."

Rusty saw agreement in the other men's faces, all but Barlow's. He leaned his rifle across the saddle and drew a bead on Oldham's broad chest. He tried to keep his voice calm. "We're liable to take more killin' than you'll want to do."

Barlow raised a hand, his palm out. "Let's don't nobody do nothin' hasty. If you say you ain't rangers anymore, I say we ought to take your word . . . for now. How about you two comin' along with us?"

"We've got plans of our own."

The Oldhams and two others cautiously moved up a little, trying to form a semicircle that would prevent escape. Rusty pivoted the rifle barrel from Clyde Oldham to his younger brother. "You-all stop where you're at."

Tanner whispered, "There ain't but five, two for me and two for you. We can share the other one."

Rusty thought it would be a poor consolation to die knowing they had won the fight. "We don't want to kill anybody."

Barlow said, "We don't either." He seemed to be speaking to his friends more than to Rusty and Tanner. "We came here to stay out of the war. Ain't no point in startin' one of our own."

The younger Oldham looked to the men on either side of him. He echoed Tanner. "Ain't but two of them. You-all afraid?"

Clyde Oldham cautioned, "*You'd* better be, little brother. You've got a rifle aimed right at your belly."

"Well, I ain't afraid." The youth's eyes gave away his intention just before he brought up a pistol and pointed it toward Rusty.

Rusty muttered, "Oh hell!" and triggered the rifle. Through the smoke he saw young Oldham jerk back as if kicked by a mule. In reflex the youth fired his pistol. The paint staggered and fell, dumping Oldham on the ground. He had shot his own horse.

Tanner shouted, "Don't anybody make a bad move. I still got a load in this gun."

Clyde Oldham left the saddle quickly and knelt over his younger brother. "Buddy!" he cried. The dying horse was kicking. Oldham dragged the youth away from the flailing hooves.

The other three men stared as if they could not believe what they saw. Tanner said, "You-all throw them guns to one side before you get off of your horses." They complied.

Rusty was momentarily in shock. He had acted by instinct. He had not had time even to take good aim. Now he saw the blood and knew it was of his own doing. He felt sick.

Tanner calmly told him, "We're still deep in the woods. You better reload that rifle or draw your pistol."

"I hope I didn't kill that kid."

"If you didn't, you taught him a hell of a lesson." Tanner moved slowly from behind his horse, keeping his rifle trained in the direction of the brush men. Clyde Oldham had laid his rifle on the ground. Tanner tossed it away and did the same with the pistol the younger Oldham had dropped. He leaned over the fallen youth, then looked up at Rusty.

"You hit him in the arm. It's a hell of a mess."

Rusty gathered his wits and reloaded his rifle. Oldham had ripped his brother's sleeve to expose the wound. The arm was shattered. The youth groaned, his face draining white in shock.

Oldham cried, "He'll bleed to death."

Rusty handed his rifle to Tanner. "Not if I can help it." He wrapped his neckerchief above the wound as a tourniquet. He twisted it tightly until the blood slowed. Anger began to rise. "Damn it to hell, I didn't want this. But he was fixin' to shoot me."

Oldham showed no sign that he had heard, or if he heard, that it made any difference. "Little brother, don't you go and die on me. Don't do it, I say."

The only answer was a deep groan.

Rusty managed to choke the blood flow down to a trickle. "I don't suppose anybody in your camp claims to be a doctor?"

Barlow said, "There's a preacher comes to see us now and again, but he ain't there right now."

"A preacher?" Rusty felt a sudden hope. "Would his name be Webb?"

"That's him. You know him?"

"From as far back as I can remember."

The more he looked at young Oldham's

89

smashed arm, the more he despaired of saving it. At this point he would not wager two bits that the youth would even survive. "Ain't much more we can do for him out here. You-all better get him back to your camp."

Clyde Oldham looked up, hatred in his eyes. "You think we'll just let the two of you ride away?"

"That's all we wanted in the first place. The rest of this was your own doin'."

Tanner stepped between the men and the weapons they had tossed away. "You can come back later to fetch these."

Rusty heard horses and looked up. Six or eight riders came loping out of the thicket toward them. His heart sagged, and for a moment he felt defeated. Then he recognized the man riding in the lead. Hope began a tentative revival.

Tanner raised his rifle. Rusty motioned for him to lower it. "James Monahan is with them."

Tanner hesitated. "Last time you and him met, you didn't part real friendly."

"He's the best hope we've got. We can't fight our way past all that bunch."

James brought his mount to a rough stop, raising a small cloud of dust. "We heard shootin'. What the hell happened here?"

Barlow jerked his head toward Rusty. "It was Buddy Oldham's fault. He tried to shoot this ranger."

James recognized Rusty. His reaction was less than cordial. "Damn it, Rusty Shannon, can't you go anywhere without takin' trouble with you?" James examined the wounded arm and looked up at Rusty, his eyes critical. "If you had to shoot him, couldn't you just crease him a little?"

Rusty knew it would be poor politics to say he had aimed at the heart. "I didn't want to shoot him at all. He gave me no choice."

James turned on Clyde Oldham, his voice severe. "You're his big brother. Looks like you could've kept him jugged and stoppered."

"He's always had a mind of his own."

"Damned pity he never used it much." James looked up at the men who had ridden with him. "Let's get him to camp and see what more we can do. Mack, we'll put him on your horse. You can ride behind the saddle and hold him on." He faced Rusty again. "Did you have to shoot Buddy's horse too?"

"He did it himself."

James nodded. "That don't come as any big surprise." He helped Clyde Oldham and

Barlow lift the half-conscious boy into the saddle. The man named Mack sat behind the cantle, one arm holding Buddy in place. James jerked his head at Rusty and Tanner. "You-all come and go with us."

Rusty saw no choice. "We're keepin' our guns."

"Be careful whichaway you point them."

Riding, Rusty studied Geneva's brother. James had been forced to leave home early in the war and live by his wits in a wild area where the only people he encountered were Indians and fugitives like himself. The strain had put a haunted, desperate look in his eyes. Rusty knew him to be near his own age, mid-to late twenties, but James had the appearance of a man closer to his forties.

Rusty wanted to ask him a dozen questions, most having to do with Geneva, but this did not seem the time.

James broke the silence. "You still a ranger?"

"Not since yesterday." He explained the circumstances under which he and Tanner had left the company.

James said, "You took a long time about doin' the smart thing."

"It wasn't smart. We just didn't see where we had any choice. We were tryin' to explain that when Buddy-Boy decided to commence firin'."

Clyde Oldham said bitterly, "He couldn't have hit you. He never could shoot worth a damn."

"I wish I'd known that."

Oldham seemed to be making an effort not to cry. "I brought him out here to protect him, to keep the war from takin' him. And now this . . ."

Rusty had no answers left. A thousand of them would not change what had happened. He asked James, "Are you the chief of this camp?"

"This camp ain't got no chief. Every man is free to come and go, to do what suits him as long as he don't hurt somebody else. We stay together for mutual protection against the Indians, the army, and the rangers." His eyes narrowed. "Especially the rangers."

"You don't need be concerned about the rangers anymore. There's not enough left to guard a jailhouse, much less to raid a brush camp. I'd worry a lot more about the Indians."

"Worst they've ever done is make a try for our horses. Raidin' parties ride a long way around a camp as big as ours."

Rusty had heard talk about a large gathering of brush men far west of Fort Belknap, near the ragged breaks that marked the

93

eastern edge of the staked plains. He supposed the fugitives moved camp from time
to time for security.

Tanner muttered, "We've got ourselves
into a dandy fix. We ought to've fought
when we had the chance."

Rusty said, "I'd've ridden fifty miles extra
to stay out of their way. All we can do now
is keep our eyes open."

The brush men rode ahead but watched
lest Rusty and Tanner turn and run. The
situation reminded Rusty of two fighting
bobcats locked in a sharp-clawed embrace
from which neither dared try to break away.

Tanner asked, "What'll we do when we
get to wherever we're goin'?"

"We'll dance to whatever tune the fiddler
plays."

Rusty smelled wood smoke before he saw
the camp. A number of horses grazed on a
rolling stretch of open prairie, accompanied
by a slack-shouldered boy who appeared to
be asleep in the saddle. Rusty's attention
went to a long-legged mule. Recognition
brought a surge of pleasure that for a moment shoved aside his concern over their
trouble. "Yonder's old Chapultepec."

Tanner said, "Looks like him, all right."

The mule looked up as the horsemen rode
past, but he went back to grazing.

Tanner shrugged. "Didn't recognize you. I suppose old mules are forgetful, like old people."

"He'd've noticed if I'd been ridin' Alamo. They always got along good together." Rusty thought about the deserter who had stolen the animal from the ranger camp. "Lancer must be here too. I owe him a busted jaw for stealin' Daddy Mike's mule."

James Monahan stopped and waited for Rusty to come up even with him. "You know that mule?"

"My old daddy brought him home from the Mexican War. A deserter named Lancer stole him awhile back. Me and him are fixin' to talk about that."

James frowned. "It won't be much of a conversation. Lancer is buried where we had our last camp." He pointed northwestward. "He was a hard man to get along with. Every time somethin' didn't suit him, he threatened to go fetch the rangers. One of the boys got a bellyful of it."

Rusty said, "I'm goin' to want my mule."

James did not reply. Rusty took that as a sign James was not sure he and Tanner would ever leave this place.

He had seen ranger camps and army camps. This looked like neither. It was a haphazard scattering of canvas tents and rude brush shelters strung along the banks of a creek. Half a dozen campfires sent up their smoke, and the smell of roasting meat made him aware that he was hungry.

Hell of a thing, Rusty thought, thinking about my stomach when I ought to be thinking about my hide.

Tanner remarked to James, "It don't look like you-all's cup has run over with prosperity."

"At least we ain't takin' orders from Richmond, or Austin either. We're still free men."

Free seemed a questionable description. The brush men were free in the sense that they were neither in the army nor in jail. But their situation hardly met Rusty's definition of freedom. Hostile Indians roamed to the north and west. To the east, the Confederate government considered them traitors. The only relatively open course was to the south, toward a distant foreign border. Those willing to flee to Mexico had done so much earlier in the war. In a sense, those who remained here were confined to a huge prison without walls. They were refugees, hiding, moving periodically lest they be discovered and overrun.

Almost immediately Rusty and Tanner

were surrounded by more than a dozen men. He knew his rifle would be useless. At best he might shoot one man before the rest swarmed over him. Tanner's expression said he was still willing to fight if Rusty gave him the sign. Rusty shook his head.

Somebody demanded, "James, where'd you find these rangers?"

Rusty did not know the speaker's name, but he remembered the face from among the men who used to loaf around the dram-shops at the Fort Belknap settlement. He looked about, hoping to see other familiar faces. Surely some of the men he remembered deserting from the rangers would be among this group.

Clyde Oldham pointed to his brother and said Rusty had shot him . . . shot him down in cold blood. Someone grabbed Rusty's rifle, jerking it from his hand before he could react. Tanner tried to hang on to his, but two men dragged him from his saddle, landing on top of him as he hit the ground. They took his rifle and his pistol.

Rusty felt hostility radiating from the men who surrounded him. He was reminded of the hatred Caleb Dawkins and other Confederate zealots had shown toward the Monahan family, hatred that had culminated in two hangings. His pistol was still in its holster on his hip, but if he tried to draw it he would not live to pull the trigger.

It would be useless to argue that the army had become too small and too weak to indulge its time searching the wide West Texas wilderness for a poverty camp like this. It was likely that most of these men had hidden out through a major part of the war. Many had probably suffered during the early period when fanaticism had inflicted injustice upon those whose loyalties were suspect. They would not easily believe that the long war had sapped the energy and resolve of even the most extreme, like the hangman Caleb Dawkins. Most Texans now simply wanted to put the conflict behind them and rebuild what they could from the wreckage of war.

James stood in front of Rusty's horse. "You'd just as well get down. I'll see that nobody does anything to you."

Though hostility was strong in the faces Rusty saw uplifted toward him, the men seemed willing to accept James's leadership. James extended his hand. "Just for safety, maybe you'd better give me your pistol."

Rusty grasped it stubbornly. "I believe I'll keep it."

He expected an argument, but James made what in other circumstances might be regarded as a faint smile. To the men around him he said, "Leave him hold on to it. He knows better than to try and do anything." To Rusty he added, "I'll give you ranger boys credit for guts, even if not good sense."

Rusty was surprised to see a couple of women and half a dozen children in the camp, families uprooted by the war.

James said, "First thing, we'd better see what we can do about Buddy."

Young Oldham was carried into a tent and laid down on some blankets. James went to his knees beside him and gave the wound a closer examination. He loosened the tourniquet to let the blood flow. It had slowed considerably from before. His face was grave as he looked up at Clyde Oldham. "Ain't nothin' holdin' that arm together but a little skin. The bone is busted into a dozen pieces. It needs to come off."

Oldham's voice went shrill. "Amputate? But what can he ever do with just one arm?"

"Live, maybe. Otherwise, he ain't got a jackrabbit's chance. If I was you, Clyde, I'd go out yonder and find somethin' to drink. You don't want to watch this."

Oldham's stricken gaze fastened on Rusty for a moment before he walked away from the tent. A friend put an arm around his shoulder and said, "Come on, Clyde. You need a shot of whiskey."

James beckoned to Rusty. "You did the shootin'. It's your place to do the cuttin'."

Rusty had treated bullet and arrow wounds, but he had never cut off an arm or leg. James held the blade of a skinning knife over a campfire, then handed it to him. Sweat trickling down his face and burning his eyes, Rusty severed what remained of the arm.

Young Oldham screamed. His brother turned to come back, but his friend held him. "We both need a drink, Clyde."

Rusty felt sick at his stomach. He fought to keep everything in it from coming up.

James said, "You'll need to tie off those veins."

"I'd better let you do it." Rusty walked out of the tent and leaned against a tree while his stomach emptied itself. Barlow joined him, kicking dirt over the vomit. "There's a spring down yonder. You can wash the blood off. Then I know where there's a jug. It ain't good whiskey, but there ain't no good stuff to be had."

Rusty doubted he could keep the whiskey down.

Barlow said, "The kid ought to live, if shock don't kill him, or blood poisonin'. Or he don't bite himself like a rattlesnake."

Kneeling by the spring, actually just a slow seep in the bank of the nondescript creek, Rusty dipped his hands into the cold water. The blood would wash away, but not the memory. "Why did that button have to play the fool?" he demanded. "This damned war . . ."

"Some people are bound to be fools, war or no war. Buddy-Boy never did have brains enough to pour water out of a bucket. You said somethin' about headin' for your farm."

"We were, 'til we ran into this outfit." Rusty looked to the west, where the sun was rapidly sinking toward the horizon. "Are we prisoners?"

"Depends on how you look at it. Some of the boys probably wouldn't want to see you leave just yet."

"Clyde Oldham might decide in the middle of the night to shove a knife between my ribs. Especially if his brother takes a turn for the worse."

"I'll keep an eye on Clyde. Anyway, if he wanted you that bad, he could follow and kill you the first time you stopped."

Rusty clenched a fist. "He could've sat on that little brother of his if he'd tried to."

"It's like I said about fools. Those two tried to kill an army recruiter. That's when they skedaddled to the brush."

James came out of the tent, his hands bloody. Rusty started to approach him, but an angry look in James's face turned him back.

Damn it all, Rusty thought, I didn't ask for this.

He wanted to ask James about Geneva and the rest of the family, but he decided it would be prudent to wait.

Somebody shouted, "Yonder comes Old Man Timpson."

Rusty squinted. He made out the figure of a rider leading two pack horses a quarter mile from camp.

Barlow took joy in the sight. "The old man brings us supplies. People here have got folks back in the settlements. They send what they can . . . flour and salt, powder and lead. And news . . . the old man is our main way of keepin' up with what's goin' on back yonder. Him, and now and again Preacher Webb."

"This is a long way for Preacher Webb to travel."

"He answers his callin'. There's some people here who need a strong dose of preachin' any time they can get it."

Rusty agreed. "There's been a right smart of raidin' and horse stealin' laid at these men's door."

"There's a few sour apples like them Old-ham brothers, but you can't blame everybody. Most of these are decent people. The war put them in a bad situation, that's all. When it's over they'll go back to where they came from and tend to their own business."

"*Most.* But what about those who use the war as an excuse, the ones who would've been renegades even without it?"

"Time'll weed them out. They'll rob the wrong citizen or steal the wrong horse."

"You could've weeded them out yourselves."

"We need them. When the war is over we won't need them anymore."

Men of the camp surged forward as Old Man Timpson rode in. He flipped the pack horses' lead rein to one of them.

Somebody shouted, "I hope you brung us some coffee."

The old man's voice was hoarse. He was weary from a long ride. "Sure enough, along with flour and salt and such." He coughed, trying to clear his throat of dust. "But I brought somethin' a lot better than any of that."

Barlow spoke up, "I don't know nothin' better than coffee."

"I brought news." The old man took off his hat and bowed his head. "Praise God

. . ." He paused, taking a deep breath. "The war is over."

Shouts erupted among the men, moving through the camp like a whirlwind as the message was relayed from one to another. Timpson dismounted slowly and carefully, then clung wearily to the saddle, his aging legs stiff. He explained that General Robert E. Lee had surrendered and the Confederacy was no more.

Rusty had sized up Barlow as a farmer, for he had the strong, broad shoulders of one used to hard and heavy work, his large hands probably accustomed to gripping the handles of a plow. Yet this big man stood without shame and let tears roll down his whiskery cheeks in front of everybody. He murmured, "I had begun to think we never would live to see this day."

He turned toward the crowd. "Friends, looks to me like we ought to join together and give thanks . . . thanks to Him who has delivered us from this terrible ordeal."

He stood with hat in hand, waiting for the remainder of the crowd to gather. The two women clutched their husbands' arms and wept. Many men knelt while Barlow said his prayer. His voice gained strength as he spoke.

"Lord, Thou hast watched over us and

brought us through four long years of misery. Now we bow to offer our gratitude. Thou hast brought us deliverance from the evil that has rent families asunder and torn our country apart. We ask Thee now to give us errant children guidance as we undertake to bind up the wounds. We beseech Thy blessings upon the widow, the orphan, the soldier crippled. Bring us together and make us whole again, we ask in the name of Him who died for our sins, Amen."

Rusty shivered as he pondered the significance of the old man's news. He had sensed the end coming, yet it seemed unreal that the years of agony had come to an end.

Barlow asked Timpson, "Does this mean we can go home?"

"It means there's no Confederate government to say you can't."

Tanner gripped Rusty's shoulder, jubilation in his eyes. "That high-and-mighty Lieutenant Billings can't have got halfway to Austin yet. Wouldn't you love to see his face when he finds out?"

Rusty felt more awed than jubilant. "This means we didn't really have to quit the ranger company."

Clearly, that idea had not occurred to Tanner, but it did not give him pause. "There may not be a company left anyhow. If there's no more Confederacy, there's no more government."

"If there's no government, there's no law." The thought brought a chill to Rusty. He could visualize criminals banding together, ranging over the country with impunity, taking what they wanted, smashing anyone daring enough to stand in their way. "There's *got* to be law."

"It's just so much paper if there ain't nobody to carry it out."

Rusty wished they had not quit the rangers. "Len, we've got to go back."

"Where?"

"To the camp at Fort Belknap. Captain Whitfield may need us now more than ever."

Tanner's face fell. "I was countin' pretty strong on goin' home and seein' my folks."

"Duty, Len. I don't see we've got a choice if we ever want to hold our heads up again."

"I never saw anybody so hell-bent on duty."

"Then go on south without me. I know what I've got to do."

"I've already had to save your life once or twice. You'll probably get yourself killed if I'm not around, so I'll go with you. But damn it, Rusty, that sense of duty will be the death of you someday, I swear it will."

Rusty felt a strong hand grip his arm. He

turned to a grim-faced James Monahan.

James said quietly, "Now's your chance to get out of camp while everybody's mind is on somethin' else."

A quick glance showed Rusty that nobody seemed to be paying any attention to him and Tanner.

"We'll catch our horses and go. But first I want to ask you . . ."

Impatiently James declared, "You ain't got time to ask questions, and I ain't got time to answer any. Git while the gittin's good."

Reluctantly Rusty had to acknowledge the wisdom in James's advice. He was bursting with questions about Geneva, but they would have to wait.

"All right, let's go, Len. But I'm takin' Daddy Mike's old mule."

James jerked his head toward the place where the two rangers' horses were tied. "Take him and be damned. But whatever you do, do it quick."

CHAPTER 5

At first the ranger camp appeared deserted. Captain Whitfield's tent was still standing. The others had been struck, the canvas folded and stacked on the ground. Wooden stakes lay in a pile.

Riding in, Rusty saw only a few ranger horses grazing free. He gave a quick, happy shout as he recognized Alamo among them. The horse nickered at Chapultepec. Rusty slipped the loop of a rawhide reata around Alamo's neck and petted the black horse before leading him into camp with the mule. "Old friend, I was afraid somebody with light fingers might've taken a fancy to you." To Rusty, a thief was a thief, whether he decorated his head with a hat or a feather.

Tanner grunted. "Place looks like everybody died."

"Bound to be somebody around."

"We might've come for nothin'. But at least you got your horse back."

That in itself was justification enough for returning, Rusty thought. "Maybe the captain's still here."

He found Whitfield taking his rest on a cot inside the stained old canvas tent. It struck Rusty that he had never seen the captain idle in the daytime. But he had never seen Whitfield take an arrow in the hip before, either.

Whitfield arose slowly, wincing in pain from the wound. He seemed drawn, his eyes dull as he shook Rusty's hand, then Tanner's. "I thought you boys took off for the tall timber."

Rusty said, "We heard about the surrender. What's happened to the company?"

Whitfield made a sweeping motion with his hand. "You can see about all that's left. Billings and the sergeant took most of them away before word came about the war. The others didn't see much point in stayin' around after we got the news. If you-all came back with any hope of gettin' paid, forget it. Even if they gave it to you, a barrelful of Confederate money wouldn't buy you a plug of tobacco."

Rusty said, "We gave up on pay a long time ago. We just thought you might need us."

"If somebody was to commit cold-blooded

murder on the street in Fort Belknap, we couldn't do anything about it. We've got no authority."

"We could still turn back Indians if any tried a raid. We wouldn't need anybody's authority for that."

"We'd need more manpower. It's all finished, boys. If you've got a home to go to, you'd just as well head thataway. I'm goin' myself, soon as Oscar Pickett fetches a wagon so I can load up the state's property and keep these rascals around here from stealin' it."

The prospects were troubling. Rusty said, "I don't see how a country can get along without law."

"Texas was part of the Confederacy. That's gone. It'll take the Federals awhile to set up their own government. 'Til then, except for maybe a little local law, everything is left hangin' between the devil and the deep blue sea."

Rusty felt cold. "So it's every man for himself."

"If I was a robber or a horse thief, I'd be pickin' in tall cotton right now."

Rusty told the captain about the brush camp, now in the process of breaking up.

Tanner said, "There's men in that bunch

would skin their grandmothers for six bits a hide."

"Not much we can do about them now."

Tanner pointed his chin at Rusty. "He done somethin'. Shot one of them, he did."

"By accident?"

Rusty shook his head. "I did it on purpose. Had to. But I'm hopin' he lives."

Tanner said, "You better hope he don't. He may come after you someday. Even with one arm, he could still blow a hole through you."

Whitfield frowned. "There was a time we might've broken up a camp like that, but I didn't want to. Most of them were just tryin' to stay out of the army. Now they're not my problem anymore. As long as they don't bother me or mine, I won't bother them."

Rusty asked Whitfield, "Do you think you can travel with that wounded hip, even in a wagon?"

"As long as it's in the direction of home, I can grit my teeth and keep goin'."

Home. The word held the warmth of spring sunshine.

"It'll be safer, travelin' in a bunch. Me and Tanner will wait here with you 'til Oscar Pickett gets back. Then we'll ride along with you as far as we can."

Rusty could see in Whitfield's eyes that the wagon's jolting hurt him, but the captain voiced no complaint. Rusty had once suffered through the ordeal of a long ride after a Comanche arrow had driven deeply into his leg. Tanner had cauterized the wound with a red-hot blade. It still pained him to remember, though the searing probably saved his leg. Healed now, the scar was still large and ugly, and it sometimes itched enough to drive him to distraction. He could imagine what the captain was going through.

Oscar Pickett hunched beside Whitfield, his age-spotted, arthritis-knotted hands gripping the reins. Two of Whitfield's horses and the mule Chapultepec trotted behind, tied to the wagon by long reins. In the wagon bed were folded tents, what few supplies had remained in camp, and Whitfield's and Pickett's personal possessions. These were too meager to strain the capacity of the canvas war bags in which they were stowed.

Rusty and Tanner rode beside the wagon, Rusty leading the unclaimed dun horse he had used before recovering Alamo. They came to a burned-out cabin, its blackened ruins slumped in a heap near a seeping spring.

"Good place to water and rest the horses," Rusty observed. He was more concerned with giving the captain a rest, but he knew better than to say so. Whitfield's pride would make him insist on traveling farther.

The captain offered no complaint. He said, "I remember the folks who lived here. Jackson was their name. Indians kept wartin' them 'til they decided to go back to East Texas. Then the Comanches came and burned the cabin. Figured that would keep the family from ever comin' back."

Rusty figured the Indian victory would be short-lived.

"If the Jacksons don't," he said, "somebody else'll claim this land. Once the soldiers start comin' home, this country will settle up again, heavier than it was before."

Whitfield made no comment.

Rusty said, "They'll need law to protect them."

Whitfield shook his head. "I've been the law long enough. I just want to go back to whatever's left of my own place and enjoy some quiet for a while."

Tanner put in, "Them's my sentiments too. We ought to think of our own selves for

113

a change. All the work we done, all the ridin' we put in, and what's it got for us?" He
held up his left arm. His bony elbow poked
out through a long tear in the ragged sleeve.
"Ain't even got a decent shirt."

So far as Rusty knew, Oscar Pickett had
no home to go back to. At his age, his
prospects appeared limited. Rusty took it
for granted that the captain would see to
the old ranger's welfare, giving him a place
to stay in return for whatever work Pickett
was able to do. Otherwise Pickett was likely
to end up in some demeaning job like
swamping out a dramshop just to feed
himself and have a roof of something more
substantial than leaky canvas to turn aside
the rain.

Rusty felt a hollowness inside as he contemplated his own future. He had the farm.
He could pick up a handful of its rich soil
and know it was something substantial,
something that was his. And he was confident that Geneva would stand by his side.
But everything else was an unanswered
question. Texas, along with the rest of the
Confederacy, had lost the war. It was only a
matter of time until the Federals moved in
troops to take over whatever remained of a
government. Where would the defeated
Confederates fit in, or would they fit in at

all? What punishments might they suffer at the hands of the victors?

Rusty had never taken up arms against the Union, yet in his own way as a ranger for the state of Texas he had been an agent of the Confederacy. Would he be subject to punishment? If so, what would the punishment be? These nagging questions ran through his mind, seeking answers but only stirring up more questions.

He voiced some of his concerns to Whitfield, who lay in the shade of a tree beside the slow-yielding spring. The captain said, "They can't line us all up and shoot us; there's way too many. Ain't enough jails between here and Cape Cod to put us all behind bars. We'll make do somehow as long as we're livin' and breathin'. Even if they burned us out like Sherman did in Georgia, there's always the land. They can't burn that up."

They had unhitched the wagon team and led them to the water. Rusty took them back for a second chance to drink after their rest, then hitched them to the wagon again. "We'd best be gettin' on. It's a long ways to the Colorado River."

He began seeing familiar landmarks he associated with the Monahan farm. They brought memories rushing back. He tried to concentrate on Geneva, but thoughts of her led to the chill of remembered violence. He relived the brutal lynching of Lon and Billy Monahan and a frightening nighttime raid that had culminated in the Monahan house going up in flames.

Tanner said, "I'll bet you're thinkin' about that Geneva girl."

Rusty had been struggling with bitter memories of Colonel Caleb Dawkins and his son Pete, but he did not feel like arguing with Tanner over technicalities. "Didn't know it showed."

Len suggested, "We could swing by the old Monahan farm, maybe spend the night there."

Rusty dreaded the feelings such a visit would inevitably stir up. "It'd add some miles, maybe cost us an extra day. Wouldn't likely be much left there anyway. Dawkins and his bunch left a lot of it in ashes."

"Been a right long while since we heard anything about Caleb Dawkins." Tanner smiled hopefully. "You don't reckon somethin' awful might've happened to him?"

"I doubt it. But he may not be gettin' much sleep."

"On account of the Federals comin' in?"

"On account of James Monahan. Now

that the war is over he's free to come and go wherever he wants to. If it was me that hanged his daddy and brother, I'd have a crick in my neck from watchin' over my shoulder."

"The captain said there won't be much law for a while. James could dice old Dawkins up into little bitty chunks, and nobody could do a damned thing to him."

"There's always his son Pete and the rest of the Dawkins people. Once a thing like that gets started, it's hard to stop 'til everybody's sick of it . . . or everybody's dead."

Tanner pondered that proposition in unaccustomed silence awhile. "If I was you, the first thing I'd do when we get to your farm would be to unsaddle my horse. The second thing would be to ask that girl to marry me. Come to think of it, I might leave the horse saddled."

"It's been more than a year since I saw her. Me and her have got a lot to talk about first."

"You've got the rest of your lives to talk."

"A thing like marryin', you've got to work up to it. You don't just ride in after a year and say, 'Howdy, girl, let's go find Preacher Webb.' "

"If it was me, I would. I'd carry her off

117

someplace where nobody could find us, and I wouldn't turn her a-loose 'til we both had to come up for air. I don't know as I'd even wait for the preacher."

"A man would if he had any respect for the girl. Or for himself." Rusty would not admit to anyone that at times he entertained such fantasies about Geneva, with or without marriage. Usually he tried half-heartedly to suppress the images, then gave up the attempt and took pleasure in letting them run free. It was guilty pleasure, but pleasure just the same.

No, he would wait for Preacher Webb. But the preacher had better not be long in coming.

Rusty and Len Tanner rode a little ahead of the wagon that carried Captain Whitfield and Oscar Pickett. The captain hunkered down on the wagon seat, enduring his pain without complaint though it showed in his pinched face, his half-closed eyes. Rusty called back to him, "Hang on, Captain. We don't have far to go."

"I'm fine," Whitfield lied. "Just fine."

Ahead lay the timber that fringed the Colorado River. A dim twin-rutted trail led toward the nearest crossing that a wagon could ford without danger of floating downstream. Rusty had ridden there many times, usually with Daddy Mike, occasionally with Preacher Webb, accompanying the minister on his circuit. It was pleasant to remember when he could keep from dwelling on the sad truth that those times were over and would never come again. Mike Shannon was gone, and age would be overtaking Preacher Webb. Rusty doubted that the minister could hold up to the rigorous pace he had set for himself in earlier times, carrying the gospel to the forks of the creek and beyond. Traveling that once had been a joy for him must now have become an ordeal. Yet Rusty knew Webb persisted, traveling more slowly and paying a price in weariness for every mile.

Rusty began to see mares and colts bearing the Monahan brand. The family had brought their horses down from the old place to Rusty's because of the certainty that they would quickly be stolen if left behind. No one had an incentive to steal cattle except an occasional one to butcher for beef. War had made horses scarce and valuable even as it resulted in an overabundance of unclaimed cattle.

He noticed several cows with calves bearing his brand. He had not been here to burn it on them, so he credited the Monahans. They had been looking after his interests as well as their own. It was a pity the cattle had no monetary value.

Sight of the fields helped lift his melancholy. They were green with growing corn, with forage for the stock. The Shannons' old double log cabin came into view. It was easy, seeing the place, to fantasize that Daddy Mike and Mother Dora would be waiting there for him as they had done so long. Rusty was tempted to put Alamo into a lope, but reality intruded. The pleasant dream was quickly gone. Familiar landmarks aroused old memories, one on top of another.

Rusty crossed a creek where he and Daddy Mike once had ridden with a band of local farmers trailing a Comanche raiding party. They had not managed to overtake the Indians; they rarely did. Farther along, Rusty had helped bury a murdered woman. The Comanches had taken the woman's small son, but no one had ever found a trace of him. He had disappeared like the Indians themselves onto the open plains of Comanchería.

Daddy Mike . . . sometimes it was hard to realize that four years had passed since he died, yet at other times, remembering the uncounted miles Rusty had traveled since, the many rivers he had crossed, it seemed an eternity. The deaths of Daddy Mike and Mother Dora had left him with an acute sense of abandonment, of being alone in the world. That feeling of isolation had brought him to bond with the Monahans. They were not truly his kin, but they and Preacher Webb were the nearest to it that he knew. When he married Geneva he would become a part of their family. He needed that sense of belonging.

At the farthest end of the field, a man followed a mule and a moldboard plow. The distance was too great for recognition, but Rusty assumed this would be Geneva's grandfather, old Vince Purdy.

A girl was hoeing in the garden. For a fleeting few moments Rusty thought she was Geneva. He spurred ahead, then drew Alamo to a stop as he realized this was one of Geneva's sisters. The two younger girls had grown up during the war years. He had hardly known them the last time he had been here.

The girl saw the horsemen and the wagon. She dropped the hoe and climbed over the log fence that enclosed the garden. Lithe as a young deer, she raced barefoot to the cabin. She was shouting, though Rusty was too far away to make out the words.

By the time he and Tanner reached the

cabin, Clemmie Monahan stood on the dog run. She was a small, thin woman of perhaps ninety pounds, so slight that she looked as if a high wind could sweep her away. Rusty knew from experience that her appearance was deceiving. She had a will of pure steel and a backbone to match it. Her two younger daughters stood on either side, beaming with delight. Rusty struggled with his memory a moment before he recalled that the older of the two was Josie. The younger was named Alice.

Clemmie had taken it badly when Rusty had arrested her son James long ago for an attempt on Caleb Dawkins's life in revenge for Lon and Billy. She had mellowed in the years since, and he hoped she had put the incident behind her. That she greeted him with a thin smile gave him hope.

"You-all get down and come in," she shouted.

Rusty dismounted and removed his hat. "Clemmie," he said by way of greeting.

"Rusty," she answered. Neither seemed to know much more to say at first. While he tried to decide how to continue the conversation, he stared at the two girls, hardly believing the change. Josie looked a great deal like her grown sister and appeared to be about as old as Geneva had been when

Rusty had first met her. Alice was a pretty girl of fourteen or fifteen.

Josie declared, "I told them it was you, Rusty. I recognized you from as far as I could see you."

He was glad she could not read his mind and know that he had had trouble remembering her name.

He said, "I expect you-all have heard that the war is over."

"We heard," Clemmie responded. "Now maybe the menfolks will be comin' home . . . them that survived." She coughed away a catch in her throat. "I'm right glad to see that you're one of them, Rusty."

Tanner was on the ground, stretching his long legs. Pickett had brought the wagon up near the cabin's dog run. He and Tanner helped the captain to the ground.

Rusty looked past Clemmie, hoping to see Geneva somewhere. "You remember Captain Whitfield, don't you? And Len Tanner? This other feller is Oscar Pickett."

"I remember them all. Welcome, gentlemen, to our house." She glanced back quickly at Rusty. "I should've said, 'To Rusty's house.' It's his, not ours."

"It's yours as long as you want it," Rusty said. He gave the girls a second looking

123

over. "My, but you two have changed a lot in a year."

Josie smiled, looking even more like Geneva. "It's been longer than a year." She studied him up and down. "You're thin. Haven't you been eatin'?"

"When I could. Been times I couldn't."

Clemmie made a sweeping motion with her hand. "Then we'd better get busy and fix you-all a good dinner. Come on in."

Captain Whitfield limped, each step bringing pain. Clemmie frowned. "What's happened to you, Captain?"

"A Comanche had nothin' better to do than to put an arrow in my hip, is all. It's healin', thank you."

"It'll heal quicker once we put some food into you."

Rusty watched her stir up a blaze in the fireplace. He could not hold the question any longer. "Where's Geneva?"

Clemmie looked up in surprise, her expression slowly turning to one of regret. "I guess you never heard."

A cold knot suddenly built in Rusty's stomach. "Heard what?"

"She's up yonder at our old place. Her and her husband."

Rusty caught hold of a chair. "Husband?"

"She's married. Been married since winter."

Pete Dawkins poked at the campfire with a dry stick, his backside prickling with impatience. Somewhere in the distance he heard a bugle, but he gave it no attention. He had heard far too many bugles since he and his friend Scully had been hustled unceremoniously into the Confederate Army. There had been no bands to play stirring martial music, no pretty women waving at the departing soldiers. They had been marched out of Austin in the middle of a driving rain without fuss and feathers and with damned little if any showing of respect. It was almost as if they were prisoners, not soldiers.

The truth was that he and Scully would have been prisoners had they not become soldiers. Pete's hard-headed old daddy had been responsible for that. All on account of a few horses. Hell, the old man had lost more to colic than Pete and Scully had taken. He would probably have considered them stolen by the Indians and have forgotten them had it not been for the nosy damned rangers and that army horse buyer in cahoots with them. What was his name? Blessing, that was it. Tom Blessing. And the rangers. One of them he had encountered before and had gotten to know better than he wanted to. Rusty, they called him. Shannon, that was the last name. Rusty Shannon. He did not know the ranger captain's name, but he would remember that face and that bushy mustache if he lived to be a hundred.

If it hadn't been for them he wouldn't be here. He would still be in Texas, raiding the reservation north of the Red River for Indian horses and making himself wealthy enough that someday he could snap his fingers in Old Colonel's face and tell him where he could go.

And what in the hell was he still doing here anyway? Word had come days ago that the war was over. What was the use in having an army if there was no longer any war to fight? But the officers were waiting for specific orders from higher authorities. They had not allowed any soldiers to leave.

Scully stared at him from the other side of the small fire. "You tryin' to poke them coals to death? You look like you're fixin' to cloud up and rain pure vinegar."

"Just thinkin'."

"They can court-martial a soldier for thinkin'. You're supposed to leave the thinkin' to them and do what they tell you to."

"Right now they're thinkin' I'm goin' to stay here and act like a good soldier, but they're mistaken. I'm fixin' to up and leave this outfit. I'm goin' back to Texas."

"They shoot deserters."

"That was when there was still fightin' goin' on. They got no reason to keep me now, and no reason to hunt for me if I'm not here when they call the roll in the mornin'."

Scully looked around furtively to be sure no one was listening. "Would you take me with you?"

Pete hesitated in answering. He felt he could make better time alone, looking out for no one except himself. On the other hand, Scully had always been useful so long as he had Pete around to do most of the thinking for him. If anything, he was a better hand than Pete when it came to handling horses. It was as if his mind were on about the same plane of intelligence as theirs.

"I guess you can go provided you keep up. I ain't waitin' for you if you fall behind or get yourself into any trouble."

Scully's reply was curt. "The only trouble I ever got into was by followin' you."

True, they had a good thing going back home when they were gathering Indian horses from the reservation and selling them in the Texas settlements to farmers or to the Confederate Army. But they had come up short after one trip up north of the river, and Pete had seen no harm in adding a few of the old man's horses to the mix. Caleb Dawkins was already richer than one man had a right to be.

Pete knew Old Colonel's temper, for he had felt the lash of it many times, growing up. But he never gave a moment's thought to the possibility of getting caught, or of Caleb Dawkins giving him and Scully a choice between the army and the state penitentiary.

Choice hell! About like choosing between getting shot and getting hanged.

If it had been anyone except Dawkins's own son, the outcome might very well have been the rope. Old Colonel was hell on hanging people. Like them Union-loving Monahans.

Scully asked, "If we left right now, how far you reckon we could travel before daylight?"

"Eight or ten miles if we hustle. A right smart farther if we was a-horseback."

Two horses were tethered on the picket line, out beyond the light of the company's several small campfires. They belonged to the captain and the lieutenant, the only men in the company allowed to ride.

Scully said, "Are you thinkin' the same thing I am?"

Pete nodded. "The officers have ridden far enough. We ain't been paid, and we ain't goin' to *be* paid. The least the army owes us is a horse apiece."

He and Scully gathered up what few belongings they had, including their rifles. Pete led the way to the picket line. He drew a bowie knife from his belt, ready to cut the rope.

His blood went cold at the sound of a gun hammer being cocked. A voice demanded, "Who goes there?"

He saw the dark shape of a guard just in front of him, too near to miss if he fired a shot. Pete shivered.

"Who are you?" the guard demanded again. Pete recognized the gruff voice of a company sergeant.

"Just me," Pete said weakly. "I was lookin' for the latrine. Guess I got turned around in the dark."

"Well, you just turn around again. Already been two men tried tonight to take the officers' horses. The next one I'll personally shoot, and I'll bury him in the ditch we dug for the latrine."

Pete backed off, bumping into Scully. His

fear gave way to frustration as he retreated. It had not occurred to him that other men in the camp were considering desertion, just as he was, and that they had caused a stiffening of the guard detail.

Scully whispered, "What'll we do now?"

"We'll walk. Sooner or later we'll find somebody careless with his horses."

He found the road that led west. Anger made his stride long and purposeful. His mind went back to the black day that the rangers had caught him and Scully with stolen horses. He wished he had Rusty Shannon here right now. He would gladly beat him within an inch of his life, then shoot him in the belly. Maybe someday.

CHAPTER 6

Rusty felt as if a mule had kicked him in the belly. He sank into the nearest chair. "Geneva's married?"

Clemmie sensed the depth of Rusty's shock. Her voice was sympathetic. "A man named Evan Gifford. She said she wrote and told you."

"I never got the letter."

She pulled a chair up nearby and faced him, taking one of his hands. "I wish I'd known. I'd've found an easier way to tell you."

"There isn't any easy way." He could not meet her gaze. He looked down at the rough floor. He lost his voice for a minute. He swallowed hard to get it back. "I hope he's a good man."

"You can take comfort in that. He is."

Both girls spoke at the same time. "He sure is," they agreed. Rusty got the impression that either would have been happy to

131

have married him.

Too bad one of them hadn't.

Clemmie said, "Evan took a Union bullet in his chest. They sent him home to die, only when he got there he found he didn't have a home anymore. He showed up here with one foot in the grave. We cared for him the best we knew how."

"Sounds like you done right good." For the moment, he wished they had not.

"When he was able, he commenced helpin' around the place. That corn and that feed you see growin' out yonder, he done a big part of the plantin', along with Daddy Vince. Branded your calves for you too."

Rusty turned so they could not see the anguish in his face. His long-nourished dreams were slipping away from him. He was powerless to grab them and bring them back. He looked through the open door. "I see Vince out yonder, ridin' a mule in from the field."

"It's early for him to be quittin'. Probably saw you-all and thought he'd better come to the house. Visitors mean trouble, oftener than not."

One in particular, he thought, by the name of Evan Gifford. "You-all've had trouble?"

"No Indians lately, but there's been horse

thieves. There's them that represent the army and give you worthless paper for them. Then there's them that don't bother with paper, they just run off whatever they can find."

"At least the army shouldn't bother you anymore. I imagine it's breakin' up fast."

"There's enough of them others, though. And there's already been soldiers cut loose afoot and hungry, tryin' to scavenge a livin' wherever they can. You can't expect them to stay hungry without puttin' up a struggle. The law is apt to be scarce, so everybody'll pretty much have to take care of their-selves."

"Who *is* the law around here these days?"

"The regular sheriff went off to the army, so folks elected a man by the name of Tom Blessing. Know him?"

"Tom Blessing." The name brought memories that would have been pleasant were he not still in shock over Geneva. "He was a friend of Daddy Mike's. And he was the man who first put me into the rangers."

Clemmie's eyebrows went up. "You're grateful to him for that?"

"It was the best thing that ever happened to me." He saw Vince Purdy nearing the barn. That gave him an excuse to get out of the cabin. Perhaps in the open air he could clear his head and get a grip on his feelings. "I'll go meet Vince and set his mind at ease."

Purdy rode the plow mule, carrying the long reins coiled in one hand. He was taller than his daughter Clemmie but built along the same spare lines. His work-toughened hands seemed too large for the rest of him. Every year of his long life was etched deeply in lines that spider-webbed his thin, weathered face.

He grasped Rusty's hand with bone-crunching strength that belied his age. "You home for good?"

"For better or for worse." Rusty figured he had already heard the worst. He motioned toward the field. "The crops look good."

"Rains've been fair enough, and we've watered them with a goodly amount of sweat. You ought to have a good harvest."

"Not me. You. You-all planted and worked the fields. Whatever comes off of them rightly belongs to you."

"With the war ended, I figured we'd soon be goin' back up to our own place."

"I don't see any need to hurry. At least you'd ought to stay here 'til the fields are cut."

"We've got fields up yonder too. Evan and

Geneva can't handle all that work by their-selves."

Evan and Geneva. Hearing the names spoken together jolted Rusty anew. "Maybe James will be able to help them, now that he's free to travel."

Purdy's eyes brightened. "You've seen him?"

Rusty told him of their brief encounter in the brush men's camp. "I expect that camp broke up fast."

Some of Purdy's years seemed to have lifted from his thin shoulders. Humming, he began removing the mule's harness. "James comin' home . . . Everything's fixin' to be fine from now on out."

Rusty leaned against a fence and turned away with his eyes closed. They burned as if he had rubbed pepper into them. "Yeah, fine from now on."

Rusty talked Captain Whitfield into staying a few days and resting before he finished his trip. His hip gave him pain enough that he was amenable to the idea. Clemmie and the girls seemed to enjoy waiting on him. Rusty rode with Tanner around the farm, search-ing beyond his own boundaries for cattle bearing his brand. He rough-counted about fifty head, double what Daddy Mike had owned and what had been here when Rusty rode off to join the rangers.

Tanner said, "Looks like the folks taken good care of things for you."

"I never had a moment's hesitation. I knew what they'd done with their own."

"I'm sorry that girl let you down."

Rusty was immediately defensive on Geneva's behalf. "She didn't let me down. She hadn't made me any promise and didn't owe me nothin'. From what Clemmie says, she didn't even know if I was still alive. None of my letters ever got here."

He brought up the subject of the calves at the supper table, thanking Vince Purdy for branding them.

Purdy said, "Couldn't've done it by myself. Evan helped me, and Preacher Webb pitched in every time he came by." He glanced up at Clemmie. "Which has been right often."

Clemmie suppressed a smile.

Purdy said, "The girls helped a right smart too. They're both good hands whether it's with a cow or a plow."

Rusty thanked them. Josie said, "It's the least we could do. You gave us a place to go, away from Caleb Dawkins and his men."

Clemmie said sharply, "We've agreed never to mention that man's name in this house. What a scorchin' he's got comin' when the devil gets his turn."

Purdy said, "It ain't no big thing, holdin' onto cattle. Nobody wants them much anyway. Not unless it's a milk cow. Our old Spot's been missin' for over a month. Somebody's probably milkin' her right now, and I'll bet it ain't no Comanche Indian."

Rusty said, "I think I remember her. Mostly white with brown spots, and a stub horn on the left . . . no, the right side?"

"That's her. I've hunted high and low. It's like she fell in a big hole and covered herself up."

"You talked to all the folks around us?"

"Nobody's seen her."

Rusty had a suspicion, but he would not voice it, not yet. "I've been neglectful," he said. "I ain't made a circle yet to visit my neighbors. I don't even know if they're all still around."

Clemmie's face wrinkled. "There's one that's been around a lot more than I would've liked."

Rusty thought he knew. "Sounds like Fowler Gaskin."

Gaskin had lived just a few miles from the Shannons for years, to their continual misfortune.

Clemmie said, "That old sneak has got it

in his mind that I ought to be in the market for a new husband. If there wasn't but one man left alive on the face of God's earth and it was him, I wouldn't let him within smellin' distance of me. And I can smell him a long way."

Gaskin had been a thorn in Daddy Mike's side, always borrowing without asking, never bringing anything back, always looking to ride instead of walk if he could manage it at someone else's expense. Clemmie said, "You ever see a pig that would wiggle in with other litters and steal milk from every sow in the pen? That's Fowler Gaskin."

Vince Purdy scowled at mention of the name. "I've had to threaten to wallop him with a singletree to make him leave Clemmie alone."

Clemmie might be well into middle age, but to her father she was still a young girl who needed protection. Though she might not weigh enough to sink in deep water, Rusty suspected she could swing a mean singletree herself if the need arose.

Rusty said, "I'll go talk to Fowler. Me and Tanner."

The last time he had seen the Gaskin cabin, part of it had been damaged by a windstorm. Repairs had been done in a makeshift manner, but now the whole cabin leaned to the south and seemed in danger of collapse.

Tanner observed, "He's propped a log against the eaves. That's the only thing holdin' it up. That and the south wind."

"He'd rather bleed than sweat. Never do for himself what he can wheedle someone else into doin' for him. Never buy anything if he can borrow it. And never remember to take back anything he borrows."

"You mean like a milk cow?"

"I'd not be surprised."

Gaskin's droop-tailed hound announced the horsemen. Gaskin stepped out through the cabin's sagging door and stood slouched in front, a long rifle in his hand. Rusty wondered idly who he had "borrowed" it from. Gaskin reminded Rusty of a scarecrow, gaunt, bent-shouldered, his tangled beard a mixture of black and gray, streaked with tobacco juice that had dribbled down his chin. His red-rimmed eyes were far from friendly.

"Rusty Shannon. Back, are you?"

It was not much to say after such a long time, but in Gaskin's case Rusty was not interested in extended conversation. "Back. I see you're still here."

It would have been too much to ask of good fortune to find that Gaskin had left the country. "I think you met Len Tanner a time or two."

Gaskin hardly looked away from Rusty. "You a ranger now, or a soldier?"

"Neither one. Our company disbanded."

"Just as well. I never seen the rangers stop an Indian raid yet, not 'til after the damage was done."

Rusty felt the burning of resentment. The rangers had turned back a number of attempted raids before they were able to materialize. Nobody other than the rangers themselves knew it had happened. "You still livin' here by yourself?"

Gaskin's voice broke into a whine. "You know I am. Them two good boys of mine gave up their lives fightin' for the Confederacy."

Rusty knew better. The Gaskin boys had been absent without leave and were killed in a New Orleans bawdy house fight. He was not sure Fowler Gaskin was aware of that. If he truly believed his sons had died on the battlefield, it was just as well to leave him that illusion. If he was lying to save humiliation, Rusty saw no point in picking the scab from an old sore.

"I don't suppose you've seen anything of a milk cow that belongs to the Monahan family?"

"They done asked me about that cow. I'll tell you the same as I told them. If I ever see the old hussy, I'll give her a whack on the rump and send her home."

Rusty heard a sound he had not encountered in a long time, the bleating of lambs. "You got sheep?"

"Ain't nothin' wrong with sheep," Gaskin said defensively. "Confederate money ain't worth nothin', but you can always swap wool for somethin' you need. Them's dogie lambs in that pen. Lost their mamas."

Rusty's faint suspicions began to take on larger dimensions. "What you feedin' them?"

"Whatever I've got. Lambs ain't choosy."

Rusty and Tanner rode down to the pen, Gaskin following suspiciously. Rusty saw half a dozen lambs. He asked Tanner, "You know anything about sheep?"

"Not much. Just that they don't smell good, is all."

Rusty would guess these lambs were two or three months old, all in excellent flesh. Whatever they had been fed, they were thriving. Over in the corner of the pen was a stanchion large enough for a cow.

Sheep manure came in small pellets. Scattered around the pen were large patties, some of them fresh.

Rusty said to Gaskin, "You must have some awful big sheep."

Gaskin looked nervous. "They're big enough."

The cabin was within easy water-carrying distance of the river, which was fringed with heavy timber and thick underbrush. Rusty saw cow tracks leading off in that direction. He saw boot tracks as well.

He told Gaskin, "Since you don't know anything about that cow, we'll be movin' along."

"You-all come back sometime." The tone of Gaskin's voice said that he hoped they never would.

Rusty and Tanner circled around and came into the timber downriver, where Gaskin was unlikely to see them. They rode along the edge of the water, back in the direction of the cabin. If they found what Rusty expected, it would not be far from the pens. Fowler Gaskin was not likely to walk any farther than necessary.

He found the spotted cow staked on a long rope that allowed her room to graze and to reach the water. She gave the horsemen a docile bovine stare as Rusty dismounted and looked her over. Examining her udder, he noted that the teats showed small tooth marks.

"Just about lamb size," he muttered. He assumed that Gaskin had been staking the cow out of sight and leading her up to the pen for the dogie lambs to suckle.

Tanner said, "I'll bet that old heifer put up a fight the first time or two he put them lambs on her."

"Probably thought they were the funniest-lookin' calves she ever saw. That's what the stanchion was for, so he could tie her up good and tight 'til she got used to the lambs."

The rope was attached to a strong sapling. Rusty untied it, coiled it, and got back on the horse. The cow followed him as he put Alamo up the riverbank and across a narrow strip of pasture.

At the front of the cabin he hollered for Gaskin. The old man came out, his jaw slack with disappointment as he saw the cow.

Tanner shouted, "Look what we found down yonder. She somehow got a rope around her neck and tied it to a tree."

Whatever Gaskin was trying to say, it caught in his throat.

Rusty said, "It's about time them lambs were weaned onto grass, don't you think?"

Gaskin found voice, and it was shrill. "I'll have the sheriff on you, takin' a man's cow."

"I'll go tell him myself and save you the trip."

Gaskin turned and reached back through the cabin door and brought out the long rifle.

Len asked, "You don't reckon that old man's crazy enough to fire that thing at us, do you?"

Rusty had not considered that Gaskin might actually be crazy. The notion was not far-fetched. "I sure wouldn't stop and ask him." He spurred Alamo and forced horse and cow into a long trot.

Clemmie beamed as Rusty led the cow into the yard. She walked around the animal, petting her, rubbing a hand along the smooth hide. "I'm sure glad to see you back, old girl."

Rusty explained the circumstances. She said, "Daddy was over at the Gaskin place a couple of times, thinkin' she might've strayed in that direction."

"She strayed all right, with a little help."

"How come you figured it out so easy?"

"With Fowler Gaskin for a neighbor, nothin' is safe unless it's nailed down tight or too heavy to carry."

He did not worry about Fowler Gaskin carrying his complaint to the sheriff. Tom

Blessing knew the old reprobate as well as Rusty did. But mention of Blessing set Rusty to thinking he should ride over and visit Daddy Mike's old friend. He intended to take Len Tanner along, but Len seemed to be enjoying himself hoeing the garden with the two girls.

He told Rusty, "These Monahan sisters are different. Somehow I can talk to them without my tongue-tyin' itself up in a bow knot."

"They're still just kids."

"Kids? Maybe you've been hurtin' so bad over Geneva that you ain't taken a close look, especially at Josie. Country girls turn into women fast. Ain't no make-believe like with them town girls, no flirty put-on."

Rusty did not need Tanner to remind him of Geneva. She was never far from his thoughts.

"Well, you keep choppin' those weeds and don't get too close to the girls. You wouldn't want their mother comin' after *you* with a singletree."

Tom Blessing was a large man whose natural leadership drew others to follow him no matter how long or difficult the trail. He had led local volunteer minutemen companies in pursuit of raiding Indians and by example had been a strong moral force in the community. Daddy Mike had always looked up to him, and Mike Shannon had not been one to give honor where honor was not due. He had always said Tom Blessing's word was like gospel. Blessing had been present when Mike and Preacher Webb had found a frightened little red-haired boy on the battleground at Plum Creek back in 1840. Later it seemed he was never far away when the Shannons needed help.

As a boy, Rusty had looked upon Tom Blessing with an awe that had never entirely left him though now he stood as tall as Blessing and could look him squarely in the eyes.

Blessing had added a wing onto his cabin since Rusty had last been there. It was typical of him that he never let "well enough" alone. He was not content with existing conditions if he could see a way to improve them.

Rusty saw him saddling a horse in a log pen beside the barn and reined Alamo over that way. Blessing reacted with surprise upon recognition but methodically finished buckling the girth before he stepped around from behind the gray horse and waved a huge hand. "Thought the Indians might've got you, or you'd plumb left the country."

Rusty dismounted and accepted Blessing's bruising handshake. "Never saw a place I liked better than here." He studied the gray horse. It took a big one to carry a man like Blessing. "Looks like I caught you fixin' to go someplace. I wouldn't want to hold you up."

Blessing frowned, considering before he spoke. "I got a message from Isaac York. Asked me to come over to his place as quick as I could. I'd invite you to go with me, but I remember that you held a heavy grudge against him."

"That was a long time ago. When I found out I was mistaken, I told him I was sorry." Rusty had long believed York had fired the shot that killed Mike Shannon. He had been almost to the point of shooting the man before he discovered that the blame lay elsewhere.

"Then you're welcome to come if you're of a mind to."

Rusty was a little surprised that York was still alive. York had fought a long and hopeless battle with whiskey. Neighbors had placed bets on when he would lose the inevitable fight with the final bottle.

"Still drinkin' as hard as he used to?"

"I'm afraid so. Last time I saw him, I doubted he'd make it home. If it hadn't been for Shanty, he probably wouldn't have."

Shanty was York's slave. More than that, he was York's friend, almost the only one the man still had after years of alienating his neighbors.

Rusty said, "I still owe Isaac for all the bad things I said about him. I'll go with you."

Blessing nodded his approval. "You show your good Shannon raisin'. Takes a strong man to admit he's been wrong." He mounted the gray horse and started off, Rusty pulling in beside him. They talked of old times, shared experiences on the trail when Blessing had headed up the local volunteer minutemen and Rusty had gone along as a green youngster eager for his first real fight. He had never been that eager again, not after seeing blood.

Blessing had helped Rusty and Captain Whitfield break up a horse-stealing ring. He had been buying remounts as a civilian representative of the Confederate Army when Caleb Dawkins's son Pete had driven a sizeable bunch into Jacksboro to sell. They proved to have been stolen, some from Caleb Dawkins's own remuda. Facing his prideful father's wrath, and a choice of prison or military service, Pete had reluctantly enlisted in the Southern Army.

Rusty said, "I hear you're the sheriff now. I don't see you wearin' a badge."

"The last sheriff lost it someplace. Anyway, everybody around here knows who I am."

"What if you run into outlaws and they don't know you?"

"They'll get acquainted with me quick enough."

York's cabin was plain, without even such embellishments as a small porch or a yard fence. York had no family beyond the slave Shanty. His wife and daughters had been killed by Comanches years ago. He had tried to drown his bitterness in whiskey ever since. He seethed with hatred for Indians, no matter their intentions, no matter their tribe, and embraced any opportunity to kill them.

A dog's barking brought a slight figure to the cabin door. Rusty recognized the aging slave. The talk was that his mother had belonged to Isaac York's father, and he and Isaac had grown up together. Some people whispered that the two might be half-brothers. Technically Shanty was York's property, but in practice he was more a caretaker and protector. Had it not been for Shanty constantly watching over him, dragging his contentious master out of a fight before it went too far, sobering him up before it was too late, Isaac probably would have gone to his grave years ago.

Shanty bowed in the deferential manner drilled into him from the time he had learned to walk. His lean body was bent under the weight of hard times. His big-knuckled hands were disproportionately large, bespeaking a lifetime of manual labor. "Mr. Blessing, it's a mercy you've come. Mr. Isaac's mighty low." The voice was soft and seemed near breaking. Shanty looked at Rusty a moment before coming to recognition. "Why, you're that Shannon boy. Been a long time. Only you don't look like a boy no more."

"Nobody stays young long in this part of the country. Sorry about Isaac."

"I'm afraid the Lord's fixin' to call him to Heaven."

Rusty was not sure Heaven was Isaac's true destination. He was about to ask if a doctor had seen Isaac, then remembered that the nearest thing to a doctor anywhere around was Preacher Webb. Primarily interested in ministering to souls, Webb had a considerable practical knowledge about healing bodies as well.

Shanty said, "Last we seen of Preacher

Webb, he was headin' west. Said he had a flock out yonder in need of a shepherd."

That might have been a reference to the brush men, Rusty thought. One had mentioned occasional visits by Preacher Webb.

Shanty's eyes reflected a deep sadness. "There's lost sheep in need of him right here. I hope he comes in time."

A weak voice called from inside the cabin. Shanty motioned toward the door. "He's been frettin', Mr. Blessing, wonderin' when you'd come."

Rusty followed Blessing into the cabin. Shanty came behind him. Rusty's eyes adjusted slowly to the gloom indoors. Isaac York lay on a cot, his face drawn, his eyes hollow and showing but little life. He extended a trembling hand to the sheriff. "Tom. I was afraid you wouldn't get here in time."

"I'm here now, Isaac. What can I do for you?"

York's gaze lighted on Rusty. He was momentarily surprised. "Shannon? Rusty Shannon?"

"It's me, Isaac."

York's voice was hoarse. "I never killed your daddy. Me and Mike didn't get along, but it wasn't me that killed him."

"I know that. I'm sorry I ever thought

151

otherwise. I wish I could take back every bad word I ever spoke about you."

"I'm glad you come. You can be a second witness."

Blessing asked, "Witness to what?"

"I want you to write me a will. I'd do it myself, only my hands shake too much. There's some paper over on that table, and a pencil."

Blessing found a sheet of paper and used the bottom of a tin plate to give it a firm backing. "What do you want me to write?"

York looked toward Shanty, who leaned his bent frame against the log wall. "I want you to say that I am of sound mind and body. Well, maybe the body ain't sound, but my mind is clear. I want you to write down that I am givin' Shanty his freedom. No *ifs,* no maybes. I want it known that he don't belong to me or to nobody else."

Rusty saw that gesture as unnecessary. Abraham Lincoln had declared the slaves free, and if they weren't already they would be when the first Yankee soldiers showed up.

"Another thing," York said, "everything I own, this farm, this cabin, the little bit of money I've got . . . it all goes to Shanty."

Blessing's eyebrows raised a little. "There's liable to be talk."

"In my shape, what do I care about talk? Shanty ain't a slave, not anymore. He's worked hard on this land. By all rights, it's his."

"You mentioned money."

"There's a can with Yankee silver in it. A little over a hundred dollars, buried out by the corner post of my cow pen."

"You don't have any blood kin that you'd want to leave somethin' to?"

"Used to have a brother over the Sabine in Louisiana. We ain't seen one another in years. He never even answered my letter when I buried my family. So to hell with him."

Blessing wrote slowly and laboriously, then handed the paper over to Rusty. "That look to you like what he said?"

Rusty glanced quickly over the scribbling. "You got it just fine."

York reached for the paper, pencil, and plate. With shaking hand he signed it. "You-all witness it. Make it to where no lawyer can mess with it."

Blessing signed beneath York's name and passed the paper to Rusty. "You've done good by Shanty. I'm proud to've known you, Isaac."

"I ought to've given him his freedom years ago."

Shanty's voice quavered. "I thank you, Mr. Isaac."

Isaac relaxed, seeming to sink deeper into the bed. "Some people ain't blessed with any real honest-to-God friends in a lifetime. I've had one, at least."

Outside, Blessing turned sharp eyes on Rusty. "You got any idea where Preacher Webb might be found?"

"Ain't seen him, but they tell me he comes by my place to visit the Monahan family pretty often."

"If he shows up, I wish you'd tell him to get over here as quick as he can. I doubt he can do much about Isaac's sickness, but maybe he can help the poor feller die with his soul at ease."

"I'll watch for him."

Blessing looked worried. "I'm afraid Isaac ain't thought all this through."

"He's leavin' Shanty a good farm."

"May be leavin' him trouble too. There's some folks won't take it kindly."

"It's Isaac's farm to do with as he pleases."

"He won't be here to take the punishment, but Shanty will."

"You're the sheriff. You can help him."

Blessing's eyes narrowed. "Maybe, maybe not. Looks to me like the state government is comin' unraveled. Maybe we can hold the county together. I'll keep tryin' to do my job 'til the Federals come and tell me I'm not sheriff anymore."

Blessing's comment was like an echo of the concerns Rusty had heard from Captain Whitfield. "Do you really think they'll do that?"

"I don't know. I've never been on the losin' side of a war before. We weren't exactly gentle with Mexico. Maybe the Yankees won't treat us kindly either."

"Captain Whitfield says they can't hang us all, and they don't have prisons enough to pen us all up."

"But they can make life pretty miserable. Best thing for a while is stay close to home and tend to business like I always did. Keep the peace the best I can 'til they tell me otherwise."

"You won't have any rangers to back you up."

"I don't even have a deputy. He went off to the war, and the county hasn't hired anybody to take his place."

Rusty considered awhile. "If you need help, let me know. I'll come runnin'."

"Thanks, but the county's got no money to pay you."

"I didn't get paid for most of my ranger service either. They sent us a little flour and salt and sometimes coffee. They allowed us a place to roll out our beddin'. That was about all."

"I hope you're not sorry I got you into it in the first place."

"No. If I'd stayed here I'd have most likely shot Isaac York, thinkin' he killed Daddy Mike. I always felt like I was doin' somethin' useful, bein' a ranger. I'll miss it."

Blessing turned wistful. "Once the Federals have been here long enough to see how bad we need the rangers, maybe they'll organize them again."

"If they do, I'll be ready."

"You've barely got home and you're already talkin' about leavin' again. Rangerin' can be a hard life, even harder than farmin'."

"How long can a man stare at a mule's hind end before he starts gettin' a little crazy?"

CHAPTER 7

Approaching home, Rusty saw Vince Purdy and Oscar Pickett with a mule in the cornfield. Tanner and the two Monahan girls were hoeing weeds at opposite ends of the garden. Tanner turned away, but not before Rusty saw a bruise on his cheek and a darkening around one eye. He asked Josie, "What happened to Len?"

She and her younger sister exchanged quick looks. "He stumbled and hit himself in the face with the hoe handle."

The younger girl giggled.

Rusty thought two and two stopped short of being four. He led Alamo to where Tanner worked. He waited for Tanner to volunteer an explanation, but none came. Rusty had to ask him.

Tanner reluctantly admitted, "I tried to kiss that Josie. You know she's got a fist like a mule's left hind foot?"

Rusty could imagine Clemmie chasing

Fowler Gaskin, swinging a singletree at his head. "She's her mother's daughter."

"All that time in the rangers, I thought we were protectin' helpless womenfolks. I pity the poor Indian that runs afoul of the Monahan girls."

Rusty returned to where the two girls stood watching. "Len tells me it wasn't a hoe handle that bruised his face."

Josie blushed. "He kissed me without even askin'."

Rusty smiled at her embarrassment. "I'll remember that if I ever feel like kissin' you."

Her eyes sparkled. "The difference is, *you* won't need to ask me."

Rusty rode Alamo to the barn. He noticed a strange horse in the pen. He tied his own horse to the fence and walked toward the cabin. Clemmie was sharing a bench with a man on the open dog run. Recognition brought Rusty a surge of joy.

"Preacher Webb!" He rushed to offer his hand. Webb had been like a foster father to him, second after Daddy Mike.

Webb stood up, carefully stretching his back as if it ached. That would not be surprising, considering the long miles he rode to carry the gospel's light to every dark corner he could reach. Rusty gripped the minister's hand so tightly that Webb winced.

"Careful, Rusty. These old bones are turnin' brittle." The knuckles were swollen with arthritis.

Rusty was taken aback to see that wrinkles had bitten deeply into the minister's face. The war had aged everyone more than its four years should justify. "Looks to me like you're still tryin' to carry the weight of the world."

"The Word is never too heavy for these arms to bear, even if one of them *is* crippled."

Webb's left arm had been broken in an Indian fight long ago. It had given him trouble ever since. He was thinner than when Rusty had seen him last. His hair seemed grayer and his eyes care-worn in spite of what he said about the joy of carrying the Word.

Rusty sobered. "I just came from Isaac York's. You're needed real bad over there."

Webb's smile died. "For doctorin', or to preach a funeral?"

"I'm afraid that depends on how long it takes you. When I left, it didn't look like Isaac had much time left."

"I've expected this, sort of." Webb turned. "Clemmie, I'd meant to stay longer."

Clemmie clutched his arm. Regret colored her voice. "Next time."

He patted her hand, then set off toward the barn. Rusty had to lengthen his stride to keep up.

Webb said, "I took a look at Captain Whitfield's wound. It seems to be healin' right well. He's anxious to go on home."

Rusty had been with Whitfield so long that seeing him leave would almost be like watching a good friend die. Distances being what they were and the farm likely to tie him down, he might not see the captain again for a long time, if ever.

Len Tanner would probably go when Whitfield and Pickett did. Rusty dreaded parting with him, for they had ridden together a long time. However, given Tanner's little run-in with Josie, it might be just as well. Staying here, being constantly reminded of his humiliation, would be for Tanner like an itch he could not scratch.

Saddling his horse, Webb asked, "How did you know about Isaac?"

"I went with Tom Blessing to witness Isaac's will."

"He's never talked to me about havin' any kin."

"He's leavin' everything to Shanty."

Webb reacted much as Tom Blessing had. He seemed troubled. "Isaac may have burdened Shanty with a load of grief too heavy for his old shoulders."

"I don't know who would bother him. These are God-fearin' people around here . . . or used to be."

"Some who call themselves God's children have notions they didn't learn in church."

"They won't hurt Shanty. There's a bunch of us will see to that."

"I'm afraid Isaac didn't realize the trouble he might be stirrin' up."

Or maybe he did, Rusty thought. York was a bitter man who had little liking for his neighbors.

Webb started to mount his horse but paused. "Clemmie says you didn't know about Geneva bein' married."

Rusty looked away. "No, I didn't."

"I wrote you. I guess you never got the letter."

"We seldom got much mail."

"Are you goin' to be all right with it?"

"I *have* to be, don't I?"

"You're still young, and there's lots of nice young women out there. You'll find one."

"I don't know that I'll be lookin'."

"Then maybe she'll find *you*."

Clemmie was still standing on the dog run when Rusty returned to the cabin. Her worried eyes were fixed on Webb, riding away toward the east. She said, "He looks awful tired. He should think of himself for a change."

"I don't believe he knows how."

"He ought to quit travelin' so much. He needs somebody to take care of him."

Like you, for instance? Rusty resisted speaking the thought aloud.

She said, "I'm afraid he'll die all alone out on some trail with nothin' but his horse and his Bible."

"He's a man of the cloth. He'd consider it a fittin' way to go."

Her mouth tight, Clemmie retreated into the kitchen. Rusty considered following after her but could not think of anything helpful he might say.

Vince Purdy and Oscar Pickett came in from the field, Vince riding the plow mule, Pickett carrying a hoe over his thin shoulder. Rusty walked out to meet them. He unsaddled his own horse, then helped remove the harness from the mule. Purdy said, "Preacher left here in a hurry, seems like."

Rusty explained. Purdy looked with concern toward the cabin. "Clemmie figured on him stayin' a day or two."

"He'll be back."

"But then he'll be gone again. She sets a lot of store by him."

"It appears that way to me."

"It ain't like she's forgot about Lon and Billy. She never will. But there comes a time when folks have got to pick up and move on, live for the livin' and not for them that's gone. What is it the Bible says? Don't look for me in the graveyard because I've gone on to a better place?"

"Somethin' like that." Rusty had never done much reading in the Book, though Mother Dora had read a lot to him when he was small. There had been times when things he saw happen around him made him wonder if the Word applied to Texas. He had seen too many good people die, like Daddy Mike and Mother Dora, Lon and Billy, while others like Caleb Dawkins and Fowler Gaskin lived on. That seemed a contradiction of the Scriptures.

Reconciling to the loss of his foster parents had taken him a long time. Even yet, something heard or seen or felt would bring them suddenly to mind. Remnants of old grief would sweep over him, reviving a painful sense of aloneness. That feeling had been renewed and intensified by his loss of Geneva. "It's easy to say we ought to put such things behind us. I wish doin' it was as easy as talkin' about it."

Captain Whitfield came onto the dog run as the men approached the cabin. He had left his cane inside. "Oscar, would you be ready to leave here in the mornin'?"

Pickett seemed pleased. He had evidently expected this. "Ready any time you are, Captain."

"We've abused these good folks' hospitality too long."

Rusty assured him, "You could stay here all summer and not wear out your welcome."

"I'm rarin' to go and make sure nobody has carried off my farm."

It did not take long for the three men to load their belongings after an early-morning breakfast. They had little to take with them. Whitfield tugged at his big mustache, eager to go, yet reluctant to say good-bye. He took a hard grip on Rusty's hand.

Rusty said, "Sir, it's been a pleasure and a privilege to serve under you."

Whitfield blinked a couple of times. "Looks to me like the state government has fallen to pieces. I don't know when it may ever decide that Texas needs to reorganize the ranger force. But if anybody asks me, I'll tell them you'd make a good officer."

Whitfield gave Rusty's hand another shake, then turned quickly and climbed up into the wagon. Oscar Pickett said, "I better

164

git too, before he runs off and leaves me."

"You take good care of him." Rusty figured the two old rangers would take care of each other.

Len Tanner hung back after Pickett set the wagon in motion. He twisted the reins in his hand and stared at the ground. "Damn it, Rusty, this is hard."

"I know. I feel the same way."

"I'm anxious to go see how Mama and Daddy are gettin' along. But don't you be surprised if I show up around here again one of these days."

"I'll be lookin' for you."

Tanner glanced toward the sisters on the dog run. "You watch out for them girls. They could hurt a man."

He gripped Rusty's hand, then mounted and spurred off after the wagon. He looked back once. Rusty could not tell whether Tanner was looking at him or at the girls.

When Rusty looked at them, he saw Geneva.

He attended Isaac York's funeral more out of guilt than out of liking for the man — that and respect for the aging Shanty. It weighed on his conscience that he had so long blamed the innocent York for Daddy Mike's death. But York had been easy to dislike for his disagreeable manner, his violent temper.

Fewer than two dozen neighbors and people from the settlement came to see York laid to rest. To find good words to say about the deceased, Preacher Webb skirted gingerly along the boundary between fact and fiction. Funerals were one place where a minister had license to stretch the truth a little.

Ropes lowered the plain wooden coffin into the grave. Rusty gazed at Shanty's solemn face and considered the infinite patience the black man must have had to live with and serve someone who had so many negative traits. Of course, as a slave Shanty had had no real choice. But even a slave's tolerance must have its limits. Now he was legally free. But Rusty wondered if at heart he could ever be free from slavery's legacy of dependence and self-doubt.

No one claiming to be a relative showed up for the service. That was to be expected, for York had never said much about his kin. He had mentioned a brother in Louisiana, but no one around the settlement knew just where the brother lived, if indeed he was still alive. The only known survivor, then, was Shanty. Only a few people filed by after the service and extended their sympathies to him. As a former slave, his feelings were not widely regarded as being of much importance.

Tom Blessing was among the exceptions. He said, "Shanty, you'll need to come to the courthouse the first chance you get. There'll be some papers need signin' before this land can be deeded over to you. Since Isaac made me executor of his will, I'll see that they're ready and waitin' for you."

"I'm obliged, Mr. Blessing."

"I'll need your last name. I don't believe I ever heard it."

"I don't recollect as I ever had one. They just called me Shanty. That was all."

"You can take Isaac's name then. I'll make out the papers in the name of Shanty York."

"Shanty York suits me fine, sir."

Fowler Gaskin pushed forward, scowling. "You'd give a nigger a white man's name?"

Blessing was taken aback. "It's an old custom for slaves to take the name of their masters."

"Not where I come from it ain't."

Rusty wondered why Gaskin had come to the funeral unless he hoped to pick up something useful when nobody was looking. Gaskin had disliked Isaac York, and York never had a good word for him. That was one point on which York and Rusty had long been in full agreement. Rusty said, "Maybe you ought to go back where you came from, Fowler."

Gaskin turned on Rusty. "You'd like that, wouldn't you? Well, I'm stayin' where I'm at. But it don't set right with me, knowin' I got a nigger for a neighbor."

"You always did. He's been there longer than you have."

"But he never owned the land. He was just what the Lord intended for a nigger to be. A white man's property."

Gaskin gave Shanty a contemptuous look and stalked away toward a lank mule he had tied nearby.

Rusty moved to Tom Blessing's side. "What Fowler Gaskin thinks don't amount to a damn."

"But look around you. Even some people who don't like him agree with him on this."

"They'll get used to it. With the war over, there's a new day comin'."

Blessing's mouth drooped at the corners. "The war is over, but I'm afraid the fightin's not."

Steals the Ponies was troubled. Two Comanche warriors returning from a clandestine visit to relatives on the reservation had brought interesting news that raised many questions but offered few answers.

He interrogated them at length, distrusting their report. Much of the word that circulated among people on the reservation proved after a time to be false. The whites were worse tricksters than the coyote.

"How do you know the white men's war is finished? Who told you?"

"My cousin," said Wolf Eyes. "He heard it from a shaman."

"Shamans are always seeing things that are not there. It is what they do."

"But this one went to the long-knife post at Fort Sill. He was told by those who heard it from the soldiers. The *teibos* of the North defeated those of the South."

Despite his distrust of whites, Steals the Ponies found the report plausible. But even if true, its meaning was uncertain and therefore troubling.

Wolf Eyes said the war's end had aroused consternation among the many peoples who lived on the reservation and in the territory beyond. Some, like those near-whites known as Cherokees, had been divided in their loyalties, many fighting alongside men of the north, others allying with the South. What the Cherokees did was always a source of puzzlement to Steals the Ponies. They walked along the white man's road in the way they lived and thought. He did not consider them to be of the same race as the Comanche.

He had been told that the whites saw all red men as being of one people, though reason proved that it was not true. Comanches had little in common with the Cherokees or the others who had migrated from some distant eastern land and tried to make themselves white. To suggest that Comanches had anything in common with the accursed Apaches was an insult. To Steals the Ponies, each tribal group was a race apart. The Comanches were *The* People, the chosen ones, a superior race. All others were allowed to live or willed to die at the discretion of the True Human Beings.

Steals the Ponies had heard old men say the world was large, that it would take many seasons to ride all the way across it on even the fastest horse. His father had told him of visiting a great water, so wide he could not see the far side. The elders said there were many more races of men than he had ever heard about, and each race had its own manner of speaking. One would reason that they must have a common sign language like the plains people so they could make themselves understood to strangers. He had noted, however, that most white men did not seem to have the same signals as The People. They moved their hands a lot as they talked, but the meanings were lost to him.

Nor could he distinguish much difference between white men, though the elders claimed they were of many races. They all looked more or less alike except that some were hairier than others. Their talk was gibberish, as empty as the chatter of the gray cranes that wintered around the many playa lakes shimmering on the plains after a season of rain. How they understood one another was beyond his imagining. It stood to reason that one had to be born white to talk that way, and one had to be born Comanche to know The People's language.

Yet, Steals the Ponies had a foster brother who was white. His father had captured him on a raid and brought him home as a small boy. At first Badger Boy had babbled in the white man's undecipherable tongue. Now nine or ten summers old, he spoke Comanche almost as if he had been born to it.

Steals the Ponies wondered if he would ever understand life's puzzling contradictions.

After lengthy consideration, he told Wolf Eyes, "The white men have fought each other a long time. It is not reasonable that they would stop now while so many on both sides still live. We shall go and see for ourselves."

Wolf Eyes was more than willing, for the ranger warrior society had thwarted the last two raids in which he had participated. "How many of us will go? Do you think we will bring back many horses?"

"There will be only the two of us. We go to look, not to fight."

Wolf Eyes became dubious. "What is the use in just looking?"

"So we will know for certain."

"And once we know, what then? Is it good for us, or is it bad, that the white men no longer fight each other?"

Steals the Ponies considered. "I fear it will not be good. If the Texans no longer war against the men of the North, they may make more war against The People. If the ranger society and the long knives make peace with each other, they may join together to fight us."

Wolf Eyes remained disappointed that a pony raid was not to be part of the expedition. "Perhaps if some *teibos* should attack us and we kill them, we may take their horses."

"It is my intention that we see but are not seen. We leave tomorrow, before the sun."

He traveled light on such trips, not wanting to encumber his horse with excess weight. He packed dried beef strips and pemmican in a leather pouch and tested his bowstring to be certain it would not break should the unforeseen force him to use it.

A boy moved up beside him in the firelight. "You are going somewhere, big brother?"

"Not far, Badger Boy. I will not be gone for long."

"Would you take me with you?" Badger Boy was always begging to go somewhere, but he was still too young for any mission that involved danger. He had earned his name by fighting to a standstill all the other boys who tried to pick on him. Steals the Ponies considered Badger Boy an appropriate name because the lad had that animal's unyielding temperament when provoked. He fought with a badger's tenacity.

"Not this time. You must grow some more." Steals the Ponies placed the flat of his hand against the top of the boy's head, then raised it. "When you are this high, then you can go."

The fire blazed up unexpectedly, and Steals the Ponies was reminded that the boy's eyes were much lighter in color than his own. In daylight they were blue. Steals the Ponies had long ago become accustomed to that fact, yet now and again it struck him as if for the first time, reminding him that he and the boy were not of the same blood.

"This is your new brother," Buffalo Caller had said when he brought the young captive home. "Teach him so he will forget the white man's ways."

At the time the boy had been four or perhaps five summers old. Steals the Ponies had resented him. He had beaten him when Buffalo Caller was not there to see. But the boy had fought back with the ferocity of a cornered bear cub, gradually gaining his adoptive brother's respect and eventually his love. Steals the Ponies had become his protector against those who would antagonize him. Badger Boy had grown strong for his age, able to exact a painful price from anyone tempted to taunt him because of his light-colored skin and blue eyes. Seldom anymore did anyone try.

So far as Steals the Ponies could determine, the lad had forgotten his white past, his blood parents, even the white man's language. He was as Comanche-born.

Steals the Ponies said, "I promise that when you are ready I will take you on a raid deep into the white men's country, and you will have many horses."

"I am ready now."

Warily eyeing the horizon for sign of anyone on horseback, Steals the Ponies rode across what had been the ranger warrior society's camp. The corrals remained as he remembered. He had stolen horses out of them more than once. Now they were empty, the gates sagging open. Where the ranger tepees had stood, he found only square areas of hard-packed earth.

Wolf Eyes suggested, "Perhaps you are mistaken. This may not be the place."

"It is the place. I have taken ponies from this corral while the rangers slept."

The two warriors had made their way here by the light of the moon, skirting the nearby settlement. He had no wish to stir up the white men and set them into pursuit. This was only a mission of discovery. Clearly, the rangers had evacuated the camp. But where had they gone? Surely they had not been killed off, for word would have spread like wildfire sweeping the prairies under a dry west wind. He suspected their removal had something to do with the end of the white men's war, but it was unlikely the rangers had abandoned their war against The People.

The last attempted raid had shamed him in the eyes of the camp. Though outnumbered, rangers had caught the warriors by surprise and routed them ingloriously. He and his followers had been forced back across the river empty-handed, with fewer horses than when they had started. The failure still rankled. Like Wolf Eyes, he itched for redemption. But unlike his companion, he could be patient when patience was called for.

Wolf Eyes suggested, "If the rangers are gone, it will be easier for us. There will be no one to keep us from going among the settlements and taking the farmers' horses."

Steals the Ponies was not so confident. Perhaps the rangers had relocated to a larger camp. If the white men were no longer fighting among themselves, more might choose to join the struggle to drive The People onto the reservation. It appeared obvious that they intended to take over all the old hunting grounds and either violate the earth with their steel-pointed plows or chase off the buffalo and substitute their spotted cattle. Such a thing was a blasphemy too profane to be tolerated.

Wolf Eyes asked, "What do you want to do?"

"We shall find if the rangers have truly left

or if they are still somewhere around. You have been telling me you want to take horses. You saw those that graze near the white men's houses?" He pointed in the direction of the settlement that was Fort Belknap.

"There did not seem to be even a guard."

"We shall rest in the timber until night. Then we shall take the horses and see if the rangers come after us. If they do not, we will know they are no longer anywhere near."

"And if they are not?"

"Then when the grass is cured and the moon is full, we shall come back. We shall take all the horses we want and show the hair-faced *teibos* that this land belongs to The People."

CHAPTER 8

It had been a long, wearisome walk for Pete Dawkins and his friend Scully. They had quietly taken leave of their company in the middle of the night without bothering to notify the officer in charge. Pete had seen no reason to disturb the captain's sleep. Everybody had been mourning the loss of the war, declaring the Confederacy crushed, complaining that no one was going to be paid what was due him. Pete saw no reason to stay around for formalities or to surrender to some damned Yankee outfit. For all he knew, the defeated Confederate soldiers might be herded into a prison camp. If he had been willing to go to prison he would not have joined the army in the first place.

He and Scully had made a futile effort to liberate two horses from the officers' picket line but had found them too well guarded. He doubted that anyone would be shot for deserting a collapsing army, but they might be shot for trying to get away with someone else's horses. The two had made their getaway afoot, hoping for better luck somewhere along the road. Pete had always felt that luck was not a matter of waiting for something good to happen on its own. A man made his own luck, grabbing whatever came to hand.

"Scully," he said, "do you remember that good little blaze-faced sorrel I had, the one we found just wanderin' around loose on the Tonkawa reservation?"

"I remember it like to've got us scalped."

"I sure wish I had that little horse now." Pete sat down at the side of the dusty wagon road, checking the soles of his shoes. "Got a hole wore almost through. I'd be about as well off barefooted." He removed the offending shoe and rubbed his foot. Its bottom was tender where the leather had worn thinnest.

Bad as they were, the shoes were no worse than the rest of his clothing. What once had been a gray uniform was now only a couple more rips away from being rags, stained, crusted with dried sweat and dirt. The knees were out of his loose-hanging trousers. Missed meals and loss of weight had caused him to punch a new hole in his belt so he could draw it tighter. The cuffs of his tattered shirt flopped open, the buttons gone.

He said, "You'd think somewhere we ought to be able to borry a couple of horses."

"Like we borrowed from the Tonkawas?"

A buyer had come along with genuine Yankee money in his pocket, and Pete had sold the horse. In his estimation it was too good an animal for a blanket Indian anyway. It had also been too good for the buyer, but Pete had been unable to track him and steal the sorrel back, though he tried.

Scully grunted. "Horses seem awful scarce around here. Reckon the war took up all anybody could spare."

"I'd settle for a hog-backed mule if I could get off of my feet for a while."

Pete had worried little about pursuit, even before they crossed out of Louisiana into Texas two days ago. He had seen many Confederate soldiers straggling along the roads, trying to make their way home. Nobody seemed to question whether or not they had deserted their companies. An army had to be fed, and the Confederacy seemed unable to continue doing that. Better that the men scatter and try to take care of themselves. That was Pete's opinion anyway, and lots of Texans seemed to share it.

Opinion was about all most of them had left to share.

Pete and Scully had been able to shoot enough game for at least a bare subsistence. True, it was hard to fill up on squirrel, and it became tiresome day after day, but it was better than starving. Yesterday afternoon they had managed to catch a farmer's fat shoat without attracting attention. They had feasted last night on roast pork several miles beyond the farm where the shoat had come from. The meat was gone now, and Pete was hungry again.

"You'd think somebody would take pity on a couple of soldiers who went and done the fightin' for them," he complained. "Ain't nobody offered us nothin'."

"Don't look to me like anybody's got much *to* offer us. This whole country's poor as a whippoorwill."

"Their own damned fault for startin' the war." Pete had no high-flown notions about the glory of the Confederacy. He and Scully had not joined the fight out of loyalty and patriotism. Pete's father, Old Colonel Caleb Dawkins, had given them no real choice after they were caught with stolen horses, some of them his own.

The memory still rankled Pete, still roused him to occasional fits of anger when he let himself dwell upon the old man's grim ultimatum. As an alternative to prison, Caleb Dawkins had sent Pete and Scully to become targets for Yankee guns.

"Redeem yourselves," he had declared. "Expiate your guilt by serving your country."

Pete had developed an elemental survival strategy. Any time the guns sounded, he fell into a ditch or crawled up against protective trees or a stone wall. He would remain there, his head down, until the firing stopped. Be damned if he intended to die for someone else's grand cause. His only loyalty, his only obligation was to Pete Dawkins.

After resting awhile, the two men resumed their weary westward march. Pete was not sure just where they were, but the wagon road showed every sign of being well used. Surely it must lead to someplace where opportunity awaited a man keen enough to recognize it.

Scully wiped sweat from his face onto his tattered sleeve. "Reckon we'll live to reach your daddy's farm?"

"We'll get there."

"If he's still down on us like the last time we seen him, we may wish we'd gone someplace else."

"I worked like a nigger on that farm when I was a boy. The old man owes me for that. And he owes us both for packin' us off to the army over nothin' more than a few broomtails we borried from him. I figure to collect, then move on west."

"Collect what? If he's like everybody else we've seen, he's got the seat hangin' out of his britches. Probably couldn't buy us a pint of whiskey if it was ten cents a gallon."

"I know better. Bad as he hated the Union, I know he buried a bucket of Yankee gold and silver under the woodpile back of the house. Seen him myself when he didn't think anybody was lookin'. That'll spend right handy when me and you get to California."

"You think he'll just stand there and let you take it? He's got the temper of a sore-footed badger. We was with him when he hanged them Monahans, remember? A meaner-eyed son of a bitch I never seen, even if he is your daddy. I think he might be just a little bit crazy."

Sometimes Pete wondered why he put up with Scully. His partner was always asking questions, always expressing doubts even when everything appeared clear as crystal. Someday, when he didn't need him anymore, Pete would ride away and leave him afoot to manage on his lonesome. Like as not, Scully would wind up in jail before the chickens went to roost.

Just at dusk they trudged into the edge of a small farming town. Pete saw no sign bearing its name, but the name did not matter. A town was a town. He observed a tired-looking woman bent over a washboard and tub. Behind her, wet clothes hung on a line, flapping in the evening breeze. He guessed she was a professional washerwoman. A regular housewife should have finished her family wash earlier in the day unless she had a terribly large family.

Pete said, "Late as it is, them clothes won't be dry enough to take in the house before dark. Ought to be somethin' there that'll fit us."

"They don't look like much."

"They're better than what we've got on. We'll circle back this way after a while."

"How far do you think we'd get, afoot like we are?"

"Maybe when we leave here we won't be afoot."

"Takin' other people's horses is what got us into the army in the first place."

"And it'll get us away from here. Stay close to me and maybe you'll learn somethin'."

"I learned a lot the last time."

From up the street Pete heard singing. He thought at first it might be from a saloon, and the thought made him thirsty. But he soon realized the music was not the kind that went with whiskey. Lamplight spilled from the open windows of a frame church. Several horses were tied on the street outside, along with a few buggies and wagons.

Scurry quickly surmised what was going through Pete's mind. "Stealin' horses is bad enough, but from a church?"

Pete smiled. "Now, where would you find more cheerful givers than in a church house?"

Scurry followed, as he always did. Pete made a hasty choice for himself and pointed to another for Scurry. "That saddle may be big for you, but you'll grow into it when we start eatin' regular again." He tightened the cinch, for the owner had loosened it to let the horse breathe more easily during the services. He mounted and jerked his head. "Come on, we don't want to be hangin' around here when the sermon is over."

"*Hangin'?* That's apt to be the outcome if they catch us."

"Ain't nobody goin' to. Dark as it is, they won't have any idea whichaway we went.

185

Let's go back and get us them clothes."

Pete was glad to find that the woman had gone into the house. Even with the help of distant lamplight, it was difficult to see the clothes and judge their size. To improve the odds, Pete picked a couple of shirts and two pairs of trousers. They were still damp. He laid them across the pommel in front of him. "Hurry up. Don't be so damned picky."

There would be time to change clothes when they were well away from town. "Let's be movin'," he said, "and put this town behind us before they take up collection down at the church house."

The Dawkins farm lay just ahead. Much as he might deny it, Pete had begun looking forward to seeing it again. He had been in his early teens when Old Colonel had built the big house. It was often an unhappy place, but home nevertheless. His father sometimes treated him as if he were a black slave in the fields. His protective mother, on the other hand, had tried to shelter him and ease his wounded pride when she thought the colonel had been too harsh. He learned early how to manipulate her. He was never able to manipulate his father.

Caleb Dawkins had been brought up to believe in supplementing the sermon with the lash. He bore scars from his own boy-hood and visited their like upon his son. He believed in bending the twig in the direction he wanted the tree to grow. But Pete had thwarted him. He grew in his own direction.

The nearer they came to the house, the more nervous Scully became. Some of that nervousness was contagious, but Pete would not acknowledge it for a hundred dollars in Yankee silver.

Pete tried to ease Scully's fears. "Who knows? He may even kill the fatted calf."

"More likely he'll meet us with a shotgun. It near tore the heart out of him to admit what you done."

"What *we* done. You was mixed up in it as deep as I was."

"But it was your idea."

"We're stayin' just long enough to get us a fresh outfit and maybe some better horses. And to dig up that can of gold and silver from under the woodpile."

"He may have dug it up already."

"He's too tight. He'd let it lay there and rust before he'd spend it. I'm takin' it for all the work I done on this place and never got paid for."

"What if he puts up a fight?"

"He's an old man, and I'm tougher than

when I went into the army. I can whip him."

"You didn't talk this brave the last time."

Pete gave Scully an angry look. Scully was getting too free with his mouth. One of these days he was liable to earn himself a good stomping. That would teach him to stay in his proper place. "I'll handle the old man, don't you worry yourself about that."

In truth, Pete had no idea what the reception would be or how he would react to it. He thought he would try being politely formal. That would please his mother and make her easy to handle. It might be unexpected enough to keep the old man off balance as well. If it did not work, military service had taught Pete a few things, like standing up for his rights so long as that stand did not put his life in jeopardy. He knew there was a time to be bold and a time to back away. He could always try boldness if being polite did not disarm Old Colonel.

One of the slaves came out from the barn and stared in surprise. "Marse Pete? Can that be you?"

"Sure as hell is, Jethro." Pete dismounted and held out the reins for the servant to take. It occurred to him that by order of the Union government Jethro was no longer a slave. It was possible no one had told him, certainly not the colonel. Pete could not imagine Jethro or any other slaves staying around here under the Dawkins thumb if they had an alternative. "Is the colonel up at the house?"

Jethro nodded solemnly. "He stays up there a right smart anymore, since old missus died."

The news struck Pete hard. The words came painfully and sounded like the croaking of a frog. "Mama's gone?"

"Taken to her bed last winter and never got up again."

Scully said, "Damn, Pete, but that's tough."

Pete turned and leaned against his horse, trying to get his emotions under control. Maybe the colonel had written him a letter but he had never received it. Or, just as likely, the stubborn old bastard hadn't even tried.

The first rush of grief passed, and anger took its place. Pete clenched his fist. If his suspicion was correct, he had found one more reason to hate his father.

He turned back to Jethro. "Ain't nothin' wrong with the colonel, I suppose?" He hoped there was.

"He's down in his mind, what with old missus dyin' and the war bein' lost. But he's a strong man. He'll do a lot better, seein' as you've come home."

Don't bet on it, Pete thought. More than likely he'll throw a conniption fit.

"Put our horses up for us, Jethro. We're goin' to the house." He walked away without looking back, knowing the servant would obey and Scully would follow. He held his gaze on the open front door, wondering if the colonel had seen him and would come to meet him. He halfway hoped for a cordial reception, though he knew it was unlikely.

He was right. He stepped through the door and stopped a moment, letting his eyes adjust to the near-dark interior. The drapes were drawn, but he could see the colonel seated in the parlor, his huge bearlike body completely filling his favorite chair. Holding a glass of whiskey, the colonel stared at him with eagle eyes that offered no sign of welcome. As always, his was a formidable presence. Pete had seen strong men shake when the colonel confronted them.

Despite his intention of taking a strong initiative, Pete felt his face warming, his heartbeat quickening.

Damn it to hell, he was still a little afraid of the old man. He hoped the colonel could not see it.

Pete walked up almost within touching distance, trying to muster voice to speak.

Caleb Dawkins spoke first, in a tone like a pronouncement of doom. "You back legally, or did you just run away?" Dawkins's scowl matched his voice.

"The Confederacy is breakin' up. Wasn't no use stayin' around for the funeral."

"I'm surprised you didn't try to run away sooner and get yourself shot for desertion."

Pete had a sinking feeling. He had hoped his father might have softened a bit. Clearly, he was still the same bull-headed son of a bitch he had always been. "I didn't know about Mama. You ought to've written to me. I'd have come."

"If you hadn't been a horse thief, you'd have been here to start with." The colonel's gaze went to Scully for only a second, then back to Pete. "I see you're still runnin' with the same trash as before."

Scully took a step backward, toward the door. Pete summoned enough nerve to command, "Stand firm, Scully. We've got a right to be here." He surprised himself a little. Emboldened, he stepped to the small table beside the colonel's chair and picked up the bottle of whiskey from which Dawkins had filled his glass. Pete tipped it and took a long swallow. "You used to buy a better brand of bourbon."

Dawkins said, "How would you know? I

never gave you any."

"I took it when you wasn't lookin'."

"Like you took my horses." Dawkins finished what was in his glass and set it down. "Where do you plan to go from here?" The implication was plain enough: he did not intend for Pete to remain.

That stiffened Pete's stubborn streak. "What makes you think I figure on goin' anywhere?"

"I don't intend to let you stay here."

"I'll stay if I decide I want to. Me and Scully both."

"I'll have the law on you."

Pete thought he sensed a weakness in the colonel's voice. It was time to play his trump card. "It's pretty soon goin' to be Yankee law, and I don't think you'll want it pokin' into what happened over at the Monahan farm. Me and Scully was there, remember?"

Colonel Dawkins tried to stare Pete down, but he was the first to pull his gaze away. He went to the whiskey bottle and refilled his glass. He drank most of it in one huge swallow. "We did the patriotic thing. Those Monahans were traitors."

"Not the way the Yankee law will see it. You sure won't want to stand in front of a Yankee judge and jury while me and Scully tell what happened."

"You can't testify against me without implicating yourselves."

"They got a word for it. *Coercion,* I think it is."

For the first time Pete could remember, he had his father pinned against the wall. He could see conflicting emotions in the old man's eyes: resentment, defiance, fear.

He declared, "Like I said, we're stayin' if we want to. The way I figure it, this farm is part mine. When you're gone, it'll all be mine."

Defiance won out, but not by a wide margin. The colonel's eyes crackled with anger. "Stay and be damned. But keep out of my sight."

"This farm ain't *that* big. You'll be seein' a lot of me. And every time you see me, remember the way you treated me when I was a boy and couldn't defend myself. I ain't a boy no more."

Dawkins met Pete's gaze, and this time he held it. "If I didn't know how good a woman your mother was, I'd wonder if you were truly my son."

"Take a hard look, because your face is a lot the same as mine. I'm yours, and I've decided I can be just as stubborn mean as you are. I worked and sweated like a field hand to make you wealthy, and now I'm claimin' my share." Pete jerked his head at Scully. "Come on. I'm takin' my old room back."

Later he had Jethro muster three of the hands and led them to the woodpile behind the big house. "You-all throw all that wood over here," he said, pointing to an open piece of ground. When the wood had been moved, he dug the toe of his shoe into the soft earth. "Grab your shovels and start diggin'."

Scully stood by with hands on his hips. "You sure you remember just where the colonel buried that bucket of money?"

"I'll remember it to my dyin' day."

Scully motioned toward the back porch. Colonel Dawkins stood there, staring. "This could *be* your dyin' day. I do believe that old man'd shoot you, son or not."

"There was a time he would've, but somethin's been took out of him. Maybe it's losin' the war, or maybe it's losin' Mama, I don't know. He acts as mean as ever, but look in his eyes and you'll see he ain't the man he was."

"I looked in his eyes, and they still scared me."

The hole was four feet deep when a field hand's shovel struck a rock. He raised up, sweat rolling down his face. "Ain't nothin' more down here."

Pete's confidence began to waver. Scully said, "Maybe your memory ain't as good as you thought it was."

Pete reluctantly admitted, "Maybe I missed it a foot or two. Dig the hole out wider, thisaway."

At last Colonel Dawkins stepped down from the small back porch and strode out to where the woodpile had been. He challenged Pete, "You think you're mighty smart, but you're making a fool of yourself."

"The hell I am. I saw you myself, buryin' a whole bucketful of Yankee money. I figure by rights it's mine because of all the work I done around here for nothin'."

"You're several months too late. I already dug it up."

Pete felt as if an ax handle had struck him across the stomach. "What did you do with it?"

"I gave it to the cause. The Confederacy needed it to buy guns in Mexico."

Pete wanted to believe his father was lying, but he knew instinctively that he was not. Though the old man would not have spent that money on himself or any of his family, he would squander it on a lost cause. "You fool! You damned old fool!"

Triumph glowed in Caleb Dawkins's eyes. "When I saw the men start digging, I knew why you wanted to stay. You weren't content just to steal horses from me. You were going to steal my money too. Well, now there's nothing here for you except a lot of hard work. So, when are you leaving?"

Pete gritted his teeth. "That'd tickle you plumb to death, wouldn't it? But this country owes me, and one way or another I'm goin' to collect. If not from you, then from anywhere and anybody I can." He turned angrily on Jethro. "Fill that hole up before somebody falls in it."

Scully said, "It looks like a grave to me."

The Colonel walked back into the house. Pete kicked a clod of dirt and broke it into a dozen pieces.

Scully said, "Seems like there ain't much use in us stayin' around here."

"At least we got a roof and beds and somethin' to eat. And I've found out the old dog barks loud but ain't got any teeth left. So we'll stay. Even a blind hog finds him an acorn now and then."

"We ain't blind hogs."

"So there's no tellin' what acorns we may find."

CHAPTER 9

Every day or two, tired and hungry ex-soldiers stopped by Rusty's farm. Most had not been released officially. They had simply declared themselves finished with war and had struck out on their own without a by-your-leave. They were ragged, hungry, and afoot, too proud to ask outright for a meal but grateful for anything offered. Some were making their way to homes farther along. Some had found that they no longer had a home and were looking for a place where they might start afresh. Open country to the west offered land almost free for the taking if a man were willing to accept the challenge of low rainfall, few neighbors, and the risk of Indian raids.

No matter where they came from, the refugees carried essentially the same reports. Hard times had fallen upon Texas with a vengeance. Confederate money would buy nothing, and Yankee money had long ago been spent. Commerce, what little there was, had to be conducted on a barter basis. Local governments were for the most part in a state of collapse.

Rusty gave what he could to the transients, grateful not to be among them. The cabin was reserved for Clemmie Monahan and her two younger daughters. Rusty and Grandpa Vince Purdy slept beneath a shed out beside the barn. Soldiers were welcome to spend the night beneath that roof. If they were too tired to go on, they were given welcome to stay and rest.

At least there was food. The spring-planted garden was yielding vegetables. Beef was plentiful and without monetary value because cattle had run free and mostly unclaimed during the war, multiplying without limits beyond those imposed by drought and the available grazing.

Rusty listened with interest to the soldiers' stories. They reminded him of tales Daddy Mike Shannon had brought home from the fighting in Mexico. Names and faces were different, but the recent war seemed much the same as the one before, bloody, frightening, and often maddeningly futile.

"Seemed sometimes like the generals was just playin' a game, and they used us soldier boys like checker pieces," said one veteran, his face scarred by an exploding shell. Using a broken-off stick, he drew a circle in the dirt at his feet and punched a hole in the center. "This here'd be a gun emplacement. We'd run the Yankees off from it, then they'd build up a little stronger and chase us back. We'd drive them away again, like a bunch of schoolboys playin' tag. Then the officers would decide we didn't need the position anyway, and they'd move us someplace else. Long as we cost the Yankees more than they cost us, the generals seemed satisfied. I never seen many of *them* bleed."

"Hell of a way to run a war," Rusty sympathized. "It was a lot that way with us rangers and the Indians. We'd cut them off and chase them back across the Red River. Then they'd get together and come again when they were ready. Nothin' ever got settled for good. Still hasn't."

The soldier's eyes seemed haunted, his hair and beard grayer than his years would justify. Rusty blamed the war for that.

Clouds had built black and threatening. Lightning streaked. A loud clap of thunder startled the soldier so that he ducked and whirled around. Sheepishly he apologized. "I didn't go to act like an old woman. I still see Yankees under every bush."

"They haven't found us out here yet." But

they would, Rusty knew. It was only a matter of time before the Federal government would send soldiers and civilian regulators past the forks of every creek, to the end of the last wagon track.

The soldier worried, "When they do, they ain't apt to look kindly on us old rebel boys. Especially after what happened to Lincoln."

It was said that Lincoln had been urging leniency toward the beaten Confederates. Now, in the bitter aftermath of his assassination, it was widely speculated that the proponents of vengeance would take over, that the Southern states were in for harsh retribution.

Rusty said, "Nothin' much we can do except wait and see. I just hope the war doesn't start all over again."

"I ain't waitin' to see. I'm travelin' west 'til I can soak my sore and achin' feet in the Pacific Ocean. And if I can catch me a boat, I may go all the way to China. Everything around here has been stood on its head. You know you got a neighbor that was a slave? Face blacker than the ace of spades, and now he owns a farm."

"That'd be Shanty. Sure, I know."

"I spent last night at his place. Treated me kind, he did. Even said 'sir.' But I was glad to get away from there without any trouble.

I know some hard-headed old boys back home who wouldn't hold still for such as that. I wouldn't want to be there when they come callin'."

"Everybody around here has known Shanty for years. They won't bother him."

"Maybe you don't know everybody around here as well as you think. I ran into an old man on the road, name of Gaskin. When I told him where I'd spent the night, he fell into a cussin' fit."

"Fowler Gaskin is all wind. Nobody listens to him."

"Well, you know your neighbors. I don't. If I was that Shanty, though, I'd sleep with one eye open."

Rusty remembered Tom Blessings's misgivings when Isaac York had dictated his will.

Maybe I'd best go talk to Tom the first chance I get, and make sure there's nothing going on that I haven't heard about, he thought.

He had known the Monahan family would not remain indefinitely. They had come seeking refuge from Caleb Dawkins's violent fanaticism. That danger had ended with the war. For a while Clemmie had been saying they should soon return to their own farm to piece together whatever remnants they could find of their past lives. Each time Rusty saw her step out onto the dog run and look hopefully to the northwest, he knew she was looking for her son James.

It was raining the night he came. Rusty had been watching the darkening clouds during the afternoon, fearing they might pass over without shedding a drop, or at least more than a light shower. But weather was unpredictable. Drought or flood, anything was possible. The farmer's life was always subject to the vagaries of wind, rain, and sunshine.

Coming in from the field, he saw the two girls harvesting vegetables in the garden, holding them in their aprons, carrying them to baskets set at the end of the rows. Sometimes their sudden appearance caught him off guard and gave him a start, making him think of Geneva. Especially Josie, who looked the most like her older sister. Josie came to meet him at the garden gate, her long hair blown by the wind.

She said, "Looks like we're fixin' to get a frog-stranglin' rain. We thought we'd better gather what we could."

"I'll pitch in and help you."

Josie smiled. "We'd like that."

An hour or so later they were seated at

the supper table. The cabin door had been closed against the damp wind that came with the rain. It was suddenly flung open, and James Monahan stood there, his clothes dripping water. Lightning flashed in the sky behind him, making him look like some malevolent apparition.

Clemmie jumped up so quickly she overturned her chair. She kicked it aside in her eagerness to reach her son. Shouting with joy, she threw her arms around him, oblivious to the fact that his clothing was soaked. The girls hugged him when their mother stepped back. Old Vince Purdy grabbed James's hand and pumped it vigorously.

Clemmie said, "We been prayin' for this day."

James said, "I wish you'd prayed for dry weather. My wagon like to've bogged down, and I'm wet to the hide." His gaze drifted to Rusty. A little of his old reserve remained, but he shook Rusty's hand. "I do appreciate you givin' the folks a place to live for so long."

Rusty shrugged. "The whole outfit might've dried up and blowed away if they hadn't been here. They took good care of things while I was away."

"I'm glad you got past the brush men all right. Some of them turned kind of peevish when they found out you'd slipped away."

"How was that Oldham boy when you left camp?"

"Alive but not kickin' much. His brother wanted me to tell him where you live. I told him I thought it was somewhere over on the Trinity River." That would be a long way from the Colorado.

"Thanks. I don't want any more trouble with them. I wasn't lookin' for the trouble I already had."

Clemmie did not know what they were talking about, or care. She demanded of her son, "The war's been over for a right smart while. Where've you been all this time?"

"Up at our old place, helpin' Geneva and Evan build you a new house. It's finished, Mama, and waitin' for you." He looked at his sisters and grandfather. "For all of you, any time you're ready to go."

Clemmie clasped his hands. "We've been ready for the longest time." She looked apologetically at Rusty. "This place has been good to us, and Rusty's been more than generous. But it ain't the same as home."

"The new house ain't as fine as the one Caleb Dawkins burned down, but it'll keep the rain off of your head."

She asked, "Is the old cabin still standin',

or did Caleb Dawkins go back and burn it?"

"It's still there, such as it is. Geneva and Evan been livin' in it." James peeled off a wet jacket and hung it on a peg. "Have you heard from Geneva lately?"

Clemmie shook her head. "Ain't been any mail since I don't know when."

"She's in a family way. Goin' to make a grandmother of you before the snow flies."

Rusty swallowed hard, then walked out onto the dog run, watching rain pound the hard-packed ground and run-off water move in small brown rivulets down toward the swelling creek. He stopped beneath the edge of the roof and felt the wind-blown spray wetting his face. He shook, suddenly cold, and wished the rain could wash away the grief that came with the slow dying of old dreams.

He was still on the dog run, sitting on a bench, when James finished his supper and came out to join him. James stood beside him, looking out into the rain.

Rusty said, "Back there in that brush camp you could've told me Geneva was married."

"I never got around to it. We had other things pressin' on us, remember? And pretty soon you were gone."

"I never thought but what she'd wait for me."

"She hadn't heard from you in a long time. For all she knew, you were dead."

"I wrote to her. The letters never got through."

"You ought to've found a way to come and see her, even if you had to desert the rangers. But you didn't, and Evan came along, lookin' like he was fixin' to die. Geneva cared for him like a nurse. You know how it is, a man and a woman together so much. You weren't here, and he was. Nature just took its course."

Rusty doubled a fist. The war, the damned war. It had cost everybody far too much.

James argued, "Evan works hard, he loves her, and he makes her smile. For a long time she didn't have much to smile about."

"The war was hell on everybody, even those who never went to it. Sooner or later, it came to *them*."

An old bitterness pinched James's eyes. "The Monahans sure suffered their share."

"It may be hard on Clemmie, goin' back where so many sorrowful things happened."

"It'll pass. She's got a will like an iron hammer." James started toward the kitchen door but stopped. "Your feelin's for Geneva will pass too, if you'll let them."

Rusty felt a deep ache. "I'd figured on askin' her to marry me."

"When a man really wants to do somethin', he'd ought to go ahead and do it. Time has a way of takin' things away from you if you wait too long."

"So I've found out."

"I used to lay awake nights, thinkin' about killin' Caleb Dawkins. But I decided that was too quick and easy for what he done, so I'm lettin' him wait and sweat over what I'm goin' to do and when I'm goin' to do it."

"What *are* you goin' to do?"

"Nothin', just let him worry himself to death. That way the revenge will last longer."

James went back into the kitchen side of the cabin. In a little while Josie came out. Her shoulders were slumped, her eyes downcast.

Rusty said, "I thought you'd be happier, seein' your brother."

"He's come to take us home."

"That's what you've been waitin' for, isn't it?"

"It's what Mama's been wantin', and Alice and Grandpa. But I like it here."

"Nothin' is as good as home."

"Too much happened there, too many bad things. Everything here has been good, 'til

207

now." She turned toward him, her eyes sad. At this moment she looked more than ever like Geneva. "You don't want us to leave, do you, Rusty?"

"I've got used to havin' you-all on the place. It'll be lonesome when everybody is gone. But I guess it had to happen sometime."

"I'd rather stay here. You'll need somebody to cook for you and sew and keep the garden."

Rusty smiled indulgently. "I'm afraid Clemmie would never stand still for such as that. You a young woman, me a man . . . it'd give folks an awful lot to gossip about."

"It wouldn't be anybody's business."

"That's when people *really* talk, when it's none of their business."

Presently James and his grandfather returned to the dog run. The rain seemed to be slacking off. That suited Rusty. He had rather not have so much that it drowned out part of the field.

James said, "First thing come mornin', me and Grandpa will start gatherin' up our horses."

When the Monahan women and Vince Purdy had moved to Rusty's place to wait out the war, they had brought their band of mares with them. Unattended at the deserted Monahan home place, the whole bunch would have disappeared in short order. As it was, their numbers had increased.

Purdy said, "Young'un, you got no idee how much trouble we had holdin' on to them. Army horse buyers kept sniffin' around, worse than the Indians. They'd offer Confederate scrip that everybody knowed wasn't worth a bucket of cold spit. At least the Comanches never bothered tryin' to lie to us. They just taken what they could find and went on their way."

Purdy tamped tobacco into his pipe. "Me and Clemmie let the buyers take a few snides now and again, but we managed to keep the best of the bunch hid out to the west of here. We'd go to talkin' about Indians, and no government people ever got the nerve to venture that far."

Rusty said, "I've seen where most of the mares are runnin'. I'll help you round them up."

James nodded. "You've got work of your own to do. But we'd be obliged."

Rusty said, "And I'll help you move your folks back home. I'll go along with you."

"We couldn't impose on you that far."

Rusty said, "I'm thinkin' of the risk. Don't you think it was kind of dangerous, you comin' down here all by yourself?"

"Durin' the war I traveled by myself a-plenty of times to visit the folks, and I had conscript officers and sheriffs lookin' to catch me. Now I don't have to fret about them no more."

"There's always a chance of runnin' into Indians."

"Done that too. I always had a faster horse than they did."

"This time you came in a wagon. What if you-all ran across Indians on your way home? You couldn't outrun them. How long would you last in a fight, just two men and three women?"

"Long enough to do them some damage." But Rusty could tell by James's expression that he was struggling with new doubts.

James said, "One more man *would* help the odds. If you think this farm can get along without you, we'd be tickled to have you come with us."

"The fields are goin' to be too wet to work anyway."

The younger of the girls rode with her mother on the wagon James had brought. Josie rode on horseback alongside Rusty and her brother James, driving the mares, colts, and a bay stallion. Vince Purdy drove a second wagon piled high with family belongings. It was one the Monahans had brought with them when they fled Caleb Dawkins.

Rusty had not heard of any Indian incursions in a while, but the possibility could never be dismissed. Another potential problem was the defeated ex-soldiers straggling across the country. Most were harmless, but some were hungry, frustrated, and desperate enough to do almost anything. Tom Blessing had told Rusty about a couple of murders supposedly committed in the course of robbery.

He would deny it even to himself, but one reason he had volunteered to join the Monahans on this trip was that he burned to see Geneva. He realized that seeing her might hurt worse than *not* seeing her. Still, the compulsion was too strong to put down. He could rationalize that the family needed the extra protection his presence would afford, but in some secret corner of his mind he knew that was not his primary reason for going.

He caught James studying him critically, and he suspected Geneva's brother saw into that secret corner.

The first day passed without incident. The mares and colts had to be held back, limited by the lumbering pace of the wagons. They would move well ahead, then the riders would stop and loose-herd them to graze until the wagons caught up.

Josie rode a sidesaddle belonging to her mother. Rusty told her, "You sit real good on that thing."

"I rode with Grandpa Vince a lot, lookin' after the mares. 'Til Evan came, I was Grandpa's main outside help except when Preacher Webb stopped by, or James slipped past the law to spend a day or two with us."

Her face was deeply tanned, for she had spent a lot of time in the sun and wind. Rusty had seen her ride horseback and maneuver a plow, though he had noted that she knew her way around the kitchen too. A Texas farm woman — or girl — was expected to be able to work like a man without forgetting she wasn't one.

He said, "Looks to me like you can do whatever you set your mind to."

She grinned. "I was hopin' you'd see that."

Rusty saw cattle bearing the Monahan brand. He told James, "If cattle were worth cash money, you'd be in good shape."

James nodded. "I managed to slip back here now and again when nobody was lookin'. Gave me a chance to see after the cattle my family had to leave behind when they refugeed down to your farm."

"Looks like they increased."

"Cows didn't know there was a war on. Kept havin' calves every year. There's cattle runnin' wild over this country, no brands or earmarks, just waitin' for somebody to put a claim on them."

"They're not worth runnin' after."

"But one day they *will* be worth somethin'. I'm figurin' to burn a brand on as many as I can catch."

The procession was nearing the Monahan home place when Rusty saw two horsemen a few hundred yards ahead. The pair quickly moved into the cover of nearby brush.

Rusty turned. "James . . ."

"I saw them." Frowning, James rode quickly to his sister. "Josie, you get back with the wagons. Tell Mama and Grandpa to keep their eyes open. Be ready to run for that ravine yonder."

She nodded soberly. "Indians, you reckon?"

"We'll find out pretty soon. We'll hold the mares here 'til the wagons catch up."

Rusty and James brought the mares and colts to a stop but did not let them spread out to graze. Rusty drew his rifle from its scabbard and placed it in front of him. He watched the brush for movement.

It came, finally. As the wagons drew up even with the herded mares, the two riders emerged into the open. James squinted. "At least it ain't Indians."

Watching the horsemen's approach, Rusty relaxed his tight hold on the rifle. He did not place the weapon back into the scabbard.

Clemmie and Vince Purdy asked no questions, but Purdy had brought a rifle up from beneath his wagon seat. Clemmie held a big Colt Dragoon in her lap. It looked as if it might weigh a quarter as much as she did. She said, "Probably just a couple of soldiers lookin' for a meal. That's all right, as long as they ain't after anything else." She jerked her head toward Josie. "You stay close by me and your sister."

James had ridden out a little way to intercept the two riders before they reached the wagons. Rusty eased forward to join him.

James muttered a low oath. "Damn! Do you see who's comin' yonder?"

Rusty was unable to recognize either rider at the distance. James growled, "It's Caleb Dawkins's son."

"Pete? Last I knew of him, the old man sent him off to the army."

"Too bad some Yankee didn't get a clean

shot at him."

"I expect Pete was careful not to offer them much of a target."

Pete Dawkins reined up short, giving Rusty and James a diapproving scrutiny before he spoke. "Thought at first you-all might be Indians with stolen horses, wantin' to add ours to the bunch. Then we saw the wagons and knowed different. Now that I see who you are, I almost wish you *had* been Indians."

Rusty waited for James to speak, but James held silent, his eyes smoldering with an old hatred. Rusty said grittily, "We're glad to see you too."

Rusty recognized the second rider as Scully, who had been with Pete when the rangers caught them stealing horses. Pete hungrily studied the Monahan mares. The thought behind his eyes was easy to read.

He said, "People been tellin' me the country is near stripped of horses. That's a likely lookin' bunch of mares and colts you got."

James declared, "We've got them, and we're keepin' them."

"Ain't you afraid some slick-fingered Comanches might run off with them?"

Rusty said, "All the slick fingers don't belong to Comanches. I remember the day we caught you two with some horses you forgot to pay for."

Pete's eyes flashed resentment while his mouth curved into a forced smile. "An honest mistake. We misread the brands."

James said, "These all carry the Monahan brand, big enough for a blind man to see."

Scully had not spoken. He seemed content to let Pete do the talking. Rusty judged him to be a follower. He would follow Pete all the way to hell if that was the direction Pete chose to go. It probably would be, sooner or later.

Pete turned his attention to Rusty. "You still a ranger?"

"There are no rangers, as far as I know. The outfit broke up."

"Ain't that a shame!" Pete's smile turned genuine. "Won't be no laws around to beat up on us hard-workin' farm boys."

James patted the palm of his hand against the rifle across his lap. Malice was in his voice. "There's still guns, and there's still rope. You remember about rope, don't you, Pete?"

Pete's smile died as quickly as it had come.

James added, "Since we won't have any regular law, it'll be up to all of us to administer justice accordin' to our own lights. I remember the way the Dawkinses did it."

"You threatenin' me, Monahan?"

"Just lettin' you know I've got a long memory. Now, if you're through visitin', we've still got a ways to go."

Pete pulled aside, and Scully trailed after him like a pup. Rusty and James set the mares to moving. Rusty turned in the saddle, making certain Pete and Scully did not follow. "I didn't like the way Pete was lookin' at your horses."

"I liked it. First time he makes a try for them, he's liable to disappear off the face of the earth, and everybody'll wonder what went with him."

"Everybody but you?"

"Everybody but me."

"Maybe it's just as well I'm not a ranger anymore. I'd hate to be the one sent to take you in."

"I'd hate it too. I wouldn't like havin' you on my conscience."

CHAPTER 10

The Monahans' new house was simple, constructed of logs and built in the traditional double-cabin fashion with an open dog run between the sections, much like Rusty's own. Clemmie's reaction could not have been more enthusiastic if it had been the governor's mansion. She leaned forward on the wagon seat, straining to see better.

"We're home, children," she exclaimed to her daughters.

Josie sat on her horse beside Rusty's Alamo. She had contrived to ride near him most of the trip. She said, "We're not children. At least I'm not."

She was not, though Rusty thought she would probably always seem that way to her mother. She was blossoming into a handsome young woman.

Some of the older mares had seemed to perk up during the last miles of the trip.

They held their heads higher and quickened the pace.

James said, "They remember. They're glad to get back."

Vince Purdy had told Rusty a few mares had caused problems in the first weeks after the original move down to Rusty's farm. They kept trying to return north to what had been their home. They became accustomed to their new range after a time but evidently never forgot where they came from. One problem now, for a time at least, would be to keep younger mares from trying to return south to the Colorado River. Horses had been known to travel hundreds of miles, following their instincts to go back where they came from. Occasionally a horse stolen by Indians would escape and turn up at the home corral weeks or even months later.

Rusty looked hopefully toward the open dog run, thinking Geneva might walk out to greet her mother and sisters. He burned to see her. But the only person he saw was a man he realized must be her husband. Evan Gifford opened a corral gate to receive the mares, then strode toward the wagons with a hand raised in welcome.

Josie said, "You'll like Evan."

Rusty doubted it.

"You-all light and hitch," Gifford shouted. He raised his arms to help his mother-in-law, and then Alice, down from the wagon. Rusty studied him, hoping to find something to dislike but seeing nothing beyond the fact that he had won Geneva while Rusty was busy elsewhere. Gifford appeared to be about Rusty's own age. The effects of war showed in his face, in the seriousness of his eyes. A narrow scar across his right cheekbone could have resulted from a saber slash or a bullet.

If a bullet, Rusty thought, why could it not have been an inch farther in? He immediately felt guilty. Such a thought was unworthy of him. He wished no one dead, least of all a soldier who fought for his country.

Clemmie looked around worriedly. "Where's Geneva? There's nothin' wrong with her, is there?"

Gifford tried to reassure her, shaking his head. "She's in the cabin, takin' her rest. Been havin' some low days. Preacher Webb says it's normal, what with her condition."

Clemmie brightened. "Preacher's here?"

"In yonder with Geneva."

Clemmie turned toward the older structure in which Geneva and her husband had made their home. It had been the Monahan family's first dwelling years ago, replaced eventually by a larger house.

Gifford asked, "Don't you want to look at your new home first?"

"It'll still be there when I'm ready. I need to see after my daughter." Clemmie hurried through the door, calling, "Geneva, we're here." Alice trailed close behind.

Rusty helped Josie dismount from her sidesaddle. Smiling her appreciation, she clung to Rusty's arm longer than necessary, then followed her mother and sister.

Still on horseback, James followed the mares into the corral. Rusty waited a moment for the dust to settle, then closed the gate behind them. He heard Vince Purdy ask Gifford, "You sure Geneva's all right?"

"Preacher don't seem worried. A neighbor lady's been comin' over regular. Geneva'll do better now that she's got her family around her. She's missed them."

"And we've missed her," Purdy said. He went into the cabin.

Rusty offered a handshake. "I'm Rusty Shannon."

Gifford accepted the gesture without hesitation. "Pleased to meet you. Geneva and her folks have spoken of you. I already know a lot about you."

"I never knew about *you* 'til just a little

while back."

Rusty hoped his voice betrayed no resentment. His feelings were badly confused. He told Gifford, "Ever since I got home, Clemmie's been itchin' to get back here and pick up where she left off."

"Nothin' will ever be the same as it was, but she'll bow her neck and make the best of what there is. These Monahans are a strong-minded bunch."

"I know for certain that James is." Rusty looked toward Geneva's brother, still in the corral busily inspecting the mares. "We came across Pete Dawkins. He been by here, him or his daddy?"

"No, they've taken wide roundance of this place. James let it be known that he wasn't lookin' for trouble, but if any came at him he'd go meet it halfway. Everybody knew he was talkin' about the Dawkinses. I imagine the word got to them."

"Pete gave the mares a long and hungry look."

Gifford's eyes hardened. "If any turn up missin', me and James will know where to look first. And we'd better not find them there."

Rusty sensed that there was no false bravado in Gifford. He meant what he said. That was a strong point in his favor.

The hardness left Gifford's eyes. "I owe the Monahans a lot. You have any idea what it means not to have anybody, no family . . . nobody?"

Rusty felt a flicker of an old sadness. "I do. I've been there myself." Still am, he thought.

"The army sent me home, so shot up they thought I'd die. But I found I didn't have a home to go back to. Ma and Pa had both passed away. My only sister had sold the place. Then she took down with the fever, and she was gone too. I was like a lost child 'til the Monahans took me in. Nursed me like I was their own. Got me back on my feet."

"Old Colonel Dawkins had killed Lon and Billy. Like as not you filled an empty space for the family."

"They sure filled an empty space for *me*." Gifford looked away, trying to find the right words. "I have a notion you and Geneva were sort of close. Close enough for marryin'?"

"We never talked about that. Anyway, it was a long time ago, before you came. That's over and forgotten about." The lie almost choked him.

"I'd like to have you for a friend, Rusty,

but I'd need to know I've got no reason to worry."

"You don't." Though his heart was not in it, Rusty extended his hand again. Gifford took it, then beckoned with his head. "Come on, let's go in. Geneva's had time to say howdy to her folks by now."

The bedroom half of the cabin was separated from the kitchen side by an opening over which a common roof extended. Rusty followed Gifford through the narrow door. He steeled himself, not sure what his feelings would be when he saw Geneva.

She sat on the edge of a bed, tinier than he had remembered, though her stomach was visibly extended. Alice was brushing out Geneva's long hair. Clemmie and Purdy had pulled wooden chairs up close. Geneva's features were as fine as he remembered. He thought her face looked pale, but it was hard to be sure because the room was semi-dark. Rusty felt warmth rise in his face, and for a moment he wished he had not come.

She smiled at him. "Welcome back, Rusty." She extended her small hand. Hesitant to take it, he held it gently as if it were an eggshell. She seemed frail.

"You look mighty good," he said. He felt anew the aching sense of loss. It used to be easy to talk with her. Now he felt awkward, especially with her husband standing beside her. He saw a look of affection pass between the two and wished for some excuse to leave this crowded room. The air seemed close and hard to breathe.

She said, "Rusty, when I didn't hear from you for so long, I thought you were probably dead. We heard about some awful Indian fights."

"There were some rangers killed, but none of them were me." He realized too late how unnecessary that sounded.

For the first time he noticed Preacher Webb standing back in a corner. Rusty suspected Webb was aware of his discomfort, for after a minute the minister placed a hand on Rusty's shoulder. "It's been a while since I ministered to my flock down your way. I hope sin has not broken loose amongst the lambs."

"Not so much that a sermon or two wouldn't fix it."

"It's time I went back down there. I may ride with you when you're ready to go."

"It'd pleasure me to have your company."

Rusty turned back to Geneva. "I know you've got a lot of family visitin' to do. I'd best go see after my horse."

Geneva took his hand again. "Don't be in a hurry to leave."

He saw nothing to stay for. He had come mostly because of a compulsion to see her again. Now he had seen her, and it still hurt as badly as *not* seeing her.

The minister followed him out onto the dog run. He looked back to see if anyone might hear. "Maybe you oughtn't to've come. It's like pickin' at an old sore after it's healed over. Or *has* it healed?"

"One reason I came was to find out. And I guess it hasn't."

"There's times a man has got to turn loose of what's past, no matter how bad it hurts."

"I know. I'm leavin' here come daylight tomorrow mornin'."

"I'll ride with you, Rusty. It'll be like old times."

Nothing would ever again be like old times, but Rusty was grateful for whatever part of them he could salvage. He thought of the occasions in his youth when he had ridden with Warren Webb on the minister's preaching circuit. "I'd be tickled to have your company."

"I'd need to stop and deliver a couple of sermons along the way."

"A sermon or two might do me a world of good."

At breakfast, Clemmie expressed sorrow

about their leaving. Rusty suspected her distress was over Webb's departure more than his own. She said, "I do wish you-all wouldn't hurry away. We just barely got here."

Webb said, "Rusty's got work to do at home, and I've got sheep wanderin' around lookin' for their shepherd."

Clemmie took the minister's hand. "You've got a flock here that loves to see you come and hates to see you go." Almost as an afterthought she added, "You'll always be welcome too, Rusty. You made your home ours for a long time. Now our home is yours."

"I'm obliged." Rusty thought he would probably wait awhile. Maybe someday he could look at Geneva without aching inside.

He was tightening the cinch on his saddle when Evan Gifford came around from behind Alamo, looking for a chance to speak without anyone else hearing. "I know you're concerned about Geneva. So am I. But Preacher says he thinks she'll be all right. Says it's pretty much normal, bein' her first baby."

"Preacher's a good doctor."

Again, Gifford seemed to fish around for the words. "I can tell by the way you looked at her, there was a lot of deep feelin's. I want you to know that I love her . . . that I'll never hurt her . . . that she'll never have reason to shed a tear over anything I do."

Rusty swallowed hard. "Nobody could ask for more than that. I hope you both live for a hundred years, and every year is better than the one before it." He put out his hand and forced a weak smile. "She made a good choice."

Gifford walked away. Preacher Webb had come up in time to hear. He gave Rusty an approving nod. "I know it hurt to say that. It takes a strong man, sometimes, to recognize the truth and to speak it."

"Then let's be gettin' started while I'm still feelin' strong." Rusty put his foot in the stirrup and swung up onto Alamo's back.

Josie stood in the open gate. Rusty saw tears in her eyes. She said, "I wish you'd stay, but I know why you can't." She glanced back toward Geneva, who stood in the dog run of the older cabin.

He said, "I'll be back one of these days."

"I know you will, because one of these days I'm goin' to marry you, Rusty Shannon." She turned and hurried toward the new house.

Preacher Webb gave Rusty a quizzical look. Embarrassed, Rusty said, "She's too young to know her own mind."

Webb smiled. "She's a Monahan. Monahans are *born* knowin' their minds."

James and Vince had turned the mares out
of the corral at daybreak. Rusty and Webb
rode through them as they scattered, the
older mares seeking out remembered fa-
vored grazing places, the younger ones
exploring their new range. Rusty caught
sight of two horsemen a quarter mile away.
The pair were still.

Webb saw them too. He squinted hard.
"Maybe they're soldiers workin' their way
home."

Rusty could not see the men clearly
enough to recognize them, but he noted that
the horses were the same colors as those
Pete and Scully had been riding. "That'd
be Pete Dawkins and his runnin' mate.
Probably hatchin' a scheme to make a run
at the Monahan mares some dark night."

"Maybe we should go back and tell
James."

"James already knows. We ran into Pete
on our way up here."

"The Monahans have already suffered too
much at the hands of the Dawkins family."

"I have a notion it's the Dawkinses' turn
to suffer at the hands of James Monahan."

The people of the band knew him as Badger

229

Boy because he had a badger's belligerent response when other boys picked on him. And pick on him they had, in the beginning, for he seemed a misfit among those near his own age. His eyes were blue where theirs were brown or black, his skin lighter than theirs. He had found that the best way to stop others from bedeviling him was to hit back stronger than he was struck, resorting to a preemptive strike from time to time to keep his tormentors off balance.

Gradually they had learned to show him respect, though it was obvious that he had not been born of The People.

He had only hazy recollections of a time when he was not living among the Comanches. He was dimly aware, more from stories heard than from things remembered, that he had been taken in a raid on a *teibo* settlement when he was no more than four or five summers old. He remembered his Comanche father, known as Buffalo Caller. No one spoke that name anymore because it was the way of The People not to voice the names of the dead lest their spirits be disturbed.

He vaguely remembered a Texan father and mother. The years had all but erased any memory of what they looked like or anything they had said. Yet, buried somewhere deep in his consciousness was a faint memory of raw terror that came to him now and again as in a dream. He knew within reason that his white parents had been killed, for they would not otherwise have yielded him up. None of The People had ever told him anything of his origins. He sometimes wished he could recall more. That remembered fear rose up as a barrier, blocking him from probing deeper into the dark shadows of his past.

Buffalo Caller had taken him as a son but all too soon had died a warrior's death at the hands of the rangers. Steals the Ponies had shouldered the responsibility of becoming both brother and father to the boy. He had taught Badger Boy how to make a boy-sized bow and the arrows that went with it, how to ride, how to hunt. He had refined the youngster's fighting skills, though most had come instinctively as a defense against other boys tempted to taunt an outsider.

Now they stepped aside rather than face his fists, or sometimes a leather quirt or heavy stick, whatever he could lay his hands on. Older people often said within his hearing that he might well become the fiercest warrior of them all. But they added that he had to wait, to bide his time and get his full growth.

He thought he had waited long enough. He had listened to his brother and other young warriors make plans for a raid on the Texan settlements, and he wanted to go.

The thought seemed only to amuse Steals the Ponies. Condescendingly he pulled one of the boy's long braids. "Your legs are still too short. You could not keep up."

"But you will be riding, not walking. My legs are long enough for riding a war pony."

"A short-legged pony perhaps."

Badger Boy felt anger rising hot in his face. Steals the Ponies took the idea as a joke, but Badger Boy was in earnest. "I would not fall behind. If I do, you can leave me. I can find the way by myself."

"The Texans would laugh at us. They would say The People must have no warriors left if they bring a boy on a mission of war."

"I hear that Mexican Talker is going. He is not but this much taller than me." Badger Boy made a gesture with both hands to illustrate the small difference. Mexican Talker, like himself, had been brought into the band as a captive, taken as a boy in a raid on a Mexican village. He was dark-skinned and black-eyed, so that strangers looking upon him could easily assume he was Comanche by blood. Only when he spoke would they know otherwise, because he still had the accent of one who had learned another language first. Badger Boy had a bit of the same problem. A few words never came out quite the way he intended. People said it was because of his Texan birth.

"Mexican Talker is older than you. He has made his quest and found his medicine. No, Badger Boy, you must wait a while longer."

Badger Boy reluctantly conceded to himself that his brother would not allow him to ride out with the others when they invaded the white men's settlements. So Badger Boy began planning how he would slip out of the encampment and go anyway.

CHAPTER 11

It took Rusty somewhat longer to get home than he expected because Preacher Webb was much in demand along the way. Isolated settlers rarely had a chance to hear the gospel unless they read it themselves.

Clemmie Monahan had once said, "Others may know the words, but Preacher Webb knows the Master."

The two stopped for the night at the house of a farmer Rusty had met and Webb knew well. The farmer seemed overjoyed.

"Preacher, I been beggin' the Lord to send you, and damned if He didn't do it. I was afraid there wasn't a chance in hell . . ."

Webb's warm smile turned to a concerned frown. "Somebody sick?"

"No, nothin' like that. My daughter needs marryin'. Her young man come home from the army about a month ago. Now, she's a good girl, and all that. Me and her mama brought her up accordin' to scripture. But her and her feller hadn't seen one another in three years, and . . . well, I'm afraid they've done planted a crop, if you understand my meanin'. It'd be a shame for it to sprout before the bonds are tied right and proper."

Rusty saw that Webb was trying to suppress a smile. He could not control his own. He turned to brush Alamo's sweaty hide.

Webb said, "Don't think bad of them, Hank. Sometimes our human nature outwrestles our convictions. Back when preachers were a lot scarcer, I can remember performin' a marriage and then baptizin' the infant, both in one ceremony."

"It's only been a month, so it ain't gone too far. But I think the Lord would be a damned sight better pleased if you was to do it up accordin' to the Book."

"Would tonight be soon enough?"

"They'd sleep with an easier conscience. Me and Mama would sleep better, sure enough."

The farmer's wife lamented that her eldest daughter should be married in a church, with nice decorations and organ music, or at least a piano. The farmer declared, "Ain't no need for a lot of folderol when the horse has already got out of the stable."

That brought a sharp retort and an unspoken promise of retribution from the wife, but the farmer seemed unfazed. He sent the younger sons and daughters out to pick wildflowers. That, he said, was decoration enough. The ceremony, short and simple, was performed in the open dog run of the family cabin. Two of the bride's sisters sang a hymn, not well but with conviction.

Webb reached that part of the service in which he said, "If any man knows a reason why this couple should not be joined in holy matrimony, let him speak now or forever hold his peace."

The farmer looked around fiercely as if expecting someone to voice an objection. The only people present besides family were Webb and Rusty. Webb pronounced the couple man and wife.

The farmer grinned, finally. "Preacher, I hope you drawed that knot good and tight."

Webb watched the couple kiss. "When I marry them, the knot always holds."

Rusty had been impatient at first, wanting to leave, but now he relaxed and enjoyed the easy-going family atmosphere. It was evident that the new son-in-law was accepted into the circle, and that he felt secure in it. Rusty envied him. These people were not the Monahan family, yet they had much in common as frontier folk facing up to whatever hardships their isolated life imposed upon them and grateful for whatever small pleasures they managed to wring from it. If they had concerns about Indians, or about whatever changes might be imposed upon them as the Federals took over in Texas, they seemed able to put them aside and enjoy the amenities of the moment.

As he and Webb retired to their blankets beneath the wagon shed, Rusty said, "They seem like contented folks. I'd hate to see anything bust up what they've got here."

"People like these won't stay busted. Their ancestors fought their way across the Alleghenies and down through the old Southern states. This generation has made it all the way out to the far edge of Texas. They've been beaten down and some of them killed, but those that survived always got back on their feet. Time and again, they've stood shoulder to shoulder with the Lord and fought the devil to a standstill."

"I guess the key to it is family."

"And you're thinkin' you don't belong to one."

"All the family I ever had is gone."

"If you're just lookin' at blood, I don't have a family either. But all the people I minister to, all the friends I've made along my circuit, even the strangers I come across

. . . they're my family. They're kin because we've walked the same ground. We've shared the same experiences. Look at it that way, Rusty, and you'll see that you've got family too. A mighty big family."

"I wouldn't count Fowler Gaskin. Or the Dawkinses."

"Fowler's like the uncle nobody wants to claim, the one they forget to invite to family gatherin's. Caleb Dawkins thinks he hears the voice of God, but he's just talkin' to himself. Still, saint or sinner, they're all our brothers in the sight of the Lord."

The first thing Rusty noticed was that the weeds had gotten somewhat ahead of him. The second was that the mule Chapultepec did not come to the barn at the usual time.

"I guess he got used to me bein' gone," he told Webb. But morning came without the mule showing up. Rusty saddled Alamo and rode a wide circle without finding sign of the lost animal.

Webb said, "Maybe he's just strayed a little farther than usual. Mules have a way of knowin' what you want them to do, and they do the opposite."

Rusty remembered the Monahan milk cow. "Any time somethin' comes up missin' around here, I see the fine hand of Fowler

Gaskin. He probably got wind that I was gone. You've got to nail everything down tight to keep him from walkin' off with it."

Webb said, "I'll ride over there with you. The mood you're in, you may say or do somethin' you'll be sorry for afterwards."

"I've never spoken a cross word to Fowler that wasn't justified. But you're welcome."

They rode in silence, for they had exhausted just about all subjects for conversation on the long and often interrupted trip back from the Monahan farm. Passing Gaskin's field, Rusty saw that weeds threatened to choke the crops.

"If Fowler took my mule, he didn't use him to plow out his corn," he said. "Probably rode him to town to get whiskey."

"Don't condemn a man 'til you know he's guilty. Be tolerant."

"When it comes to rascals and thieves, I don't see where tolerance has got much place."

Rusty's first impression was that the old cabin leaned a little farther than the last time he had seen it, but he decided that was his imagination. Were it not for a couple of logs leaned up at an angle to brace one wall, it probably would have collapsed by now. Fowler Gaskin sat in a wooden chair beside the front door, a jug at his feet.

He started to arise, then sat down heavily as if his legs would not support him. He blinked, trying to clear his eyes. "You come makin' trouble again, Rusty Shannon? And who's that you got with you?" He blinked some more. "Oh, howdy, Preacher. Didn't know you right off. Sun got in my eyes."

Rusty did not waste time. "I come lookin' for my mule. You got him?"

Rusty's sharp tone brought an equally sharp reply. "You see him anywhere around here? I already got one old wore-out mule. What would I want with another?"

Webb spoke softly. "Rusty doesn't mean to accuse you, Fowler. He's just worried about Chapultepec. I don't suppose you've seen him wanderin' around?"

"Ain't seen him and ain't lookin' for him."

Gaskin's voice was relatively calm. Rusty thought the old man might be telling the truth, for once. Usually the guiltier he was, the more loudly he protested his innocence.

Gaskin reached down for the jug. He let the stopper fall from his hand but made no move to retrieve it from the ground. "You been over to the York place and asked that nigger Shanty?"

Rusty said, "No, you were the first one that came to mind."

"You're like your old daddy . . . always

quick to accuse a man." Fowler scowled. "I been tellin' everybody: there ain't nothin' safe around here as long as that Shanty stays amongst us."

"Shanty's never hurt anybody."

"No? Them niggers are always sneakin' around, stealin' whatever they can find. I'd bet a gallon of good whiskey that you'll find your mule over at his place."

"I don't believe Shanty would steal from me."

Gaskin dragged his sleeve across his mouth. "He may not be around here much longer to steal from *anybody.* I heard that some fellers rode over there last night to tell him he'd be a sight healthier somewheres else. It ain't fittin', a nigger ownin' a farm same as a white man."

Webb showed a sudden concern. "What fellers?"

"I ain't sayin'."

Rusty demanded, "Where were *you* last night?"

"You ain't a ranger no more. I don't have to tell you nothin'."

Rusty was instantly convinced that Gaskin had been with whomever had visited Shanty's place. "If you did that old man any harm . . ."

"You're accusin' me again. Go over there,

why don't you? Like as not that's where you'll find your mule."

If I do, Rusty thought, it'll be because you put him there. He said, "Let's go, Preacher." He reined Alamo around without waiting.

The minister had to push to catch up with him. "I can read your mind. You're thinkin' Fowler might've taken the mule over there to make Shanty look like a thief."

"I didn't know it showed so plain."

"I doubt Fowler has that much imagination."

"Maybe I *am* blamin' him too quick, but I don't put anything past that old reprobate."

He felt a special responsibility to the former slave, partly, at least, because he had wrongly accused Shanty's former owner, Isaac York, for so long. Crossing the land that had been York's and now belonged to Shanty, Rusty saw no sign of his mule. He had hoped he would not. That would have provided ammunition to those who agitated against Shanty's presence, even though Rusty would not have believed the passive-natured old man to be a thief.

He saw Shanty in his field, plowing with a mule much younger than Chapultepec. The corn stood tall, and the cotton looked green and promising. The farm was in sharp contrast to what Rusty and Webb had seen at Gaskin's.

Webb said, "This shows what a man can do when he's on the good side of the Lord."

"Shows what he can do if he's willin' to work." Rusty reined Alamo toward the field.

Seeing them, Shanty appeared apprehensive. He reined the plow mule to a stop and took off his hat, lifting and holding it to shade his face and block out the sun's glare. He looked ready to turn and run. Recognizing the visitors, he resumed plowing to the end of the row, then halted the mule and stepped to the rail fence to greet them.

He took off his hat again and bowed in the deferential manner he had learned in boyhood. "Good afternoon, Mr. Preacher, Mr. Rusty."

Rusty saw an ugly welt across Shanty's dark face. It appeared to have been left by a quirt or a whip. Anger seized him.

"Who did that to you?"

Shanty blinked as fear came into his dark eyes. "I'm all right. Ain't nothin' been done that won't heal."

Webb dismounted. With thumb and forefinger on Shanty's chin, he turned the black man's head one way, then the other, examining the mark closely. "That cut deep enough to bring blood. Have you put anything on it?"

"Some bacon grease with a touch of salt in it. That's all I had."

Anger made Rusty tremble. "Anybody who'd do a thing like that . . ."

Shanty shrugged with the resignation to which he had been conditioned all his life. "They just figured to scare me some, is all. And I reckon they done that."

"Warned you to get off of this place?"

"That seemed to be the main thing on their mind. Said I don't belong here, and if I don't want somethin' worse than that whip I'd better leave. But I got nowhere to go."

"This place belongs to you fair and square. They've got no right to run you off."

Soberly Webb said, "Rights don't matter when the devil's at work. Don't forget what happened to Lon and Billy Monahan."

"Tom Blessing's the law. I'll go talk to him. No tellin' what they might do the next time."

Webb said, "It wouldn't be a bad idea if you took Shanty home with you where you can watch out for him. I'll go see Tom."

Shanty demurred, gently but firmly. "I thank you gentlemen, I surely do. But I got crops here and a few critters to see after. I can't just be goin' off and leavin' them."

Rusty said, "It's dangerous for you here 'til we get this thing squashed."

Shanty shook his head. "Ain't nothin' happens without the Lord's will. I'll talk to Him about it."

Rusty considered a moment. "You're dealin' with people who don't spend much time listenin' to the Lord. But they'll listen to me or pay the price. Who were they, Shanty?"

Shanty looked down, avoiding Rusty's eyes. "They come at night. Had their faces covered."

"I'll bet Fowler Gaskin was amongst them."

"Like I said, I didn't see no faces. I wouldn't want to bear false witness against nobody. The Commandments is plain on that."

"Damned cowards, whippin' an old man that can't afford to defend himself. Let's see them try and whip *me*."

Webb warned, "Better get ahold of yourself. The mood you're in, you might shoot somebody."

Shanty pleaded, "I wouldn't want nobody killed on my account. This little old place ain't worth that."

Rusty realized Webb was right; in his present state he just *might* shoot somebody. He had come frighteningly close once with Isaac York, and he would have done it the night the Monahans were lynched if he could have reached Caleb Dawkins. On both occasions he had felt chilled afterward, realizing how near he had come to doing murder.

Webb said, "You talk to Tom Blessing. I'll stay with Shanty. I don't think anybody would molest him with me as a witness."

Rusty felt more like staying, but he recognized Webb's wisdom. "I'll go see Tom."

He wondered how much legal authority the sheriff had since the breakup of the Confederacy. But Tom Blessing's challenging presence bespoke authority whether backed by law or not. He had only to walk into a crowd to draw its full attention.

Rusty had not visited the settlement since his return home. Physically it had not changed much. It was a farming community with a plain two-story stone courthouse, a cotton gin, a general store, and three dramshops. The dirt streets were quiet, though he noticed an unusual number of men loafing in front of the store, the saloons, and a blacksmith shop. Some wore remnants of Confederate uniforms. Most had a hungry look, for they had come back from the war to find employment scarce and money scarcer. A couple of strangers gave him a hostile stare for no good reason he could think of except perhaps that he seemed to carry purpose, and they had none. To a barefoot man, the owner of an old pair of boots appears rich.

He had ridden first by the Blessing farm, where Mrs. Blessing had told him her husband was in town. Rusty entered the sheriff's office. The high windows were open, but the breeze outside was not strong enough to carry through the room. The place was oppressively warm.

Tom Blessing worked at a stack of papers, his face beaded with sweat. He laid them aside and stood up, shoving out his big, rough hand. "I hope you brought a few dollars to town, Rusty. This place ain't been blessed with fresh money in six months."

"I haven't got ten cents."

"If somebody was to spend a hundred dollars in Yankee silver it'd circulate from one hand to another and wipe out most of the town's debts before dark."

Rusty did not feel like making small talk. "There's been trouble out at the York place."

"Shanty?"

Rusty told what he and Webb had found. "They're liable to kill him next time, or try to. But that farm belongs to him. They've got no call to run him off of it."

Blessing listened, his blue eyes troubled.

"Ever since Isaac left him that place, I've been afraid of somethin' like this."

"What're you goin' to do about it?"

Blessing turned up his work-roughened hands. "I could camp out at Shanty's shack and hold off trouble for a while, but I couldn't stay forever. There's just one of me. They'd wait me out and hit him after I left."

"What's the use in havin' law if it can't be enforced?"

"I'm not sure how much law there is. Governor Murrah has gone south to Mexico and taken a bunch of state officials with him. He figured when the Yankee troops move in they'd put him in irons. Like as not, they would. For all I know, they may come and put *me* in irons."

" 'Til they do, you're still sheriff."

"Even if I throw somebody in jail I couldn't take a case to trial. I don't think the Federals recognize any Texas courts right now."

"Kind of like havin' an empty gun and no shells."

"It's quiet here compared to some places. There's been riots in Austin and San Antonio, places like that. A lot of soldiers came home with empty pockets and feel they've got a right to whatever they feel like takin'.

Been folks killed fightin' over property that don't amount to a damn."

"The Confederate government never paid much attention to us out here except for the conscript officers. Maybe the Yankees won't either."

"We won't know where we stand 'til they move in and take over."

"We may not like it."

"It's what we get for losin' the war."

It never was my war in the first place, Rusty thought. He knew Blessing had felt allegiance to the Confederacy, so he did not give voice to what was in his mind. "This still doesn't answer what we're goin' to do about Shanty."

Blessing studied him intently. "You were a ranger, Rusty. A good one, from everything I saw and what I've heard. How would you feel about bein' a deputy sheriff?"

"You just said you don't have much authority left. A deputy would have even less."

Blessing walked to a wooden rack attached to the wall. He selected a rifle and lifted it out. "Even if the government goes all to pieces — and it might — there's still authority in this."

Rusty was hesitant. "I don't know . . ."

"The rifle is yours if you want it. I doubt you'll ever get any cash wages."

"When I was a ranger I got paid mighty seldom and mighty little. But why would I want to be a deputy sheriff?"

"For one thing, there's Shanty. In case of trouble, the backin' of my office might keep you out of jail."

Rusty saw some points in favor of the proposition. "I wouldn't want to be away from my farm too much."

"I'm at mine most of the time."

Rusty feared if he gave himself a chance to consider he might decide against it. "I'll do it."

"Good." Blessing fished in a desk drawer and brought out a badge. "This came from a county over in Arkansas, but if anybody gives you trouble you'd best hit him before he has time to read it anyway. Raise your right hand."

Blessing administered a short oath of his own making, then shook Rusty's hand. "Anything you feel like you need to do, tell them I told you to." He smiled in satisfaction. "Once the word gets around that you're a deputy, maybe nobody'll have the nerve to steal your old mule again."

Rusty was surprised. "What about my old mule?"

"You've missed him, ain't you?"

"Yep. I figure Fowler Gaskin's got him hid out."

"Fowler's guilty of enough stuff to earn him his own hot corner in hell, but not this time. A stranger came ridin' in the other day on Chapultepec and tried to swap him. Everybody in town knows that mule. Been plannin' to take him out to you but haven't had time to do it."

"Where's the thief now?"

"In jail. Thought I'd give him a few more days to repent, then turn him loose. There's not likely to be a session of court 'til the Yankees come."

Rusty warmed with remorse. "I'd've taken a paralyzed oath that Fowler Gaskin done it."

"You can bet he's done worse things we don't even know about. Someday when he's called to Judgment he'll have more use for a fire bucket than for angel wings."

Leading Chapultepec, Rusty arrived at Shanty's cabin a little before dark. Preacher Webb sat on a bench in front, watching. Rusty saw no sign of trouble, but he asked, "Anything happen?"

Webb stared at the badge on Rusty's shirt but made no comment about it. "Nobody's goin' to do anything in the daylight. Two men came within a couple of hundred yards and stopped to look. Then they rode on."

"Recognize them?"

"My eyes aren't what they used to be. If they ever were." Webb shifted his attention to Chapultepec. "Where'd you find your mule?"

Rusty told him. Webb nodded in satisfaction. "I don't think either man I saw was Fowler Gaskin."

Rusty realized Webb was indirectly preaching him a little sermon about rising too quickly to judge.

Shanty was in the cabin, starting to fix a small supper. He was quick to see the badge. "You the sheriff now? What happened to Mr. Tom?"

"He's still the sheriff, at least 'til the Yankees come. He made me a deputy. Said that'd give me a stronger hand in case of trouble."

"I don't see why anybody'd trouble theirselves over this little old place. It barely growed enough to make a livin' for me and Mr. Isaac."

Rusty saw no tactful way to explain that the land itself was not the issue, but rather the fact that it was owned by a black, a former slave. He suspected Shanty knew the real reason he was being harassed but was trying to deny it to himself. "These are mean times. There's people who would kill a man for a pair of shoes, much less a farm."

It went against Shanty's kindly nature to think the worst about anyone. He was probably trying to delude himself as well about the danger he faced. "I'll be all right. Ain't no need you-all puttin' yourselves out on my account."

Rusty brushed the comment aside. "Me and Preacher will sleep in the shed. It's too late to go back to my place tonight."

Shanty made no further argument. "We'll be havin' somethin' to eat directly."

After supper Shanty took down an old banjo from the wall and played a couple of pieces. As the room darkened he lighted a candle and asked Webb to read to him from the Scriptures. Webb held the Bible open, but Rusty sensed that he was reciting from memory. He knew the text so well that the Book was more for display than for reference. Shanty listened, nodding in silent agreement.

Shanty said, "If I wasn't so old I'd learn myself to read. It'd be a comfort, knowin' I could go to the Good Book any time I wanted to."

Webb said, "You can talk directly to the Lord any time you want to. He's always listenin'."

Rusty stood up, turning his right ear toward the open door. "I hope He's listenin' right now, because I hear horses."

Webb blew out the candle. "I suppose it means trouble."

Rusty said, "I don't remember the last time anybody brought me good news at this hour of the night." He picked up the rifle Tom Blessing had given him. "Shanty, if there's any shootin', lay flat on the floor. Whatever you do, don't come outdoors." He turned to Webb. "You got a gun?"

"I prefer to use the Word."

"If these are the same old boys that whipped Shanty before, they ain't likely to listen to no sermons. But they'll pay attention to this rifle."

For a minute or so Rusty did not hear the horses moving. He wondered if he might have been wrong, that the riders might simply have been travelers passing by. Then he saw several small points of fire bobbing about.

"What in the world?"

Webb said, "They've lighted torches. They intend to burn this cabin."

Rusty counted six horsemen and a man on a mule. He thought on Len Tanner, who would have liked these odds. He wished he had the fight-loving Tanner at his side instead of the peaceable Preacher Webb.

He heard a hammer cock and looked back in surprise at a pistol in the minister's hand. "Thought you didn't have a gun."

"I said I *prefer* to use the Word. But sometimes you have to get their attention before they'll listen."

Rusty heard a shout, and the horses moved into a run. The men screeched and yelled as they came on, the torches weaving and dancing. A man in front fired a pistol toward the cabin. Their aim was to terrify Shanty into submission.

Rusty wondered that he felt no fear. Instead his earlier anger returned, rising like a brush fire. He lifted the rifle to his shoulder. When the leading horse was fifty feet away, he squeezed the trigger. Propelled forward by momentum, the stricken animal tumbled. He spilled the rider onto the ground almost directly in front of Rusty. Rusty dropped his rifle and jerked a pistol from its holster. He grabbed the hooded man by the collar and jammed the muzzle against his head, hard enough to break skin.

He shouted, "The rest of you stop where you're at or I'll splatter his brains all over you. If he's got any."

The other riders reined up. One cried out angrily, "Who the hell are you?"

"I'm a deputy sheriff, and I'm placin' all of you under arrest." It was a bluff. If they decided to ride him down they could do it in an instant. But about one thing he was not bluffing. He hoped they believed he would blow the lead rider's brains out, because he meant it.

The downed horse kicked a few times. By the flickering light of the torches Rusty saw a whip tied to the saddle. He knew it was intended for Shanty.

He had no time for regret over killing the horse. He had shot Indian mounts to set their riders afoot. A horse was a surer target than the man on its back. Remorse could trouble him later when he had leisure to indulge in it.

The men still in the saddle hesitated, uncertain. All wore sacks over their heads with holes punched to see through. A familiar voice growled, "You think you can stop us all by yourself?"

Preacher Webb moved into the torchlight, holding the pistol up where they could see it. "He's not by himself."

"Preacher? Who the hell told you to butt in? This ain't Sunday meetin'."

"I declared war on Satan a long time ago, and it's his work you're about tonight."

Another horseman glanced at his fellows,

still uncertain. "We didn't come here to do battle with a preacher, or even a deputy sheriff. It's got nothin' to do with you. We come to put a nigger in his place."

"We're all children of God, Shanty no less than the rest of us. A hand raised against him is a hand raised against a child of God."

The man on the mule said, "We didn't come here to listen to no preachin'. We come to do a job." He pushed forward.

Rusty jabbed the pistol against the leader's head hard enough that the man shouted in pain. "Boys, back off. He'll kill me sure."

Grittily Rusty said, "As sure as hell." He raised the muzzle toward the horsemen. "Whatever guns you've got, drop them on the ground."

The men looked at one another, each waiting for someone else to start. One said, "Don't you let your finger twitch on that trigger, deputy. That's my cousin you got there." He dropped his weapon, and the others followed suit, all but the mule's rider.

Rusty jerked the sack from the head of the man he had been holding. He recognized the face, though the name would not come to him. He said, "The rest of you, take off those hoods. I want to look at you."

He had to put the pistol back against the leader's head before the others complied.

The man on the mule wheeled about and beat a hasty retreat. The animal's tail switched furiously as the rider quirted him.

Rusty knew the mule. He had seen Fowler Gaskin riding it lately. It was like Gaskin to start a fight, then step back and let others take the consequences.

Most of the men who remained were strangers to Rusty. "Do you know them, Preacher?"

"Most of them." Webb looked regretfully at the leader, who still had the muzzle of Rusty's pistol near his ear. "I'm sorry to see you here, Jedediah Hoskins. As many times as we've prayed together, I thought better of you."

Rusty could not have called Hoskins by name on a hundred-dollar bet, but that was natural, considering how long he had been absent in the ranger service. He said, "I didn't know most of you before, but I'll know all of you the next time."

He stepped back from Hoskins, who turned on him angrily. "Since when did the law go to sidin' with niggers?"

"Black or white, right is right and wrong is wrong. It doesn't make any difference."

"Makes a difference to us. You can't be here all the time, deputy. We'll be comin' back."

"If you do, I'll know who to go lookin' for."

"What about our guns?"

"I'll sack them up and take them to Tom Blessing. When you work up the nerve, you can get them from him." Along with a sermon stiffer than Preacher Webb ever gave, he thought.

Hoskins frowned over his dead mount. "That was a good horse. It'll be hard to find another."

Rusty said, "It was either him or you. I figured you'd rather it was him."

Hoskins and his cousin struggled to retrieve the saddle, having to lift the animal's dead weight. Hoskins handed the saddle up to another rider and mounted behind his cousin. He looked back angrily as they rode away.

Preacher Webb moved over beside Rusty. "We didn't make any friends here tonight."

"I don't need friends like them anyway." Rusty turned toward the cabin. "Who was the feller I had ahold of?"

"Jed Hoskins. He and his cousin Mordecai took up farms to the south yonder a ways. It was after you went up to Fort Belknap."

"I want to remember them two."

Shanty had ventured outside. He gave the dead horse a moment's sad scrutiny. "Pity for an innocent animal to die like that."

"Might've been better to've shot the man who was on him," Rusty said, "but there would've been all kinds of trouble."

Webb said, "There's trouble anyway. You can see now that you're not safe here, Shanty. They'll keep comin' at you 'til you leave . . . or 'til somebody's dead, most likely you."

Shanty seemed finally to accept the minister's judgment. "Best that I be goin'. But this is home. Won't no other place ever be the same."

Rusty said, "I told you before, you can stay with me. It's not far. We can ride over here and work your farm together. I'll help you with your fields, and you can help me with mine."

"That'd be a kindness, but you don't owe me nothin'."

"I owe Isaac. Since you're his only heir, I owe you."

Preacher Webb nodded approval. Shanty said, "I'll tote my share of the load, and that's gospel."

His thin shoulders did not appear capable of carrying a heavy load, but Rusty knew better. He had seen him work. "You'll do fine, just fine."

Shanty went into the cabin and began to

throw a few things together. "Be all right if I fetch my old banjo along? I'll try not to be no bother with it."

"Bring it. That cabin could stand to hear some music."

CHAPTER 12

Badger Boy sat with the children at some distance from the fire. He listened to the drum and watched the dancing by his elder brother and fifteen warriors who had volunteered to accompany him on his raid. Resentment gnawed at him like hunger in an empty belly. Steals the Ponies had belittled his pleading that he be allowed to go along. His shadow was not yet long enough, his brother had said. That in itself was humiliating, but the fact that Steals the Ponies said it with a laugh only compounded the wrong.

No one could say with certainty how many summers Badger Boy had lived, but the best guess was nine or ten. The top of his head came to his brother's shoulder, and Steals the Ponies was relatively tall by the standards of The People. Badger Boy had seen warriors smaller in stature ride out to strike the Texan settlements or to invade the scattered ranches and tiny pueblos of northern Mexico. Perhaps they *had* been a little older, but that did not mean they were better riders, better fighters.

Badger Boy could not help wondering if his brother's reluctance had to do with the fact that the boy was Texan by blood, not Comanche. But he felt Comanche. All he knew was Comanche ways. Whatever he might once have known about the white man's world had been forgotten or at least pushed back into some deep corner of his memory where he could not reach it.

The dance was meant to strengthen the warriors' *puha,* the mystical power that would improve their chances of success. It was also intended to bolster their resolve and confidence. They did not lack for exuberance. They sang and shouted as they danced to the strong beat of the drum. Consternation and terror would tear like wildfire through the lodges of the Texans before these men returned to the encampment.

Badger Boy had heard pessimistic old men lament the passing of the good times. They were saying, though others strongly disagreed, that the white men were coming in ever-increasing numbers and that the days of The People as free-roaming hunters and raiders would soon be over. Wolf That Limps, highly honored for past brave deeds but too arthritic to ride far anymore, had told of a vision in which he saw the buffalo only as scattered bones. White men's spotted cattle grazed the buffalo range, thick as fleas on a camp dog. He saw no Comanches anywhere, just white men with their plows and cows.

"I do not know what we have done to offend them," Wolf had said, "but the spirits have turned against us."

Steals the Ponies contended that Wolf was an old man whose stomach had soured, that he had eaten spoiled meat and his vision had been nothing but a bad dream. Badger Boy wanted to believe that, but the dark predictions filled him with foreboding nevertheless. If he waited until he was as tall as his brother, it might be too late. There might be no more raids. He wanted to go now.

Wolf had not said where The People had gone in his vision, simply that they were no longer here. Perhaps they had returned to the place from which tradition said they had come, a hole deep in the earth. If that were so, the spirits might never call for them to emerge again, and Badger Boy's chance at being a warrior would be gone forever.

He wanted to go now, and go he would.

Later he lay awake, listening to his brother snoring nearby. He did not understand how Steals the Ponies could sleep so soundly, knowing that sunrise would find him on his way to the settlements. He supposed his brother had already ridden the war trail enough times that it no longer stirred the high excitement it once did.

Badger Boy wanted to sleep but could not. He squeezed his eyes shut, trying to force sleep, but soon he found himself staring up at the stars through the smoke hole in the tepee's top. His skin prickled with eagerness to be on his feet and moving.

Steals the Ponies and his companions made plenty of noise about their pre-dawn leaving. They had no qualms about awakening the entire camp. On the contrary, they wanted everyone to know. A major benefit of being a warrior was the acclaim one received. Reticence was not a virtue among fighting men.

Badger Boy watched his brother and the others mount their war horses in the pale light that preceded sunrise. Steals the Ponies rode over to him and leaned down for a final few words.

"Do not grieve. You will be going with us sooner than you think."

"Sooner than *you* think," Badger Boy said, too softly for his brother to hear.

He watched the men walk their horses through the center of camp, receiving the cheers and plaudits of those who could not go. They led a few extra horses to be used as remounts in the event any of those they rode were worn out, crippled, or killed.

While most of the crowd was watching the spectacle and vicariously riding with the warriors, Badger Boy entered the tepee and picked up the items he had laid out: his bow, his quiver and arrows, a leather lariat, and a supply of dried meat sufficient to last him many days provided he did not eat much. He slipped out the back side, where the bottom of the buffalo hide covering had been rolled up to allow circulation of air at ground level. He glanced around quickly to be sure no one had seen him, then trotted toward the horse herd.

He stopped twice, turning to look back, making sure he was not followed by anyone who might try to stop him. He could still see the tepee he shared with his brother. He feared he might not share it much longer, for Steals the Ponies had taken a strong fancy to a young woman of the village. He was talking about marrying her when he returned from the raid, for he was confident he would bring back many horses. Her father would be pleased to accept a new son-in-law who brought him many horses.

Badger Boy did not see why a man needed a wife. From observation he was aware that a man had physical need for a woman, but he knew a woman's favors were not difficult to obtain for one honored as a warrior. He had awakened many times deep in the night to find that a young woman had voluntarily entered the tepee and joined his brother upon his blankets. A man did not *have* to marry. He did not have to put his brother out of the tepee just so he could bring in a woman to stay.

However, since that appeared to be the probable outcome and Badger Boy would soon be living alone or perhaps sharing with other youths too young to ponder marriage, it seemed all the more appropriate that he be allowed to participate in the raid. And if he could not have his brother's approval, he would go without it.

He had planned this for some time. For several days he had slipped out before full daylight and studied the horse herd. He had found that most horses formed habits of behavior. At night, each had its own place to sleep within the group. Though the herd was moved frequently from one area to another for fresh grass, daylight would find each animal in more or less the same location relative to the others.

Steals the Ponies had taken his best war horse with him. But Badger Boy had long thought his brother might be overlooking the merits of a particular roan he had brought back from an earlier foray. This roan could usually be found near the perimeter of the herd each morning, on the north side near two other geldings with which it had formed a bond.

Stealthily, like the wolf, Badger Boy had practiced slipping among the horses and catching the roan without stirring up the rest of the herd or the two sleepy-eyed boys who stood night watch. So far he had not been caught. He did not plan to be caught today.

The roan had become accustomed to Badger Boy's morning routine. It pointed its ears toward him as he approached but showed no sign of concern. Badger Boy quickly had one arm around the horse's neck and fitted a rawhide bridle over its head. Though surprised, the roan did not resist or try to turn away.

Badger Boy held still a minute, making sure where the two night guards were. He located both on the far side, paying no attention that he could see. He felt sure one was asleep, and the other was not far from it. He led the roan to the edge of the herd in a slow walk. The roan's two friends followed. He stopped and raised his hand quickly. The pair halted, their ears following him as he continued leading the roan away.

He kept looking back over his shoulder, trying to keep the roan between him and the two guards so they would not easily spot him if they should happen to look in his direction. Only when he had reached a stand of small timber did he begin to breathe easily. Only then could he feel confident that he was getting away with his plan.

He had reconciled himself to the certainty that Steals the Ponies would be unhappy with him. He knew he was probably in for verbal and perhaps even physical abuse at his brother's hands and from his brother's companions. But by the time they saw him and knew what he had done, it would be too late to send him back. He planned to follow unseen until they were in the settlements. From that point, Steals the Ponies would see that it was safer for him to remain with the warriors than to try to find his way back alone through the white man's country.

He mounted bareback, his bow and quiver

and the lariat slung over his shoulder. He wore no decoration, no feather in his hair, for he had not yet earned the right. He had not yet been on the customary vision quest during which a young man waited for a guardian spirit to visit him, to endow him with the medicine that would guide him on his life's journey. He had asked the shaman to advise him, but the shaman had said he did not yet have enough years to seek power.

Badger Boy had a feeling the shaman had never liked him, probably because of his lighter skin, which he considered a mark of impurity. The shaman was given to strong counsel against bringing outsiders into the tribe, diluting the blood that made the Comanches *The* People, superior to all other races, white or red. If it were in the shaman's power he would see that Badger Boy never received a vision, never received the intercession of a guardian spirit. He might even try to saddle the lad with a dark spirit that would work against him.

Badger Boy felt that he could do well enough for himself without the aid of that evil-eyed old man, his potions and talismans and witchery. He had seen the shaman perform his rituals over the sick. Sometimes they recovered and sometimes they did not. In a few cases he suspected the old man had willed them dead, and they had died. There was a question in Badger Boy's mind whether the shaman had allied himself with benevolent spirits or with those of the darkness.

Unfortunately the shaman's negative views were shared by some others influential in the band, like the warrior Tonkawa Killer. Badger Boy hoped his participation in this raid would demonstrate that his white skin was not a liability.

His first impulse was to ride hard and get himself some distance away from the village in case someone should miss him and come to fetch him back. But who was likely to miss him? If he rode too fast he might overtake his brother and the war party prematurely. He would almost surely suffer punishment for his transgression, then be sent back, shamed.

Steals the Ponies had always counseled him that patience was essential, that haste too often led a warrior to a downfall. Though Badger Boy itched to move with more speed, he slowed his pace once he felt he was well clear of the village and any strong likelihood that someone would come after him. He knew Steals the Ponies and the others would not push their horses hard and risk wearing them down. The time to push would be on the return, when there was likely to be pursuit.

In the beginning the trail was easy to follow. The riders made no effort to conceal it, for here in the heart of Comanchería there was no enemy to elude. He knew that as they moved closer to the settlements the tracks would challenge him. Fortunately his brother had taught him much about trailing, whether it be for game or for enemies.

Badger Boy sometimes boasted that Steals the Ponies could trace the shadow of a hawk across bare rock.

For three days the trail led southward. Badger Boy began to wonder if his brother might have changed his mind about the Texan settlements and be heading for Mexico instead. He was disappointed, for he had much more curiosity about the Texans than about Mexico. However, the fourth day the trail abruptly shifted eastward. His brother's strategy became clear. He had remained well west of the settlements until he had led his fighters as far south as they needed to go. Now they were riding directly toward the Texans' farms. Badger Boy found anticipation exhilarating.

He was also feeling hunger. He began to understand what he had been told about the rigors of the war trail. He had eaten too deeply into his short supply of dried meat the first days. Now he had but little left. He summoned a strong will against a temptation to eat it all, to quell at least for a while the pangs that seemed to tie his belly into a knot. He realized he must not succumb to a desire for momentary relief at the expense of the larger goal.

He managed to put an arrow through a rabbit, which he roasted for a while over a tiny fire, then eagerly consumed half raw.

The first log cabin stopped him cold. He tied the roan on the far side of a small hill, out of sight, then lay on his belly in grass atop the hill. He studied the farm with an insistent curiosity. The sight prompted fleeting memories, so quickly come and gone that he could not quite grasp them and hold them for inspection. He vaguely remembered that he had lived in such a cabin once, not much different from the one he observed now. He remembered playing in the yard, riding a long stick and pretending it was a horse.

He could almost see a man and a woman in his mind's eye, but they were as elusive as the other memories. Hard as he tried, he could not bring them into focus.

Perhaps it was just as well. That was

another life, gone forever. He had attuned himself to a different life among The People. Those others, whoever they might have been, were strangers to him. The spirits probably preferred that they remain so.

He saw a wagon standing empty beside a shed. He remembered riding in one long ago. It had to have been before his time with the Comanches, for he had never seen a wagon since Buffalo Caller had taken him. He had seen no Texans either, except a couple of captives. One had been a boy younger than himself, kept to raise by another band. The other had been a woman. The last he had seen of her, some warriors were dragging her away. He could only imagine what had become of her. He remembered being strangely affected by her screams as if he had heard them before. A wizened old grandmother had warned him not to show concern, for unwarranted sympathy might mark him unfit to be trained as a fighting man. Nothing that happened to a Texan woman could ever be punishment enough for injuries the Texans had done to The People, she said.

He studied the wagon a long time, wishing he might ride in it. Then perhaps he could summon a clearer memory of the last time. He noted that the wagon had four wheels. He had seen ox-drawn carts with two big wheels, brought out onto the plains by Mexican *Comanchero* traders from somewhere west. In them they brought all manner of fascinating trade goods. Later they would return to wherever they came from, the trade goods exchanged for cattle, horses, and especially mules the warriors had taken from the Texan settlements. Comanches had little use for mules, considering them much inferior to the horse, but they had found them valuable for trading.

He understood that the Mexicans did not like the Texans. Steals the Ponies said they had warred and the Texans had won. He wished he could have seen the fight. It was claimed that they had great guns many times larger than the rifle for which Steals the Pony had once traded a horse and three mules to the *Comancheros.* It was said these guns made a noise louder than thunder. That was hard for Badger Boy to imagine.

He saw a woman come out into an open passageway between the two sides of the cabin, her long hair flowing in the wind. At the distance he had no idea if she were young or old, but something about her gave him pause, stirred unexpected feelings he could not understand. Curiosity would have carried him closer for a better look, but caution won out. In a field some distance beyond the cabin he could see a farmer at work. It was likely he had a rifle that could wound or kill at a much greater distance than Badger Boy's bow and arrows.

The raiders had made their trail much more difficult to follow once they reached the edge of the settled country, but Badger Boy knew they had passed this way. More than likely his brother had marked this place to be struck on the return journey. Then perhaps Badger Boy would get a closer look. He eased down the far side of the hill and remounted the roan. He set him into a gentle trot.

His mind turned back to the cabin and the people who lived there. He tried to reconcile them with fleeting wisps of memory that had long haunted him, tiny fragments of a past life.

An uneasy feeling came upon him. He had long recognized that he had strong instincts, premonitions about things not yet seen. Even forewarned, he almost rode upon a man and a boy in a wagon. Badger Boy saw them at about the same time they discovered him. His heart leaped. He could never explain to Steals the Ponies how he had been so careless. The man reached quickly behind the seat and brought up a firearm.

The sound of the blast indicated it was a shotgun. Dust kicked up where the shot fell short. Fortunately Badger Boy was out of range. He hoped the man did not also have a rifle, for it could carry death much farther.

Badger Boy jerked the roan horse around and kicked him into a hard run, trying to get into the cover of a wooded draw before the *teibo* could fire again. As he reached the thick brush, he heard another shot. It was no more effective than the first, but the sound made his heart pound hard. Never before had anyone attempted to kill him. He found himself sweating, his mouth dry.

Warriors were not supposed to know fear, but Badger Boy was afraid. He looked back, thinking the man might come after him. He realized the wagon made pursuit difficult, for the roan could travel where wheels could not. He began to get a grip on his nerves, though he still felt as if his thumping heart had risen high in his chest, almost in his throat.

Steals the Ponies would be ashamed of him. He was ashamed of himself.

Later, when he had time to gather his wits, he realized he had made a mistake that could endanger the raiders. By allowing himself to be seen he might have started an alarm that would move more quickly than the warriors. The Texans might be ready and waiting.

He was so weighted down with anxiety and remorse that he allowed himself to become careless again. Riding through an oak thicket, he sensed movement on both sides, a rush of hooves. Horses charged at him, and he heard a battle cry. A warrior raised a club over his head. He checked himself, but not in time to prevent his horse from colliding with Badger Boy's. The roan staggered. Badger Boy grasped desperately at the mane to keep from being knocked off the horse's back.

An angry voice lashed him like a whip. "Badger Boy! Why are you here?"

He looked into the furious eyes of Steals the Ponies. He could not find voice to speak. His brother repeated the demand.

Struggling for breath, Badger Boy managed, "I wanted to ride with you."

"I told you many times, you cannot."

Tonkawa Killer pushed up close, a quirt in his hand, fury in his face. "Do you not know that you have endangered us all? What if you had been seen?"

Badger Boy swallowed. He had rather take a beating than admit what he had done, but to hold his silence would be the same as lying. "I was. A man shot at me."

The fear that had plagued him was confirmed in the accusing faces of the warriors who surrounded him.

Tonkawa Killer shouted, "You are a fool!," and swung at him with the quirt. Though the quiver of arrows absorbed some of the force, the lash bit deeply into his flesh. He cried out in pain before he could catch himself. A warrior was supposed to bear punishment without complaint. He bit his tongue as the quirt burned him a second time.

Steals the Ponies pushed between him and Tonkawa Killer. "That is enough. We cannot undo what has been done."

Tonkawa Killer said, "He is not one of us. He has the pale skin of a Texan, and he always will."

Badger Boy fought against a rising of tears. He looked into his brother's eyes, searching for sign of forgiveness but finding none.

"Some of us may be killed because of your recklessness. Now we have to decide whether to go ahead or turn back."

Tonkawa Killer scowled. "Go back without horses? The village would laugh at us."

Steals the Ponies shook his head. "That is better than hearing the women cry because some of us do not come back at all."

Tonkawa Killer made a quick search of the warriors' faces. "Perhaps you should take your Texan baby back to the village. I will lead however many want to continue the raid."

Steals the Ponies had to concede the obvious, that most were not ready to give up what they had begun. They had invested too many days and nights already. "Either we all go back or we all go ahead. I can see that most of you want to go ahead, so that is what we will do."

Tonkawa Killer demanded, "What about that boy? He may already have spoiled our medicine. We cannot take him."

"We have no choice. We are too far into the Texan country to send him back alone."

Badger Boy began feeling better. This was what he had counted on all along, that they would have to let him remain with them. "Give me a chance to fight. I will do whatever you say."

Steals the Ponies glared at him. "Yes, you will, or I will let Tonkawa Killer wear out his quirt on your back."

His back already burned severely. Though he could not see it, Badger Boy sensed that the quirt had cut deeply enough to bring blood. He had been willing to shed blood on this raid, but he would have expected it to result from battle, not from punishment. Shame made him realize how small he really was, how badly out of place here among men who had proven their maturity and earned the right to go against the Texans.

Steals the Ponies frowned at him, then looked at the roan. "You are disobedient and you are foolish. But at least you have good judgment about horses."

That was small comfort, but even a grudging compliment was welcome in the face of so much blame. Badger Boy made it a point to ride close to his brother and as far as possible from Tonkawa Killer.

Steals the Ponies sent out "wolves" to scout the white men's farms for horses as they rode eastward. On their return they would pick up as many as they could gather without undue risk. The scouts brought back reports that they were not finding many horses. They brought back other reports that visibly disturbed the raid leader. The Texans were gathering what horses they had and holding them in corrals or herding them under guard. Moreover, the settlers seemed to be banding in numbers at certain points as if for defense.

Steals the Ponies called the men together in council under a bright, full moon. "The Texans act as if they know we have come among them. I do not know how they learned this" — he glanced at Badger Boy — "but our risk is greater now."

Tonkawa Killer did not mince words. "It is because of that child." He pointed at Badger Boy. "He allowed himself to be seen. We had as well have an owl in camp."

The owl was considered a malevolent spirit, a harbinger of misfortune, even death.

Steals the Ponies argued, "It could be that some sharp-eyed Texan noted our tracks. It is impossible to cover the trail of so many, however we may try."

Tonkawa Killer was not placated. "Our medicine has gone bad. Kill the boy and perhaps it will be good again."

Steals the Ponies was shocked. "Kill one of our own?"

"He is not one of us. He is a Texan. You cannot turn a mule into a horse."

Badger Boy drew close to his brother. He searched the faces of the warriors, wondering if any seriously considered what Tonkawa Killer said. He was unable to read their expressions in the moonlight. Steals the Ponies pushed himself protectively in front of Badger Boy. "This boy is Comanche now. If there is to be killing, let it be of the *real* white men, not my younger brother." He put extra emphasis on the word *brother.*

Killing of Comanche by Comanche was almost unheard-of. But if it did occur, it would call for vengeance by the victim's kin. Steals the Ponies made it clear he considered Badger Boy to be of his blood.

Tonkawa Killer made a placating motion with his hands. "I will not hurt him. But if the spirits move against him, I will not interfere."

Steals the Ponies looked up at the full moon. "The light is good. Let us see how many horses we can gather."

CHAPTER 13

The exhilaration of the raid overrode Badger Boy's shame. Though Steals the Ponies ordered him to remain a safe distance behind, he was able to hear the commotion. Scouts had found horses corraled in a log pen. It appeared that several farm families had gathered for mutual protection. The first inclination had been to pass the place by because of the difficulty of getting at the guarded animals, but the challenge was too strong for proud men to ignore.

Steals the Ponies and two others crept to the corral and cut the rope that bound the gate. They had pushed most of the horses through the opening before one of the Texans woke up to what was happening and fired a futile shot. Steals the Ponies leaped upon one of the stolen horses bareback and pushed the others into a run. The rest of the raiders fell in behind, whooping, shouting to bring the horses to a full gallop.

Badger Boy was among them, yelling as loudly as any.

Several warriors dropped back to intercept any Texans foolish enough to pursue. Badger Boy would have joined them had they not included Tonkawa Killer. Instead he remained with the main body, driving westward. The bright moon yielded light enough for them to see where they were going.

From far behind, Badger Boy heard a few shots, followed by silence.

Steals the Ponies ordered the horses slowed so they would not exhaust themselves and be unable to make the long trip to Comanchería. After a time the rear guard caught up.

Tonkawa Killer was disappointed. "They turned back when they saw us. They never gave us a chance to kill them."

Steals the Ponies replied, "There will be others. They are like flies on the buffalo."

The night yielded a dozen more horses from a field. Two men on horseback stood guard, but they fled toward a cabin when the Comanches charged at them. Tonkawa Killer and two of his friends managed to overtake one and knock him from his horse. Once he was on the ground, the struggle lasted but a moment. The man's scalp and his horse were taken as prizes.

In the false dawn that preceded sunrise, the raiders came upon another cabin. There appeared to be only two horses, both in a corral. Steals the Ponies ordered Badger Boy to remain with the main group and help hold the horses already taken. Badger Boy itched to follow his brother, but he had disobeyed once. He would not do so again.

Tonkawa Killer and two friends crept to the cabin. Light showed from inside. Badger Boy heard a desperate shout, then a woman's scream. It began in fright and escalated into agony.

He felt cold inside. As had happened the time he heard a captive woman's cry, he trembled for a reason he could not quite fathom. The scream aroused a memory, a clutch of long-subdued fear. He had heard such a scream before but did not know when or where. He remembered a feeling of panic, and some of that gripped him now. It was like trying to recall a dream after morning's sunlight has driven it deeply into the shadows. He found his hands shaking and puzzled over the source of his fear. It was not for himself, and it was not for the white woman dying in that cabin. But he could not remember who it *was* for.

He must not let anyone know. He must conquer this weakness lest it diminish him in the eyes of the others.

Steals the Ponies brought the two horses to add to those already taken. Tonkawa Killer caught up shortly, showing off two fresh scalps. One had hair long as his arm.

Steals the Ponies asked, "Do you feel better now?"

Tonkawa Killer grunted. "She was young. I wanted to bring her with me, but she got a rifle. I had to kill her." He held the weapon in front of him. "The rifle will be of more use."

Surprise was the Comanche's favorite tactic of war. But now and then the white man applied it against the Comanche with equal success. Badger Boy had heard old men tell of a great raid that took a huge war party all the way to the big water and left a coastal town in flames, yet was smashed by a smaller Texan force that caught the retreating column by surprise.

He was unprepared for the sudden *teibo* attack upon the stolen horse herd. Steals the Ponies had taken most of the raiding party to sweep a couple of farms a little way off the line of march. He had left Badger Boy and half a dozen warriors to continue driving the horses so no time would be lost. It was obvious that the countryside had been aroused, for some farms had been found suddenly deserted and others too heavily defended to risk frontal attack.

Tonkawa Killer was in charge of the horse guard. Badger Boy wished it had been somebody else — anybody else — for he was convinced that Tonkawa Killer meant him harm.

The horses moved along in a steady trot, and all seemed to be well with the world. Even so, Badger Boy was vaguely uneasy. His instincts were trying to tell him something, but he could not analyze what it was. He tried to put his fears behind him by imagining how it would be when they reached the encampment. Though he was yet a boy and had joined the raid against orders, surely he would be allowed to share in whatever honors the village might bestow upon the party. He had proven himself worthy to ride with men.

In a heartbeat the world turned upside down. He did not see where the Texans came from. Suddenly they were there, shouting, shooting, racing at him. The loose horses panicked and turned back, breaking into a hard run. Instead of being behind them, gently pushing, he was in front of their wild stampede, in some danger of being knocked down and trampled. He waved his arms and shouted, trying desperately to turn them, but he made no more impression than did the quail which flushed from tall grass before the pounding hooves.

He gave way to panic, as on the day the white man fired at him from the wagon. This time there were many white men, more than he had time to count, and it seemed they were all firing at him.

The roan horse did not wait for Badger Boy to decide what to do. It turned and broke into a hard run away from the shooting, away from the stampede. Badger Boy pressed hard with his knees and clung to the mane to keep from falling off. He knew he should stand his ground and fight. That was what Steals the Ponies would do. But he had no control over the horse. He freed his grip on the mane and brought his bow down from his shoulder, drawing an arrow from the quiver and fitting it to the string. He found a white-man target coming up swiftly beside him. The roan jumped a small bush just as the arrow flew. Badger Boy knew he had missed.

He saw a flash from the white man's pistol and braced himself for a bullet that did not come. The Texan missed too. While Badger

Boy struggled to fit another arrow, Tonkawa Killer raced alongside the Texan and dealt him a strong blow with his war club. The Texan fell and rolled. Looking back, Badger Boy saw him jump to his feet and begin dodging the oncoming horses. Then he was lost in the dust.

Because he was watching behind him, Badger Boy did not see the fallen tree ahead. The roan horse attempted to leap over it but struck a hind foot on the dead trunk. He went down head first and rolled over. Badger Boy cried out involuntarily as the horse's weight slammed upon his leg. He heard the bone snap and felt a stab of pain more terrible than anything he had ever known. The roan stepped on Badger Boy's stomach as it staggered to its feet. The air went out of his lungs. He gasped for breath.

For a moment, through the dust, he saw a dark figure looming over him and thought it must be a Texan come to finish him. He was too numb for fear.

The face was Tonkawa Killer's, and it was malevolent. "You have spoiled our medicine, white boy. Now die!" Tonkawa Killer swung his club. Badger Boy turned quickly aside so that the blow missed his head but struck his shoulder. Then Tonkawa Killer was gone.

Badger Boy heard the horses race by on either side of him, going around the downed tree that had caused the roan to fall. Hooves kicked dirt in his face and barely missed him. He tried to crawl farther under the tree but could not move. He felt paralyzed, his lungs burning in a desperate search for air, his broken leg ablaze with pain.

Then he saw another horseman, this time not a Comanche. He looked up at the Texan, at the rifle in the man's hand, and he closed his eyes, waiting to die.

Rusty Shannon had hoped he had seen the last of Comanche raids. Tom Blessing said it had been more than a year since hostiles had penetrated this far down the Colorado River. Now that the war was over and new settlers were occupying regions farther west, it seemed that this area should be well buffered. Yet Tom Blessing had come to him on a sweat-lathered mount and shouted, "Grab your rifle and saddle your horse. There's Indians about."

Preacher Webb was among a dozen men who rode with Blessing. He looked tired and old.

The black man Shanty had been staying at Rusty's, sleeping on the open dog run so long as the weather was favorable, working his own farm only when Rusty could be with him. He said, "I'll fetch our horses, Mr. Rusty." He turned toward the corral.

Blessing raised a hand to stop him. "Catch your horse, Shanty, but you won't be goin' with us. The women and children are gatherin' at my place. They'll need every man we can spare to protect them."

Shanty was too old and stove up to be out chasing Indians on horseback, though he could fire a rifle and take up a defensive position as well as anyone. "Yes sir, Mr. Tom, if that's what you'd rather I do."

"I'd be much obliged."

Rusty appreciated that Blessing was protecting Shanty's feelings, first by telling him he was needed and second by not making a point of the old fellow's age and limitations. Blessing's large frame and commanding presence masked a benevolent spirit.

Jed Hoskins rode with the group. Rusty remembered him from the aborted raid on Shanty's place. Hoskins grumbled, "Damned darkey won't be any help. They could scalp every last woman and child before he'd come out from under the bed."

Shanty gave no sign that he had heard, though Rusty knew he must have. A life in slavery had taught him to endure indignity without protest lest indignity turn to physical violence.

Rusty knew nothing he might say would alter Hoskins's opinion. He asked simply, "Your ear still sore?" That was a reference to his having jabbed the muzzle of his pistol against Hoskins's ear at Shanty's place.

Hoskins did not answer.

Rusty wished Preacher Webb would stay with the women and children too, for he was looking none too strong. But Webb's medical experience would be needed if anyone was wounded on this mission.

A milk-pen calf was kept confined so its mother would come to the barn twice a day to be milked and to let the calf suck. Rusty turned the calf out to find her so it would not starve in case he was gone for several days. It stared in bovine confusion at the unaccustomed freedom and nosed at the closed gate, trying to get back in.

Shanty observed, "Freedom can be a hard thing to get used to. But it's harder yet to give up, once you've had it."

As he rode, Blessing explained that a farmer farther west had come upon an Indian and fired at him with a shotgun. He was too excited to aim straight.

Rusty asked, "Was he sure it was an Indian?"

"Said he wasn't wearin' much but breechcloth and moccasins, and he had a bow slung across his shoulder. Afterward some of the neighbors went scoutin' and found tracks. Looked like there might've been twenty or thirty passed by, goin' east."

"Goin' for where they expect to find the most horses," Rusty guessed. The invaders might be disappointed, for the war had taken away large numbers. Years would pass before they could be bred back up to earlier levels. "Any notion where the Indians have got to?"

"Somewhere east. We'll keep ridin' 'til we run into them."

That happened sooner than Rusty expected. A farmer came toward them, vigorously kicking a saddle mule's ribs, pushing for all the speed the animal could muster. The man waved his hat and shouted. Foam formed around the bridle bits, and the brown hide glistened with sweat.

"Comanches! Must be a hundred of them!" The farmer's eyes seemed to bulge. He turned halfway around in the saddle, pointing behind him. "Drivin' a bunch of horses. Must be a hundred of those too."

From past experience Rusty suspected that the man's excitement caused gross exaggeration in the numbers, both of Indians and of horses. The earlier report had indicated there might be twenty or thirty Indians.

Blessing wasted no time on foolish questions. "How far?"

"Two, maybe three miles behind me. They been killin' folks right and left. Must've killed a hundred by now."

Blessing's expression indicated that he too suspected the account was exaggerated. "We'll see if we can head them off. You want to go with us?"

The farmer looked over the group. Blessing had picked up several men, bringing the number to eighteen. "There ain't near enough of you. There's a hundred of them, maybe two hundred."

Blessing nodded as if he believed. "Tell you what to do: you keep ridin', spread the word so nobody gets caught unawares."

The farmer needed no further encouragement to set the mule into a run again. He was quickly gone, dust rising behind him. Blessing turned to the men. "You heard what he said. I don't think there's near as many Indians as he claimed, but anybody who wants to turn back is free to do it."

Rusty looked at Preacher Webb, hoping he might, for the minister was obviously weary. But neither Webb nor anyone else showed an inclination to leave.

Blessing was pleased. "Then let's go find us some Comanches."

They were easily found. Rusty saw the horse herd first. A rough count showed him about twenty head, a fraction of the farmer's wild estimate. For the Comanches, this raid had been slim pickings. Moreover, only half a dozen Indians rode with the horses. Rusty suspected the raiding party consisted of considerably more, but the others were probably away looking for additional horses.

Blessing said, "I don't believe they've seen us yet. Let's don't give them time to think about it." With a wave of his hand, he led the charge.

Rusty took a quick look around to locate Preacher Webb. He wanted to keep the minister in sight, lest he get off to himself and end up in trouble.

The Indian horse guards were taken by surprise. They tried to come together, but the Texans were among them too quickly. To one side a small rider on a roan horse tried to join his companions. He was cut off by Jed Hoskins, who gave chase. The rider loosed an arrow at Hoskins but missed. Hoskins in turn fired his rifle but without effect. A second Indian cut in from behind, swinging a war club. Rusty gave chase, hoping to ward off the warrior, but he was too late. The club struck the farmer and knocked him off his horse. The Indian whirled about to finish the job but saw Rusty coming and changed his course.

The fallen Hoskins pushed shakily to his feet.

Rusty shouted, "You all right?"

Hoskins waved Rusty on. "Go get them!"

The farmer might lack tolerance, but he had nerve. Rusty continued the pursuit. The smaller Indian, out in front, turned to loose another arrow. His horse tried to jump a fallen tree but did not quite clear it. The roan went down, tumbling over its rider. It got up, shook itself and ran on, limping a little.

The second Indian paused a moment, leaning toward the one who had fallen. Rusty thought for a moment that he tried to strike the one who had fallen, but that made no sense. The warrior rode away, abandoning his companion.

Hell of a friend, Rusty thought. Usually Comanches did everything they could to rescue their own.

The downed Indian tried to crawl away, dragging a broken leg. A quiver had spilled most of its arrows in the fall, but the Indian grabbed at one, then felt around desperately for his bow. Not finding it, he flopped over on his back, grasping a knife in one hand and an arrow in the other. He jabbed them threateningly at Rusty.

"Figure on goin' out fightin', do you?" Rusty said, knowing it was unlikely the warrior understood him. Then, in surprise, "You're nothin' but a shirttail kid."

The Comanches trained them early, but this one appeared too young to be out on a raid. The boy's skin was lighter in color than most Comanches. Wide blue eyes tried to show defiance but betrayed mortal fear.

Rusty's spine tingled. "You're a white boy!"

He stepped down from Alamo. Again the boy jabbed at him with the knife, but Rusty remained out of reach. He waited until the arm was extended full length, then grabbed the wrist. Twisting hard, he took the knife from the lad's hand and broke off the arrow.

"Boy, who are you? And how come you ridin' with Comanches?"

The youngster shouted harshly, the words alien to Rusty.

Hoskins trudged through the dry grass, his legs moving heavily. Sweat rolled down his face. "You got you one, Shannon. How come you ain't killed him yet?"

"Look at him. He's no Comanche."

Hoskins leaned over for a close look. The boy struck at him with his fist. The farmer stepped back. "He's got a white skin sure enough, but underneath it he's pure Comanche."

Rusty tried again. "You got a name, boy?" The lad made no sign that he understood.

A wisp of faint memory touched Rusty like the brush of a transient breeze. "Comanches stole me from my real folks a long time ago. Like as not, that's what happened to him."

"Maybe so, but raise a dog pup with wolves and you can never get the wolf out of him. Better if he was to die right now."

"But he won't, not unless a broken leg can kill him."

"They've turned him into a savage."

Sympathy welled up in Rusty, deep enough that pain came with it. "I could've been where he is if Mike Shannon and the preacher hadn't grabbed me."

"The way I heard it, the Comanches didn't keep you long enough to hurt you much. Looks like they had this young'un long enough to ruin him for life."

Rusty heard horses and looked up, hand tightening on his rifle until he recognized Preacher Webb and Tom Blessing. Blessing leaned partway out of the saddle for a better view of the boy. "Looks like you've caught yourself a bear cub."

"Take a close look at him. He's white."

Preacher Webb dismounted heavily, fatigue pressing down on his thin shoulders. The boy stared up at him with frightened eyes that no longer tried to show fight. Plainly, he expected to be killed.

Rusty asked, "Remind you of anything?"

"Reminds me of you, a long time ago back at Plum Creek. But you were a lot younger than this." Webb knelt over the youngster. "Do you speak English, son?"

The boy did not reply.

Webb tried again. "Do you have a name? Do you remember your mother and father?"

The blue eyes flickered. Rusty thought the words might have registered, at least a little.

Webb pressed, "Your mother? Do you remember your mother?"

The boy's lips tried to form the word, though no sound came.

Webb looked up. "I believe he understands the word *mother*. Maybe he can remember more if we keep at it."

Tom Blessing dismounted, excitement rising in his face. "I think maybe I know who he is. Remember the time, Preacher — you were there too, Rusty — when we trailed after Comanches who had taken a woman and a boy? That was before the war started. We found the woman dead, but we never did find the boy."

It had been the first time Rusty had seen the results of murder. He remembered the shock, the stomach-turning sight of a woman butchered, her scalp taken.

Webb said, "I'd ministered to the family, even baptized their baby boy. Their name was Pickard. I even remember the name they gave their boy. Andrew. They called him Andy. Andy Pickard."

The boy's eyes widened at the name. His lips moved as he tried to form a word. He made a couple of efforts, then managed, "Andy. Andy." He drummed fingers against his chest. "Andy."

A chill ran all the way down to Rusty's boots. "Then he's the one we hunted for but never found."

Blessing said, "Looks like it. You were lucky we found *you* so quick. He wasn't as lucky."

"Maybe his luck is fixin' to change. Preacher, what can we do about that broken leg?"

"Set the bone if we can, and tie a splint on his leg so it stays set. It'll hurt him real bad for a minute."

Rusty nodded at Hoskins. "Me and you

will hold him while Preacher sets that leg."

Hoskins was dubious. "He's liable to bite. A man could get hydrophoby."

Blessing said, "I'll hold him, me and Rusty. You see if you can find a broken tree limb that'll do for a temporary splint."

The boy cried out and struggled as if he thought they meant to kill him. Rusty and Blessing held him tightly.

Webb said, "Now." He jerked the leg. The boy convulsed, then went limp. "Fainted dead away. It's just as well. He won't be fightin' me while I brace up his leg."

The farmer found nothing suitable. Webb placed Rusty's rifle flat against the leg and bound it with strips of cotton cloth torn from a jacket he had carried behind the cantle of his saddle.

Blessing asked, "What'll we do with him?"

Rusty said, "If somebody'll go fetch a wagon, we'll take him to my place. Me and Shanty'll look after him."

Hoskins warned, "Like as not you'll wake up dead some mornin' with a knife between your ribs."

Rusty said, "I don't see how I can do anything else." He turned to the minister. "I've been where this boy is. I look at him, and I see me layin' here in his place. Do you understand, Preacher?"

"I do. But this boy is not you. He's been raised to fight. Like as not he's been raised to hate you and me and everybody white. He may never get past that."

"You're a preacher. No matter how bad a sinner may be, you give him a chance, don't you?"

"That's part of the callin'."

"I'm a long ways from bein' a preacher, but I've learned a lot from followin' you around. I've got to give him his chance, like the Shannons gave me."

Distant shots told Steals the Ponies that the horse guard had come under attack. To their disappointment, he and the warriors he had taken with him had managed to find only six more horses. The Texans seemed not to have many, and most of those were too well protected to take without higher cost than the raiders were willing to pay. He had begun to worry about the reception they would receive when they returned to the encampment with less booty than expected.

Now a darker worry burdened him. He had left his brother where he had thought he would be safest. It appeared his judgment had been terribly wrong. He felt a fear for Badger Boy that he had never felt for himself.

"Leave the horses," he shouted, and turned in the direction from which he had heard the shouts. Most of the other warriors objected. It seemed cowardly to abandon the few they had obtained. "Had you rather lose them all?" he responded with anger.

Several men stubbornly held to the stolen horses. Steals the Ponies led the rest toward the sound of the shots. He had left Badger Boy in the care of Tonkawa Killer, as fierce a fighter as he knew. Tonkawa Killer hated the boy, but surely he would live up to the responsibility Steals the Ponies had placed upon him.

Driving the horses, the warriors stayed in or near timber as much as they could. Steals the Ponies could only guess how much opposition the Texans had mounted against them. From the cover of trees he watched a considerable number of Texans moving westward, driving a dozen horses before them. That represented about half the ones the raiding party had left under guard. He assumed that Tonkawa Killer, Badger Boy, and the rest had gotten away with the others. He felt a little better, though much anxiety lingered.

A wagon appeared to carry someone covered by a blanket. A Texan, he thought, perhaps wounded or, more to be preferred, dead, as all Texans should be.

He reasoned that the horse guard must be somewhere to the north, more or less where he had left them. When the Texans had passed out of sight he signaled the men behind him to move on. He pushed his horse into an easy lope, well out in front of the others.

He hoped to find that Badger Boy had not only survived unscathed but had acquitted himself in a manner befitting a warrior. If so, the other men should no longer chastise him for his disobedience.

He neared a tree-lined creek. A horseman rode out from the timber at some distance upstream and signaled. Much as Steals the Ponies looked forward to seeing that his brother was all right, he dreaded facing up to the fact that they had only six horses to show for their foray, plus whatever number the guard had managed to keep. This would reflect badly on his leadership and perhaps make it more difficult for him to recruit warriors for future raids.

Riding down to where the horse guard waited in the bed of the creek, he knew by their hang-dog look that they were ashamed for having failed him. But he felt that he had failed himself. To redeem his standing he would have to do something spectacular the next time.

He did not see Badger Boy. His throat tightened.

"Where is my brother?"

Nobody answered. The men who had stood guard on the horses looked away from him, most staring at the ground.

"Tonkawa Killer! Where is my brother?"

Tonkawa Killer sat up straight and defiant on his horse. "The last time I saw him, he was running away."

Angrily Steals the Ponies pushed his mount against Tonkawa Killer's, forcing the warrior to back away. "You lie! He would not run."

"I told you many times, he was never one of us. He is a Texan. Perhaps he ran to the Texans."

"He would not do that. Never would he do that." Steals the Ponies swept the other horse guards with eyes fierce as an eagle's. "Did anyone else see him? Did anyone see him run away?"

No one answered. Most looked off as if he were lashing them with a whip. He felt fire in his face. He *would* lash them if he had something more formidable than a quirt.

"Perhaps you let the Texans kill him, and you did nothing to help."

Tonkawa Killer remained defiant. "Go

look for yourself if you do not believe us."

The rest of the warriors arrived with their six horses. Steals the Ponies chewed on his anger a minute. "Go on, the rest of you. See if you can keep these horses, at least. I am going to look for my brother."

Tonkawa Killer said, "Look for him in a Texan lodge, among his *true* brothers." His tone was charged with contempt.

Heart heavy, Steals the Ponies began back-tracking the horse guard's line of retreat. He was aware of the danger that he might suddenly confront Texans doing the same thing in a reverse direction, but he had no choice. He must take that risk.

After a while he saw a horse grazing alone. Holding his breath until his lungs burned, he closed the distance quickly. He recognized the roan Badger Boy had been riding. The horse looked up, alert ears pointed forward.

Steals the Ponies grabbed the trailing rein, then circled the roan, looking for dried blood that might indicate his brother had been shot. He saw none. That raised his hopes a little. His anxious gaze scanned the countryside, searching for Badger Boy.

Shamans sometimes claimed they had heard animals talk, but Steals the Ponies never had. He wished the roan could talk to him now.

"Where is he? Where did you leave him?"

The roan tried to lower its head to graze again, but Steals the Ponies held the rein too closely. "You will lead me back to where you lost him."

He tried to pick up the roan's trail, but it was lost amid the tracks of so many others. He reasoned that all had come more or less the same way, so he followed the broader trail. He checked every brush motte, thinking a wounded Badger Boy might have dragged himself to the shade. He found nothing.

He came finally to a set of wagon tracks. Boot marks and crushed grass indicated that several men had moved around afoot. The wagon had circled and retreated in the same general direction by which it had come. He thought it probably was the one he had seen earlier, carrying some wounded Texan.

He had no interest in wounded Texans. The more of them, the better. Dead ones would please him most of all.

For a fleeting moment he considered the possibility that the Texans had found Badger Boy and carried him away. He dismissed the notion immediately. It was the way of the Texans to kill any Comanche where they found him and leave him lying where he fell, meat for the scavengers.

The sun touched fire to thin clouds stretched along the western horizon. Steals the Ponies realized darkness would be upon him soon. He urged his horse into a faster trot, tugging sternly at the rein by which he led the roan. Somewhere his brother lay injured, perhaps even dead. Steals the Ponies had to find him.

But he did not. He spent a sleepless night beside a small seep and at first light was up again, searching in ever-widening circles. For two full days he rode back and forth, looking for tracks, watching for Texans.

Not until late evening of the third day did he yield to the inevitable. Badger Boy was almost certainly dead. Otherwise Steals the Ponies would have found him by now.

It was painful to think of his brother's body being set upon by wolves or by the buzzards that seemed to await patiently the death of every living thing. But he did not know what more he could do. He felt he had searched every piece of ground where the warriors and the Texans had ridden.

Shoulders hunched, his head low, he turned northward. It was a long way to the Red River, and beyond it to where the encampment lay. He would think of Badger Boy every step of the way.

It was good that his father Buffalo Caller was not here to witness his failure. He would be ashamed, as Steals the Ponies was ashamed. Stronger even than the shame was grief for a brother lost.

Chapter 14

Rusty knew the jolting of the wagon must cause the boy intense pain, and he imagined he could feel it himself. He turned in the seat. "Grit your teeth, Andy Pickard. We'll be home after a while."

Jaw clenched, the boy stared up at the sky and made not a whimper. The Comanches had taught him stoicism. Rusty wondered what else they had taught him.

Because so many men had sent their families to Tom Blessing's place for mutual defense, it was agreed that the procession would go there first. The Texans drove before them those stolen horses they had managed to recover. The ones lost would have to be regarded as a tax of sorts, payment for living where Indian raids had to be accepted as a cost of business.

From a distance Rusty could see no one at Blessing's. Then, as the inhabitants recognized that the oncoming horsemen were not Indians, they began emerging into the open. Several riders spurred ahead, anxious to see about the women and children they had sent or left there for safety. Among them was Jed Hoskins. Whatever his shortcomings, Rusty decided, he was devoted to his family. Relieved men embraced wives and children. Rusty had no one there except Shanty. The old man limped out to meet him.

"Who's that you got in the wagon, Mr. Rusty?"

"A boy by the name of Andy Pickard."

Shanty's eyebrows lifted in surprise. "How come he's dressed up like an Indian?"

Rusty explained. "We're takin' him home with us 'til his leg mends, and 'til we can get word to his kinfolks to come and fetch him."

Tom Blessing had said he was fairly sure the boy's father had relatives down on the lower Brazos River, somewhere around old San Felipe.

Shanty leaned over the wagon and reached in as if to test the binding that held Rusty's rifle in place as a splint against the broken leg. The boy struck at him and shouted defensively. Shanty drew back. "He snaps like a young pup that's been beat on."

Rusty heard a familiar voice call his name.

312

"Rusty Shannon! Damned if your hair ain't got redder than it already was."

Rusty knew the speaker before he turned and saw him. "Len Tanner, I thought you'd gone back home for good."

The lanky former ranger grabbed Rusty's hand so hard he made the knuckles hurt. "The trouble with home is that after you've been gone too long it ain't home anymore."

"How come you here at Tom Blessing's?"

"Joined in with some fellers trackin' Indians. This is where we ended up." He peered into the wagon bed. "Just heard about your Indian boy. He don't look so fierce."

"Don't lean in too close. He's liable to take a chunk out of you."

"How you goin' to talk to him? You don't speak Comanche."

"He seems to recognize some words. I figure the language will gradually come back if we talk to him a lot."

Tanner said, "I'm better at talkin' than you are."

Rusty could not argue with that. "Then come home with us, why don't you?"

"Us?"

"Me and Shanty." He pointed toward the black man. "He's been stayin' at my place."

Tanner hesitated, then extended his hand.

313

It was not common for white to shake hands with black. Old ways faded slowly.

Jed Hoskins walked up, his face solemn. "Shanty, I want to talk to you."

Rusty stiffened, expecting trouble. He thought of his rifle, still tied to the boy's broken leg. But he had his pistol on his hip.

Hoskins said to Shanty, "My wife told me what you done."

Rusty prepared himself to step protectively in front of Shanty.

Shanty said, "I didn't do nothin' much."

"Saved my young'uns. I'd call that a right much."

Rusty stared in disbelief as Hoskins stuck out his hand toward the black man. Hoskins had a shamed look. "I've said some mean hard things agin you. I take back every one of them."

Surprised, a little flustered, Shanty accepted the handshake.

Hoskins turned to Rusty. "Wife says my young'uns and some others got restless bein' cooped up like chickens. They went outside to play and strayed off too far. All of a sudden a bunch of Comanches showed up. Of course they was mainly lookin' for horses, but they'd take a scalp from a kid if they couldn't get one from a grown man.

"Shanty was out there keepin' an eye on

the children. He put himself and his rifle between the Indians and the young'uns 'til they got back in the cabin. Like as not he kept some of them from bein' killed or carried off."

Rusty did not know what to say. Shanty seemed struck dumb too. He made a slight grin and shrugged his shoulders.

Fowler Gaskin had waited out the Indian danger with the women and children. He listened in angry disbelief. "What he done wasn't so much. I'd've done the same thing."

Hoskins turned on him. "You was here. Why didn't you?"

Gaskin stammered. "I . . . I didn't have no rifle."

"There was rifles around. You could've got you one. But they say you hunkered down in a corner and covered your head." Hoskins turned to the larger group of men. "I want everybody to understand: from now on, anybody who bothers this boy" — he pointed at Shanty "— has got me to whip." He turned a fierce face toward Fowler Gaskin.

Rusty thought it ironic that old Shanty was being called *boy*. But it was the way of the times. He voiced agreement with Hoskins. "What he said goes for me too."

Shanty seemed embarrassed by the attention. He looked at the ground.

Rusty told him, "That means you can go home if you want to, but you're welcome to keep stayin' at my place. Me and you have worked right good together."

Shanty welcomed the offer. "I reckon I'll stay at least 'til we get the crops in. Looks to me like you'll need help takin' care of that Indian boy." He pointed his chin toward the wagon.

"He's not Indian."

"But he thinks he is."

"He's liable to be a handful, sure enough."

Shanty held up both palms. "I've got two hands, both of them strong."

Preacher Webb said, "I'd better stay with you too, at least a couple of days. Got to watch that youngster's broken leg."

It was in Rusty's mind that the Comanches might set enough store in the boy to come looking for him. "The more of us the better." Himself, Shanty, Webb, and Tanner . . . they could make a good showing should it come to that.

Crowd opinion was that the Indians were unlikely to return, but it seemed the better part of valor to be prepared. Trying to outguess Comanche tactics was risky. Most agreed it was wise to remain at the Blessing farm overnight and not begin scattering until morning. No one wanted darkness to catch him halfway home.

That gave Webb plenty of time to remove the makeshift splint. He returned the rifle to Rusty, replacing it with two thin strips of pine. The Pickard boy bore the treatment in sullen silence.

Webb said, "The leg's swollen and hot. Goin' to be right painful for a while. Got a black bruise on one shoulder, too. Probably from the fall."

Everyone, particularly the children, showed a strong curiosity about the boy. They clustered around, studying him, commenting at length. The youngster tried to show them a fierce face, but his eyes betrayed fear and pain.

Webb said, "I think he's still got it in his head that we may kill him." He addressed the boy directly. "Nobody's out to hurt you, lad. We mean you well."

Tanner remarked, "You could put him in a circus and advertise him as the wild boy. He'd draw a crowd."

Rusty felt compassion. "All this attention is keepin' him agitated. We need to get him away from the crowd. Then maybe he'll settle down."

The next morning, still using the borrowed wagon, they set out for Rusty's farm. The women had made a sympathetic fuss over the Pickard boy, which seemed to distress him. The children were mainly inquisitive, some trying to talk to him, others simply chattering about him. All seemed only to add to his confusion. The boy appeared relieved to be getting away from so many strange people.

Rusty drove the wagon. Len Tanner rode close beside him on a bay horse. It was a long-legged animal, befitting its rider. Rusty said, "I didn't expect to see you back, especially so soon."

Tanner shook his head. "It don't take long to catch up on kinfolks. After about a week everybody seemed to be sayin' the same things over and over again. Even Mama and Papa. I'd figured I could help them through their old age, but they got too much family helpin' them as it is. And then there's them Yankee occupation soldiers. They got this far up the river yet?"

"Ain't seen them. I guess they've gone to the more settled places first." Rusty had heard that Union troops were scattering across the state, imposing Federal authority through martial law.

Tanner spat. "They'll get here soon enough, then you'll wish they'd never left

Ohio or Massachusetts or whatever foreign country they come from. Insolent, over-bearin' . . . you'd think they never won a war before."

"I notice that bay horse you're ridin' has got a U.S. brand on him. Bought him from the government, did you?"

"Not exactly. Borried him, you might say. I needed to leave in a considerable hurry, and I seen him tied to a hitchin' post. Saddled and all, like he had Len Tanner's name on him."

Rusty put mock accusation into his voice. "Stealin' horses. And you used to be a ranger."

"I don't lay any claim to him. If the government wants him it's welcome to come and get him. I won't give them any trouble."

"Sounds like you're already *in* trouble."

"Just a little difference of opinion with a Yankee sergeant, is all. I was sittin' in the grocery quiet and peaceful when he come in and wanted to see my parole pass. I told him I didn't have one because I never had been a Confederate soldier. Told him I'd been a ranger. He couldn't see no difference. Said if I couldn't show him a pass he was fixin' to drag me off to the Yankee compound.

"Well, after a polite discussion he ended up on his back, all covered in flour. Barrel got turned over durin' the commotion. He said he'd see to it that I saw the front end of a firin' squad. Acted plumb serious about it. This horse looked faster than the plug I'd been ridin', so I taken the borry of it. Thought it was a good time to go visit some of my old friends."

"You're welcome to stay here as long as you want to."

" 'Til the first Yankee soldiers show up. I've seen enough of them to last me awhile."

Badger Boy felt strange lying in a bed that stood on legs. He stared up at a ceiling of wood instead of buffalo hide. It did not even have a smoke hole in the center like the tepees to which he was accustomed. He vaguely remembered having lived in a cabin much like this one. He conjured up a hazy image of hard-packed dirt floors, of climbing a stairway into a loft above an open dog run. And there had been people. He wished he could remember them better, but when he reached for them they faded like dust carried away on the wind.

He wanted to get up and move around, but his leg was immobilized by the splints the Texan shaman had tied against it to hold the broken bone together.

He knew the man must be some sort of shaman. A number of people had stood with him, heads bowed, speaking to whatever guardian spirits watched over the Texans. Badger Boy reasoned that theirs must be different from those of the Comanches. How could the same spirits serve both The People and their enemies?

He longed to escape this trap that had snared him, but his leg was tightly bound and so painful he could not move. He realized that if he untied the splints the leg would collapse under his weight. They had taken away his breechcloth and moccasins and had given him a long cotton shirt much too large. To him it resembled a woman's dress, no fit garment for a fighting man.

His early fears had subsided, but he remained distrustful. Despite these Texans' display of concern, it was possible they were holding him prisoner until they were ready to torture him to death, as he had seen Comanches ceremonially torture captives, especially Apaches. If this came to pass he was resolved not to cry out or let them see fear. He could be at least as brave as any Apache. He was determined to die with the dignity worthy of a warrior. Somehow, he felt that Steals the Ponies would know.

Perhaps his adoptive father, Buffalo Caller, would look down from the spirit world and know too.

The red-haired man who had captured him walked into the small room. Badger Boy had heard others call him Rusty. He had no idea what the name meant. He sought but did not find any sign of hostility in the man's countenance. On the contrary, the Texan seemed worried about him. This was difficult to understand in an enemy.

Rusty said, "We'll have dinner directly. You hungry?"

Badger Boy recognized some words here and there. He knew *dinner* meant food. He understood *hungry.* He reasoned that he had known the Texan language before he became a Comanche. Bits and pieces came back to him as he listened to the men talk. When no one was in the room he tried to speak the words to himself. Some came easily. Others twisted his tongue.

It did not really matter whether he remembered the Texan language or not. If they did not kill him, he intended to escape. When his leg mended enough that he could walk without the splints, he would steal away and return to his true people. At times he entertained a fancy that Steals the Ponies would find him and take him away, though this hope did not stand up well when he thought soberly on it. It was probable that his brother had given him up for dead. His only hope for freedom lay in his own efforts. Time, then. He had been taught patience, necessary to a hunter and a warrior. He would bide his time and wait for strength.

Meanwhile he observed the four men who held him captive, trying to figure out who and what they were. The old one they called Preacher was, of course, some manner of shaman, for he spoke often to his gods. The tall, skinny one they called Tanner talked a lot, though Badger Boy had difficulty understanding enough words to find meaning in the one-sided conversation. The old man with the black face and hands puzzled him considerably. He could not remember ever seeing a skin so dark, not even among the Mexicans who sometimes came from the far west to trade among The People. The black man played for him on an instrument he called a banjo. The music was strange, yet he remembered hearing its like before.

Most worrisome of all was the one called Rusty. His red hair troubled Badger Boy. Steals the Ponies had told him about a warning from Buffalo Caller not long before his father's death. The old warrior had told of a Texan with red hair, carrying medicine stronger than his own. Years earlier, Buffalo Caller had captured a small Texan boy who had hair the color of rusted iron. Some days afterward, disaster had fallen upon Buffalo Caller and all The People with him. Texans had recovered the boy. From then on, Buffalo Caller had regarded red hair as a dark omen, a hostile power to be avoided. Steals the Ponies had seen a red-haired Texan in the fight that gave Buffalo Caller his fatal wound.

Badger Boy wondered if this might be the same man. Of the Texans he had observed since his capture, this was the only one who fit the description.

Often when one or more of the Texans came to look at him, he feigned sleep. Not when they brought him food, however. Once the pain diminished, his appetite returned with a vengeance. He did not recognize much of what they brought him to eat, but he found it mostly flavorful.

When Tanner told him, "You're startin' to fatten up, boy," Badger Boy understood. He was beginning to understand more words every day. He reasoned that they had been buried somewhere in his memory. Hearing them now was bringing them back into his consciousness. He began speaking some of the words, like *dinner, supper, water, meat.* After a few efforts he was able to say them easily.

One day Rusty, Tanner, and the black man Shanty brought him a pair of long sticks carved from limbs of an oak tree. Each had cloth wrapped as padding around a fork at its tops. Rusty placed the sticks beneath his own arms, demonstrating their use. He said, "These are crutches, so you can start gettin' around a little."

Badger Boy did not know the word *crutch,* but he realized the purpose of the sticks.

Len Tanner declared, "It ain't good to lay on your back too long. You'll petrify."

The old black man carefully lifted Badger Boy to a sitting position. Rusty and Tanner then positioned themselves on either side of him and brought him to his feet. Badger Boy felt weak, the room swaying around him, his leg hurting. But the two men's strength gave him confidence to remain on his feet and place the crutches beneath his armpits.

Rusty said, "Now take ahold," showing him how to grip the handles firmly attached by rawhide at arm's length. "All right, now, walk. We'll hold on to you. We won't let you fall."

Badger Boy understood the meaning and

most of the words. "I walk," he said. He took a step and would have fallen had the two men not had a firm grip.

Rusty said, "Try again. You'll get the hang of it."

This time Badger Boy took a step without feeling that he was about to fall. Gaining confidence, he took another and another. The two men relaxed their holds, though they did not relinquish them altogether.

Shanty declared enthusiastically, "You're doin' fine, boy. The Lord is lookin' down and smilin' on you."

Badger Boy reasoned that the Lord must be one of the Texans' gods. He had heard Preacher Webb talking to him from time to time, though he had never heard a reply. The Comanches' spirits often spoke to them in the voices of birds and animals. He reasoned that the Texans' gods must dwell farther away, though if that were the case he did not understand how they could hear Webb speak.

They were a strange lot, these Texans.

After a few steps the men released their hold entirely, though Rusty remained near enough to catch him if he fell. Badger Boy ventured out onto the dog run and felt the coolness of the breeze. The bright sun made his eyes pinch at first, though he found the light pleasant once they had accommodated to it. He had spent too many days in the room's close confinement.

Tanner said, "Beats hell out of stayin' indoors, don't it?"

Not sure of the proper reply, Badger Boy said, "Beats hell."

Rusty grinned at Tanner. "Good thing Preacher Webb has gone away to sermonize. He'd scorch you good for corruptin' an innocent boy."

Tanner said, "First things I ever learned as a young'un was the cusswords. A few *damn*s here and there don't hurt anything. Sometimes they're like a tonic."

Badger Boy understood only the general meaning of what they were saying, but he sensed that it was in good humor. He allowed himself a faint smile. It had been awhile since he had felt like smiling about anything.

Tanner noticed. "He's tryin' to grin. Some people don't think Indians have got any humor at all."

Rusty said, "They just don't know."

"The trouble is, what an Indian is most apt to grin about don't bode no good for a white man."

Shanty was not smiling. "Preacher Webb wouldn't like to come back and hear this boy usin' mean language. We need to teach him proper so he'll find favor in the eyes of the Lord."

There was the Lord again, Badger Boy thought. If these Texans put so much store in Him, perhaps he should learn a little about Him too. He needed all the gods and beneficent spirits he could summon, for he would require help to get away from here and return north where he belonged.

In time he more or less had the run of the place, within the limits imposed by his broken leg. He was able to get out of bed by himself, tuck the crutches beneath his arms, and go as far as the barn and livestock pens. He stayed away from the hog pen, for the mud-loving hogs had a smell like something four days dead. He saw that Rusty owned cattle, but those did not interest him. They were smaller and appeared more vulnerable than the buffalo. He found their meat less flavorful. Perhaps worst of all, they seemed dependent upon the Texans' care. Buffalo did not depend upon anybody. They ranged proud and free. They were brother to The People, like the wolves and the other wild animals of the plains.

The horses interested him a great deal more, partly because he loved horses in general, but more importantly because they were his hope of getting away from here as soon as he healed enough to ride. He noted that Rusty's favorite was a large black horse he called Alamo. He was not young, but he appeared sound, and strong enough to carry a rider all the way to Comanchería without stopping often for rest. Then there was the long-legged bay of Tanner's. From conversation he had been able to understand, he gathered that Tanner had stolen it somehow from the blue-coated soldiers. That elevated Tanner's standing in his eyes. A good horse thief was to be admired.

It pleased him to think how proud Steals the Ponies would be if Badger Boy came riding into camp on a fine Texan horse after having escaped from captivity. His brother might even stop calling him Badger Boy and give him a name befitting a man.

He leaned against the fence, staring northwestward, trying to visualize the way he and the other warriors had come. He had noted landmarks along the way, though a lot of the country had a monotonous sameness that led to confusion. He wondered if he could find his way home without getting lost.

A big worry would be the possibility of recapture, or even of being killed by the first whites who saw him. He had heard reports among The People that the white men had ended their long war against one another. He had understood enough talk by Rusty and the others to know it was true. He gathered that the warrior society known as rangers had been disbanded, which he considered especially fortunate. The People had always respected them more than the soldiers because when they engaged in a battle they clung like wildcats, with tooth and claw. The tall man Tanner talked about damnyankee soldiers, expected to arrive at any time. Badger Boy understood the word *soldiers,* but he was unsure about *damnyankee.* Tanner used the word as if it were an obscenity.

One afternoon while Badger Boy sunned himself in front of the cabin, Preacher Webb rode in. He had been absent for several days. He tied his horse and walked directly to Badger Boy, smiling. "Sunshine is the Lord's great healer, son. You're lookin' better every day." He leaned over close, reaching out as if to touch Badger Boy's long braids. He had tried more than once to persuade the lad to cut his hair white-man style. Badger Boy had resisted firmly each time, fighting off the scissors. The Texans had taken everything else that marked him as Comanche. He did not intend to let them cut his hair.

Webb said, "You need a good washin'. You've got company comin' tomorrow."

Washing, Badger Boy understood. *Company,* he did not.

"Somebody comes?"

"Kin of yours. I located your uncle down by San Felipe."

"Uncle?" Badger Boy did not understand.

"Your father's brother. His name is Pickard, like yours. Jim Pickard."

Badger Boy spoke the name. He had easily become used to being called Andy, for he dimly remembered having been called that before. He was less sure about the name Pickard. "Jim Pickard," he said, trying to find something familiar in it.

"Maybe you called him Uncle Jim."

"Uncle Jim. Uncle Jim." Nothing aroused any memories.

"Maybe when you see him. He's your family."

"Not my family. My family Comanche!"

"Well, we'll get you cleaned up in the mornin'. We don't want him to see you lookin' like a wild . . ."

Webb broke off, and Badger Boy had no idea what he had been about to say.

"Where this San Felipe?"

Webb pointed to the east. "Yonderway."

"Far?"

"Pretty far. Took me most of two days to get back."

"My uncle, he takes me?"

"I expect he will. We all figure the best place for you is with your own kin."

Rusty came in from the field. Badger Boy heard Webb tell him, "The boy's uncle stopped off at Tom Blessing's to rest his team tonight. I thought I'd better come ahead and let you know he's on his way."

Rusty stared at Badger Boy, his thoughts unreadable.

Webb went on, "Tom's not the sheriff anymore. The Federals turned him out. Appointed one of their own."

"Then they're takin' over lock, stock, and barrel."

"There are soldiers everywhere east of here, settin' up provisional local governments. They've appointed their own man governor in Austin."

"If Tom's not the sheriff anymore, then I reckon I'm not a deputy. Never saw a dime anyway, so it's no big loss." He turned back to Badger Boy. "First thing in the mornin' we'll get you shined up for your uncle."

Badger Boy bordered on panic but tried to keep from showing it. He was already a long way from The People. A trip to this place San Felipe would take him even farther and vastly increase the odds against his reaching home without being caught.

He had not intended to make the break quite this soon. His bad leg needed more healing time. But a change in circumstances was forcing his hand.

"Tomorrow. Tomorrow I get clean."

He lied. By tomorrow he intended to be a long way from here.

CHAPTER 15

Badger Boy ate hardly any supper. His stomach was in a turmoil. He watched the evening shadows lengthen and wished darkness would hurry.

Tanner noticed, for he could put away a prodigious amount of food himself. "You ain't eatin', boy. Sick?"

Preacher Webb said, "Probably excited. He seemed awful surprised when I told him about his uncle."

Rusty had said little. Mostly he had stared at his plate, picking at his food. "I know it's the right thing, sendin' him back amongst his own. But I'd like to know they'll take good care of him. What did you think of his uncle, Preacher?"

"It's hard to tell about a man the first time you see him. I noticed a family Bible on the table, and it was not dusty. That speaks well for him, I think."

Tanner declared, "I've seen some Bible

thumpers you couldn't turn your back on. Present company not included, Preacher."

Rusty said, "I've gotten used to havin' Andy here. Place'll seem different when he leaves."

Badger Boy wished they would quit talking and go to bed.

They did, eventually. Badger Boy made all the motions of bedding down, but when the room was dark he sat on the edge of the bunk, staring into darkness. He listened for snoring. It seemed forever in coming. When it came he recognized it as Tanner's.

He knew he should wait a little longer, to be safe, but anxiety gnawed at him like a wolf gnawing a bone. Before dark he tried to find his breechcloth and moccasins without arousing suspicion, but Rusty had put them away too well, or perhaps had even destroyed them. He had to content himself with wearing the long shirt. He was used to riding almost naked anyway. The question was whether he could ride, or even mount, with the splints on his leg. He knew he must try.

He moved slowly lest the crutches make a noise and awaken someone. He moved out of the room and onto the dog run, stopping often to listen. He could still hear Tanner's snoring. Shanty had been sleeping in the dog run, and Badger Boy circled around him carefully. He reached the barn, wondering which horse had been kept penned for the night. It was Rusty's habit to keep one up so he would not be afoot the first thing in the morning. Badger Boy hoped it would be Alamo.

He was disappointed. He found Tanner's long-legged bay instead. Well, the bay would have to do. At least those legs ought to carry him a good distance in a hurry. The main problem would be getting on him, for his back was a long way from the ground.

Badger Boy did not bother with a saddle. He was used to riding bareback, tucking his knees under a rope tied loosely around the horse's chest. He had a little trouble with the bridle, for he was not accustomed to dealing with the steel bits. Their sound, grating against the horse's teeth, was disconcerting.

Ordinarily he would grab a handful of mane and spring up onto the back, but the splints kept one leg immobilized. He tried a couple of times but could not achieve enough height. He led the horse close to the fence and attempted to climb far enough up the rails that he could slide over onto the back. That too proved futile.

He saw but one alternative, and it was

risky. He had to remove the splints. He hoped the bone had knitted enough to handle the strain. Leaning against the fence, he untied the wrapping Webb had put around his leg. The pine slats fell to the ground.

Gingerly he tested his weight. The leg felt as if someone had driven a spear through the bone. Cold sweat broke out on his face, and he found his palms were wet as well. He dried them on the long shirt and pulled the horse up close to him. Taking a deep breath, then gritting his teeth, he tried to spring up onto the bay's back.

He did not make it. He felt himself sliding down but was unable to stop. He intended to let the good leg take the impact as he struck the ground, but the broken leg caught much of it. It collapsed, and he fell on his stomach. The sudden movement spooked the horse. It jerked away from him and ran halfway across the pen before stopping to look back, snorting in its excitement.

Badger Boy did not know if he had rebroken the bone. The pain was excruciating. He lay helpless, unable to push up from the ground far enough to gather his legs under him. He wanted to cry out in agony but would not allow himself the weakness.

A shadow fell across the moonlit pen. Looking up, he saw the outline of a man with a rifle or shotgun.

"No shoot! No shoot!" he called.

The voice was Shanty's. "Andy, is that you layin' there? What in the Lord's good name you tryin' to do?"

Shanty knelt at Badger Boy's side. "You done taken all the wrappin' off. Wouldn't surprise me none if that leg is busted plumb in two again."

That was Badger Boy's fear too.

Shanty stood up and cupped his hands around his mouth. "Mr. Rusty! Preacher! You-all needed out here by the barn."

He started to help Badger Boy to his feet but thought better of it. "We better leave everything like it is 'til the preacher man looks at you." He shook his head, showing disapproval. "Tryin' to skedaddle, wasn't you? I figured some Indian was tryin' to take Mr. Tanner's horse. Guess I wasn't all that far wrong."

Badger Boy hurt too badly to try to decipher all Shanty said. He knew the gist of it.

Rusty, Webb, and Tanner all arrived at the same time. Webb picked up the fallen splints and leaned them against the fence, then carefully ran his hand up and down Badger

Boy's leg. Badger Boy winced. He tried not to make a sound, but an involuntary groan escaped him.

Webb said, "Maybe the bone held together. It's God's mercy if it did. Let's carry him back up to the cabin. Real careful now. That bone's as flimsy as an eggshell."

Rusty demanded, "What did you do it for?"

Badger Boy ground his teeth together in an effort to fight down the pain. "No want to go with uncle. Want to go home."

Tanner tried to make light of it. "Don't you know they hang horse thieves?" Badger Boy had surmised that Tanner stole the bay from the bluecoats, but he hurt too much to appreciate the ironic humor.

Badger Boy lay awake most of the night, the leg throbbing, allowing him no mercy. Webb had wrapped the splints around it again after satisfying himself that the bone had not broken anew. He had said, "The Comanches raise their boys to be tough. Anybody else, that leg would be in two pieces."

Badger Boy was unable to hold breakfast in his stomach. After a couple of tentative bites, he quit.

Webb said, "We'd best be about gettin'

you cleaned up."

Badger Boy would much prefer to bathe in the creek, but the splints and his injured leg precluded that. He took his bath out of a tin pan, slower and less satisfying. Done, he put on a clean shirt that Rusty brought him. It was much too large. The sleeves were considerably longer than his arms, so he had to roll them up. The tail of the shirt reached past his knees. He had seen boys at Blessing's cabin wearing long shirts and nothing else, no trousers, not even a breech-cloth. To him it still looked like something for a woman, not a man.

"Why uncle come?" he asked. "I no know him, he no know me."

"You're blood kin," Shanty said. "Everybody ought to be with their blood kin."

Badger Boy had seen no one else whose face was black like Shanty's. "You got blood kin?"

Shanty seemed taken aback. "Someplace, I expect. I was sold away when I was just a young'un. But you got a chance to be with your own folks now. You'd ought to be happy."

Badger Boy would be happy only when he got back with The People. Since last night's failure, he knew it would be somewhat longer than he had expected. Now that he had grudgingly accepted his situation, he began to feel some curiosity about the man who was his Texan father's brother. Brothers often looked much alike. He wondered if seeing his uncle would help him remember his Texan father's face.

"When uncle come?"

Rusty stood on the dog run, shading his eyes. "I see Tom Blessing on horseback, and somebody in a wagon. Let's get Andy out here in the daylight." They moved him to a chair on the dog run, the splinted leg extended straight out. Rusty gave Badger Boy a quick inspection. "Now, you be on your best behavior, and smile."

Badger Boy could not smile on command. He had to feel like it, and he did not feel like it. Anxiety put his stomach in turmoil. His uncle was coming to take him away, farther than ever from the Comanche stronghold. Hampered by his leg, Badger Boy would not be able to put up much resistance. His hands shook. He tried to hide his nervousness by folding them together.

Tom Blessing trotted ahead. The other man hauled up on the lines and stopped a team of mules that pulled his wagon. Blessing dismounted to greet his longtime friends first, then turned to Badger Boy. "Got somebody who's traveled a long ways to see you. Andy Pickard, this here is your Uncle Jim, come to fetch you home."

It was the white man's way to shake hands, but Badger Boy did not want to. He did not want anyone to see how his hands were shaking. He managed a noncommittal nod to the man who climbed down from the wagon and approached him.

Uncle Jim stopped a bit short to give Badger Boy a critical study. He did not speak directly to his nephew. "Can't say I see much of my brother in him. Maybe a little around the eyes. I'm afraid he's taken after his mother a right smart more."

Preacher Webb offered, "I remember his mother. She was a handsome woman." Most women looked handsome to old bachelor Webb.

"If you like them skinny. I always liked to see a good stout corn-fed woman myself. They can usually outwork a skinny woman two to one."

Webb seemed a little put off. "If a work-horse is all you're lookin' for."

"Just bein' practical, Preacher. Life is hard in this country, and a weak woman can't tote her share of the load. Good looks wear off pretty soon. Strong hands and a strong back, that's what a Texas woman needs."

Badger Boy listened intently, trying to understand. He stared at Pickard's face, hoping to see something that would bring back a memory of his father. The voice had a faintly familiar quality, but he saw nothing in the face to bring patchy old images back into focus. He gathered that his uncle was saying something unfavorable about his mother. Though he barely remembered her, he felt a rise of indignation.

No Comanche would insult his own mother or allow anyone else to do so. His face warming, Badger Boy tried to think of the Texan words to express his disapproval. All that came to him was Comanche, and he used that in an angry voice.

Pickard narrowed his eyes in disapproval. "He's speakin' Comanche. How come you-all ain't taught him to talk civilized?"

Rusty's voice was sharp. "It's comin' back to him a little at a time. He can talk some when he wants to."

"And how come he's still got those Indian braids in his hair? I'd cut them off first thing. He may still *be* a heathen, but he don't have to look like one."

Webb said, "We've tried to cut his hair. He won't let us."

"Since when do you let young'uns set the rules? If he gave me any sass I'd quirt the

343

heathen out of him. And I'd start with that hair." He stepped closer to Badger Boy and pulled a skinning knife from a scabbard on his belt.

Badger Boy feared his uncle meant to stab him. He recoiled, wishing for a weapon. Pickard caught one of the braids. Badger Boy realized he meant to cut it off. He jerked free, then lunged at Pickard's throat. He knocked Pickard's hat off before the splinted leg betrayed him. He fell forward, his hands striking the ground first, his chin following an instant later. He was stunned.

He heard Rusty's angry voice. "Back off, Pickard. Leave the boy alone."

"You saw how he came at me. Damned savage, that's what he is."

Webb lifted Badger Boy to his feet and helped him fit the crutches beneath his arm. "The boy's still confused. The Indians have had him since he was little."

Pickard's face was flushed with rage. "There was murder in his eyes. He's past all salvation. Keep him around white folks and he's apt to kill somebody."

Rusty said, "You've got to give him time."

Pickard picked up his hat and dusted it against his leg. "Time for what, to do murder? He'll never change. Maybe we'd all be better off if you'd shot him in the first place and put him out of his misery."

Tom Blessing seemed to swell up even larger than his natural large size. "We'll have no talk about killin'. And this boy your own kin!"

Pickard pointed. "Look at him. He ain't white anymore, he's got the killin' heart of a Comanche. If he ever was any kin of mine, he ain't no more."

Anger flared in Rusty's eyes. "I've changed my mind. I'm not lettin' you take him with you."

"I don't *want* to take him with me. Think I'd let him slit the throats of all my family? Or maybe ravage my daughters? And even if he didn't, what would my neighbors think, me keepin' a wild savage and callin' him kin? I'd probably have to chain him up like a dog."

Fists clenched, Rusty moved close enough to breathe in Pickard's face. "Then maybe you'd better get in your wagon and go back where you came from."

"I'll do more than that. I'll tell the blue-coat army about him. I'll tell them to come get him and put him on the reservation where he belongs. He'll never be nothin' but a wild Indian."

Webb and Tanner and Blessing all moved toward Pickard. He backed off, his hands raised defensively. His eyes cut from one man to another. "Four against one ain't a fair deal."

Rusty growled, "The others are stayin' out of it. It's just me and you, if you want it that way. The boy's no animal to be put in a cage."

"That's just what he is, an animal."

Badger Boy was amazed that the two men would threaten a fight over him. He had not understood all that was said, but he knew his uncle meant him no good and Rusty had come to his defense. That did not seem logical inasmuch as his uncle had a blood tie to him. This reinforced his long-held acceptance that Texans were a strange lot. Trying to make sense of them could give a man a headache.

Tom Blessing pushed between Rusty and Pickard. His was a formidable presence when he was aroused. "Now, men, you're liable to do somethin' you'll both hurt for tomorrow." He took a viselike grip on Pickard's shoulder. "Mr. Pickard, I think you'd best get in your wagon and start home. It's a long ways to San Felipe."

Pickard stomped toward the wagon and climbed up onto the seat. "That boy's a menace. My advice is that you send him back to them wild Indians where he belongs.

Or give him to the Yankee army. They've probably got a place for the likes of him." He whipped the mules into a trot.

Tanner gave Badger Boy a look of pity. "Might be better he *was* back with the Comanches."

Rusty shook his head. "Don't say such a thing where he can hear it. You'll give him more notions like he had last night."

"He's still got them. It don't take a smart man to know what he's thinkin' when he stares off to the north and shuts you out like you wasn't there."

Rusty turned to Tom Blessing. "You don't really think the Yankees would take him away and force him to the reservation, and him white?"

"There's no tellin'. They might. Or they might try to turn him into a bluecoat Indian scout."

"He's just a young'un yet."

"There was many a young'un killed in the war. In any case they won't bother askin' me or you what we think. They didn't ask me my feelin's when they took my sheriff's job away; they just slammed the door. We're a defeated enemy."

Rusty fixed a worried stare on Badger Boy. "Andy Pickard, I don't know what we're goin' to do with you."

Badger Boy wondered too.

Preacher Webb walked up beside Rusty. "That boy doesn't seem half as disturbed over this as you are."

"He's too young yet to know how it can hurt, not havin' any kin in the world. But I know."

Rusty walked halfway out to the shed and stood awhile, staring at nothing in particular. When he came back, he appeared to have come to a difficult decision. "Tanner's right. You'd be better off runnin' free with your Comanches than penned up with strangers on a reservation. Soon as you're fit to travel, I'll take you."

Webb said, "He won't be able to ride for a while yet."

"We'll wait 'til he can."

"You can't take him all the way back to the Comanches. They'd almost surely kill you."

"How else can I get him there?"

"You can take him as far as the Monahan farm, and maybe as far as the Red River. He can make the last part of the trip by himself."

Rusty frowned, studying the proposition. "In the long run this may be the wrong thing to do, but in the short run I can't see any other way. Bein' a captive on the reservation would be like dyin' an inch at a time."

"Sometimes you have to get through today the best you can and trust tomorrow to the Lord."

Rusty looked toward his field. The crops were almost all in. "Won't be much for somebody else to take care of if I'm gone for a while. Len, you've got nowhere to go. Wouldn't you like to winter here?"

Tanner shrugged. "It's better than campin' in some brushy draw when the northers come down. But hadn't you rather I'd come with you?"

"I'd rather you were here, watchin' over the farm."

Shanty said, "I ain't in no hurry about movin' back home. I can stay here with Mr. Tanner and look after my own place just the way I been doin'."

Rusty nodded his gratitude. "I don't know how long I may be gone."

Tanner said, "It won't matter. This place'll be waitin' for you when you get back. Me and Shanty won't let old Fowler Gaskin tote it away."

In another week Webb removed the splints. "Test your weight real careful and trust in the crutches."

Badger Boy was delighted. He found that

he could move the knee a little. Though it caused pain, it was a welcome pain. He had feared that the leg might remain stiff forever. "Pretty soon no more crutches."

"Don't get in too big a hurry. Rome was not built in a day."

Badger Boy wondered who Rome was.

Shanty and Tanner both grinned to see Badger Boy without the splints. Rusty was not smiling. If anything, he appeared regretful. "Why you not glad for me?" Badger Boy asked.

"I am, in a way. But I'm not anxious to see you leave us. I was hopin' maybe you'd change your mind if you stayed here long enough."

"My mind not change."

Getting rid of the splints meant a change of clothes. Webb said, "He can wear somethin' decent now instead of that long shirt."

Badger Boy was ill at ease in the white man shirt and trousers Rusty gave him. A floppy old hat dropped down to his ears and had to be stuffed out with strips of newspaper to fit comfortably on his head. He kept his moccasins because they fit his feet better than anything the men could offer.

Webb observed him with reserved satisfaction. "Except for the braids, he looks like a farm boy from anyplace. Nobody'd take him for a Comanche."

"I *am* Comanche," Badger Boy declared. "Clothes no change." He turned to Rusty. "When we go?"

"Another week. Maybe two. We've got to know you can stand a long ride."

Badger Boy sensed that Rusty continued to hope he would change his mind and stay. But when the north wind blew at night he imagined he could hear the voices of his People, calling. Nothing was going to change his mind.

Three saddled horses and a pack mule stood waiting. Rusty shook hands with Shanty, then Tanner. "In case somethin' drastic comes up, Len, you know where I'll be."

Tanner smiled. "Tell them Monahan girls Len Tanner said howdy. And kiss them for me, if you've got the nerve."

The Monahan girls. Mention of them brought the image of Geneva, and the pain that went with it. "Kissin' the girls is more in your department."

Shanty was somber. "Be watchful, Andy, and take care of yourself."

Tanner gripped the boy's hand. "You ever get tired of that Indian life, come see me. There's lots more things I can teach you."

"Damn betcha."

Webb said dryly, "I think you may have taught him too much already."

Rusty was able to follow a well-defined wagon trail for better than half the day, but then he had to turn off of it when it shifted due westward. He angled across country, toward the northwest.

Webb rode alongside him, Andy trailing a little way behind, Indian style. Webb said, "Years ago, the first time you ever rode with the volunteers, we followed Indian raiders along this same route."

Rusty nodded solemnly. "That's right. We camped for the night yonder where the trail crosses the creek. But we're not stoppin' there this time. I've got another place in mind for tonight's camp."

Webb's voice became anxious. "You sure you know what you're doin'?"

"I'm takin' a chance. He's been havin' trouble rememberin'. This may jog his memory."

"Some memories are best left buried."

"Not when you need them to tell you who you are."

Webb shook his head in doubt.

For a time Rusty feared darkness might catch them before they reached the place he was aiming for, but then he saw the line of small trees and knew he had reached the creek crossing he remembered with such terrible vividness.

Andy had sat slumped in the saddle, looking as if he might even be dozing. Now he sat up straight, looking around with serious interest. "This place. I think I been here."

He pointed to a tree that apparently had been bent out of shape as a sapling and had grown crookedly into something like a question mark. "That tree. I remember."

"One tree looks about like another."

"Not that one." Badger Boy's face became increasingly grave. "Bad place."

"Bad? How so?"

"I don't know. Feel bad spirits here. Damn bad."

Preacher Webb frowned. Tanner's teachings had left an indelible mark on the boy's speech.

Rusty said, "We'll camp here for the night."

The lad's eyes looked fearful. "Something happen here. Something bad."

"Do you remember it?"

Andy shook his head but kept looking around anxiously as if he saw or felt something the men could not.

Webb suggested, "Maybe we ought to move on a little farther."

Rusty said, "There's wood here, and water. Been others camped here before." He helped Andy down from the saddle and handed him a long stick whittled into a rude cane to aid him in walking now that he had left the crutches behind. The boy seemed reluctant to venture out.

He leaned on the cane and kept watching as if he expected something awesome to rush at him out of the trees.

Rusty and Webb took what they needed from the mule's pack. Webb built a small fire while Rusty led Badger Boy to a small pile of rocks beneath a tree. Rusty's skin went cold as he remembered. "I came this way once with Preacher and Tom Blessing and a bunch of others, trailin' a Comanche war party. They had taken a lot of horses. But worse than that, they had stolen a woman and a small boy."

He waited, watching for a reaction. He was not sure he saw one. He said, "They killed the woman here. This is where we found her, and where we buried her. We never found any sign of the boy."

Andy remained silent. Rusty was not sure he understood until the youngster asked, "That boy . . . him me?"

"Yes."

"How come I no remember?"

"You were young. And maybe you tried hard *not* to remember."

Andy seated himself on the ground, favoring the weak leg. He sat staring at the unmarked grave. He said nothing. Rusty waited for him to react, to speak, but no words came.

Eventually Webb called, "Coffee's ready if you are."

Looking back over his shoulder, Rusty walked to the fire and poured coffee from a blackened can into a tin cup.

Webb asked, "He remember anything?"

"Can't tell. It's like he's in a trance or somethin'. Indians have got a way of sensin' things they can't see. He may have gotten that from them."

Rusty's cup was half empty when he heard something, a sort of low whine, then a wail. He turned quickly to see the boy bent over, face in his arms, his body trembling. Rusty dropped the cup and hurried to him.

Andy cried out in anguish. "Mama! Mama!" He wept bitterly.

Rusty knelt and put an arm around him. "It's all right, Andy. It was a long time ago."

Preacher Webb tried to squat down on the boy's other side, but his knees were too stiff. He remained standing.

Rusty said, "Seems like he finally remembered."

"A boy so young couldn't stand lookin' into hell. He put up a high wall to shut it out. Now you've made him see over that wall."

Later, Andy stared into the small blaze of the campfire. Rusty and Webb had finally prevailed on him to eat a small supper. "This place . . . they stop here with us. They eat a horse. Then they take Mama . . ." He squeezed his eyes shut. "Many times she screams. I try to go to her, but they whip me. Long time . . . no more screams. I cry, they whip me. I make myself not cry. They don't whip me no more."

Rusty said, "At least now you remember who you are."

"I am Andy Pickard. All the same I am Badger Boy. How can I be two people?"

Rusty had no answer.

Webb said, "I knew your mother, Andy. She was a good woman. Your daddy was a good man, too."

"Not same as uncle?"

"Not the same as your uncle."

"Good. Damn uncle. No like."

Before they left camp the next morning they stood beside the grave. Rains had caused some of the rocks to roll away, and

Rusty had replaced them neatly.

Badger Boy was solemn. "My mother . . . why my people do this to her? Why they kill her but keep me?"

Rusty shook his head. "They're different from us. There's a lot us white people will never understand."

"I am white, but I am Comanche also. Why I not understand?"

CHAPTER 16

They were a couple of hours short of the Monahan farm when Andy said, "Something moves, there." He pointed to the west.

Rusty could not see anything. "Where?"

Andy pointed again. "Somewhere there. I feel it."

"Feel it? You sure it's not your imagination?"

Then Rusty saw horsemen straggle from a ragged row of trees a few hundred yards away. He reined up. "He's right, Preacher. See them?"

Webb had his own reins drawn tight. "Not until just now." He glanced at Andy with wonder. "Son, you've sure got sharp eyes."

"Not see." He touched his hand to his chest. "Feel it here."

Rusty asked, "Indians?"

Webb frowned. "Can't be sure at the distance."

Andy said, "Not Indians. White."

"If it's holdup artists, we haven't got much worth stealin'."

Webb said, "We have three horses and a mule. For some, that would be enough."

Rusty studied the terrain. It was open in all directions out to the trees. "If they come at us, this is a good place as any to stand them off." He dismounted. "Come on, Andy, I'll help you down."

The boy seemed unperturbed. "We fight?"

"Not unless they bring a fight to us." Rusty checked his rifle. Webb stood behind his horse, resting his own rifle across the saddle.

The horsemen hesitated briefly, perhaps discussing the situation, then moved cautiously across the open prairie. Rusty counted five. As they closed the distance he could see three blue uniforms. He lowered his rifle. "Soldiers. One's hunched over like he's hurt."

Webb said, "Andy, you might ought to stick those braids under your hat. We didn't bring you this far to have the army take you away from us."

Two riders were in civilian clothes. They sat awkwardly, hands tied to their saddles. Two soldiers held rifles ready for action. The third straightened up with some difficulty. Rusty recognized the uniform of a lieutenant. He lowered his rifle and stepped forward.

"You-all come on in. We're peaceful."

The two enlisted men were black. One wore sergeant's stripes. The officer's dusty coat showed a dark bloodstain on the shoulder. A bulge indicated a heavy bandage beneath it. The lieutenant's face was drained to a pale clay color.

Both prisoners were heavily bearded. Rusty looked a second time before he recognized them. "Pete Dawkins!" The other man was Dawkins's running mate Scully.

The lieutenant glanced apprehensively toward the two enlisted men. He seemed reassured to see they had not relaxed their stance with the rifles. He asked Rusty, "You know these prisoners?" His cautious manner told Rusty it would be better to deny any acquaintance.

"I wish I could say I don't. It's been my bad luck to know them for several years."

The officer eased a bit, though the two troopers remained stiffened for a possible fight.

Rusty asked, "What've they been up to this time?"

Cagily the officer said, "I hope you have no interest in setting them free. My men would drop you in a moment."

"No need to worry about us. I arrested Pete myself once, when I was with the rangers. He was stealin' horses."

"Then he's still at the same trade. He's just not very good at it."

"Who'd he hit this time?"

"A good Union family just north of here. Horse people."

"By the name of Monahan?"

"That's right. The Monahan men fought them off, but this Dawkins wounded one."

"Which one? Do you know the name?"

"Evan Gifford. Are you acquainted with him?"

Rusty grimaced. "I know his wife. Good woman. They're good people, all of them. How bad was he hurt?"

"They said he was wounded worse in the war and got over that. He will recover from this."

Rusty knew his compassion should be for Evan Gifford, but most of it was for Geneva. He imagined how it must have shaken her to see her husband brought in shot, again. "Damn you, Pete, haven't you Dawkinses caused the Monahans grief enough?"

Sullen, Pete Dawkins looked past Rusty as if he could not see him. Scully's head was down, his shoulders pinched in an attitude of despair.

The lieutenant said, "We had some trouble capturing these two. They killed one of my troopers and put a bullet through my shoulder."

Rusty said, "You look like you could use some help. We'd be glad to be of service to you."

The officer's eyes were hopeful. "You say you're a ranger?"

"Used to be. They cut us loose when the war ended. I'm Rusty Shannon. This here's Preacher Webb. The boy's Andy Pickard."

"My father knew the rangers in the Mexican War. He said they would charge hell with half a bucket of water."

"They did, several times. Where are you headed with these two?"

"Back to the Monahan farm to get positive identification."

"The Monahans'd gladly hang Pete for you . . . by his toes, by his neck, any old way you want it done. And I'd be glad to help them."

"Any hanging will be up to a court."

The lieutenant seemed about to slip out of his saddle. He grabbed his horse's mane to steady himself.

Rusty stepped forward to catch him in

case he fell. The two black soldiers instantly aimed their rifles at him. The sergeant warned, "Don't you touch Lieutenant Ames."

The lieutenant coughed. "It's all right, Bailey. He's trying to help."

"Yes sir," the sergeant said, but he did not shift the rifle's muzzle away from Rusty.

Rusty knew it would be wise not to make any more quick moves. "Lieutenant, you'd better get off of that horse and rest awhile. When you're up to it, we'll escort you to the Monahans'."

"I've come this far. I can go the rest of the way. We ask for no favors."

"We were headed there ourselves. You favor *us* by takin' Pete Dawkins away." He explained how Colonel Caleb Dawkins, Pete, and some hired help had lynched Lon and Billy Monahan early in the war for the family's pro-Union sentiments.

Ames glared at Pete. "A rebel hangman. He has that much more to answer for."

"You sure you're strong enough to keep ridin'?"

"I'm strong enough. Two Johnny Reb bullets didn't kill me at Chicamauga. I'll survive one from a bushwhacking horse thief."

The lieutenant pulled in beside Andy as

Rusty climbed back onto Alamo. "I've forgotten what he said your name is, young fellow."

The youngster gave Rusty a querulous look. "Andy."

Rusty feared Andy's halting use of the language would give him away, but the boy said nothing more.

The sergeant poked his rifle in Pete's direction. "Move out, you back-shooter."

Pete growled, "I don't take bossin' from no nigger."

The lieutenant snapped, "Then you'll take it from me. Move out, like he says, or I'll shoot you myself."

Scully was usually a follower, but he started first.

Pete said defiantly, "You ain't hanged me yet. My old daddy's got influence. Ain't no jury around here will ever convict me for killin' a nigger."

The lieutenant said, "It won't be a local jury. You killed a soldier, so you will be tried by a military court."

Clearly, Pete had not considered that possibility. He looked as if the officer had struck him with a club. Scully slumped lower in his saddle.

Rusty felt a glow of satisfaction. "Pete's not worth the price of the rope that hangs him. But I'd be glad to make the invest-ment."

"The government will provide the rope."

"I haven't seen many soldiers yet, but they tell me you-all are spreadin' out across the state."

"As rapidly as we can. It's our job to begin the Reconstruction of this country and to keep the peace no matter how many we have to shoot."

Rusty nodded in the direction of the sergeant. "Are all your soldiers black?"

"A lot of them."

"Then peace may not be easy kept. Black soldiers will be like a red flag to some folks."

"I'm afraid that's the idea, though I am not proud of it. The powers that be are determined to humiliate the defeated rebels. One way is to place former slaves in a posi-tion of authority over them."

"They'll get a bunch of soldiers killed."

"The shameful part is that the officials don't care. No price is too high, so long as someone else has to pay it."

"You know who'll pay the most. The blacks."

"Yes, just as they carried the burden of slavery."

The Monahan farm broke into view. Pete Dawkins became agitated. "You ain't goin' to let them Monahans at me, are you? They're crazy . . . James and that hateful old woman. They'd kill me and not bat an eyelash."

Preacher Webb's face reddened. "You'll not speak ill of Clemmie Monahan in my presence."

"Put a curse on me, why don't you?"

"I am a minister. I do not practice witchcraft. Any curse that's on you, you've put it there yourself."

With a lifetime of help from Colonel Caleb Dawkins, Rusty thought.

The lieutenant said, "No one is going to kill you, Dawkins, not until the duly appointed time. Then it will be the army's responsibility."

Andy waited until the lieutenant and the two troopers were out of hearing. He whispered, "Those soldiers, they Shanty kin?"

Rusty realized the boy had seen few if any blacks. "I'd hardly think so."

"Same tribe, look like."

All the way up from Rusty's farm, Geneva had weighed heavily upon his mind. She had carried him to the extremes of high anticipation, then of dread. Hearing about her husband's injury had only complicated his feelings. He wondered how well she was

366

coping with what must seem an overabundance of bad luck.

He hoped his own hurt had healed enough that he could look at her without falling apart inside.

Andy was being stoic, but Rusty could see in his weary eyes that his leg pained him, that only willpower kept him in the saddle.

The lieutenant said, "I've been trying to draw your boy into conversation. He doesn't talk much, does he?"

"The trip's worn him out. He needs a few days of rest before he goes on."

"Goes on to where?"

"Back to his folks." Rusty hoped Ames would be satisfied enough to stop asking questions. He seemed to be, for he fell quiet. He looked even wearier than Andy. That wound in his shoulder was wearing him down.

Vince Purdy, the grandfather, was the first person Rusty saw. Working in the garden, he paused and leaned on his hoe, staring at the incoming riders. Rusty's attention went to Josie Monahan, picking tomatoes and holding them in her apron. She hurried to the new log house.

"Mama! We got company comin'!" She emptied the tomatoes into a basket on the dog run, then turned to watch the visitors' approach. "I see Preacher Webb. And Rusty Shannon. Looks like soldiers with them."

Clemmie Monahan stepped out past the dog run, shading her eyes with one hand. She beamed at sight of the minister and gave Rusty a tentative nod. The smile died as she recognized the two prisoners. Reining Alamo to a stop, Rusty heard her declare, "They'll not bring Pete Dawkins into this house!"

Webb dismounted and embraced her. "Pete's a prisoner. He can't hurt anybody."

"But I may hurt *him.* Put him in the barn out yonder, or the shed. Even the root cellar. But not in this house where I've got to look at him."

The lieutenant gave her a weak salute. "We'll not trouble you with him more than we have to, ma'am. We'll keep him out of your sight."

Clemmie stepped into the yard. Her agitation over Pete turned to solicitude for Ames. "You're hurt. Come on into the house and we'll see what we can do for you."

"I'm obliged, ma'am, but first I have to see to my men, and to my prisoners."

Rusty climbed down. "I'll help your troopers, Lieutenant. You go with Clemmie . . . Miz Monahan."

Clemmie put her arms around Webb

again. "It's good to see you, Warren. Come on in. Josie, go unsaddle Warren's horse for him."

Josie's eyes shone as she stared at Rusty. The glow was infectious. The resemblance to her older sister grew stronger each time he saw her.

Clemmie noticed Andy still sitting on his horse. "Get down, boy, and come in." She asked Webb, "Who is he?"

"His name's Andy Pickard. I'll explain about him later."

Clemmie called again, "Come on down, Andy."

Andy seemed shy. "Rusty, I stay with you."

Rusty saw that the attention made the boy nervous. "You can help me unpack the mule, but be careful about that leg." He helped Andy to the ground. He shouted to Clemmie, "We'll be comin' along directly."

As he turned, he found Josie standing in front of him, blocking his way. She asked eagerly, "You stayin' awhile?"

"It all depends."

"You can stay for a hundred years as far as I'm concerned. I was afraid you'd forget about us."

"You know I could never forget the Monahans."

"Does that include me?"

"You're a Monahan."

"But I'm *Josie* Monahan. I'm not Geneva."

He thought he knew where the conversation was going, and he tried to head it off. "I hear Geneva's husband got in the way of a bullet again."

"He's laid up over in the old house."

"How bad is he hurt?"

"He's in considerable pain, but he'll heal."

"And Geneva?"

"She's in pain too, for him."

"A bad piece of luck for both of them."

"But they've got the baby. That makes up for a lot. Geneva had a boy, you know."

"Nobody told me."

Rusty was not sure what he ought to feel. Geneva was a mother now. That put her even farther beyond his reach. He had known of her pregnancy since last spring, yet he had never accommodated to the hurt, the feeling of loss. He had tried to put it aside and not deal with it. Now, one way or another, he *had* to deal with it.

Josie said, "You'll want to see the baby. It's beautiful."

"That's no big surprise. It has a beautiful mother."

"And a good-lookin' daddy. It takes two, you know."

"They get along well together, Geneva and Evan?"

"He worships the ground she walks on. And he should. After all, she's my sister. I'll want my husband to worship the ground *I* walk on, someday."

Unexpectedly he felt like smiling. "Then you'd better be careful where you step. There's been horses by here."

Sergeant Bailey asked Rusty, "You know a safe place where we can hold these prisoners for the night? I expect the lieutenant will want to travel on come mornin'."

Rusty pointed toward a shed. "Ought to be a couple of good stout posts you can tie them to. It may not be comfortable."

"They ain't got no comfort comin' to them." Bailey prodded Pete with the rifle.

Pete complained, "You wouldn't tie me to a post, would you? I wouldn't be able to sleep at-all."

Bailey was not impressed. "You'll soon be gettin' all the sleep you ever need. Come on, Private Cotter. I'll let you do the tyin'."

Josie said Evan and her brother James had come across Pete and Scully driving off some of their horses. In the gunfight that followed, Evan had taken a bullet in his arm. Another bullet had creased James's leg. "Didn't hurt him much. It was just enough to make him good and mad. He'd have followed Pete and Scully all the way to hell if he hadn't had to take care of Evan. Lieutenant Ames came along with his patrol and took over the chase."

"Knowin' James, I expect he's still mad."

"Mad enough that we'd better keep him away from Pete Dawkins."

"Pete has spilled it for good now, killin' a soldier. Old Colonel Dawkins is liable to take this mighty hard."

Bitterness crept into Josie's voice. "He's got it comin' to him for the grief he's caused this family. But the word is that he disowned Pete. Drove him off of the place with a blacksnake whip."

"You've got to feel a little sorry for the colonel, all by himself now on that big farm."

"The word we're hearin' is that it won't be his much longer. The Federals are layin' taxes on him that he can't pay. They've got it in for him because he preached so strong for the Confederacy and rode roughshod over everybody who didn't agree with him."

"Sounds like some people are still fightin' the war."

"In some ways, I'm afraid the war's barely started. Texas is in for a lot of grief."

Andy's limp was so severe that Rusty told him to sit down. The boy slumped on a wagon tongue, his eyes dull and weary.

We ought to've waited another week before we started, Rusty thought.

He turned the horses loose and fed them. Beneath the shed he found Pete and Scully sitting on the bare ground, their arms behind their backs and tied to two sturdy-looking posts.

Pete complained, "This ain't no way to treat a white man."

Rusty grunted. "It's no way to treat any man. But then, you're not much of one."

Sergeant Bailey's eyes crackled with hatred. "Pity his mama didn't take him out the day he was born and drown him like a sack of kittens. Private Wilkes was a good soldier. Didn't deserve to get shot in the back. Lieutenant didn't deserve a hole in his shoulder, neither. And all for a no-account like this."

It struck Rusty that Pete had better keep still, or he might be in more danger from Sergeant Bailey than from any of the Monahans.

James Monahan strode into the shed, his

face clouded for a storm as he sought out Pete Dawkins. He towered over the bound prisoner. "Pete, I ought to cut your throat right where you're sittin'."

Pete's eyes went wide in fear.

Sergeant Bailey said sternly, "He's the army's business now. You dassn't touch him."

James fumed. "I know, and I won't. But I'd like to." He stuck his finger in Pete's face. "I hope they send out invitations to your hangin'. I'd ride five hundred miles bareback to watch it." He strode angrily back toward the house.

Rusty said, "Andy, we'd just as well go too."

The boy pushed himself up from his place on the wagon tongue. Rusty was disturbed to notice that the braids had slipped from beneath Andy's hat and lay on his shoulders.

Bailey noticed too. "I've seen some light-skinned Indians. Is this boy half Choctaw or somethin'?"

Andy took offense. He thrust out his chest. "Not Choctaw. Comanche."

The sergeant's suspicions rushed to the surface. "You ain't fixin' to sell him or make a servant out of him, or somethin' like that, I hope. Lieutenant Ames, he wouldn't stand still for nothin' of that kind."

Rusty saw it was too late to put the cork back in the bottle. "Andy's white, but the Comanches raised him. He wants to go back to them. I'm helpin' him get there."

Andy nodded, silently vouching for Rusty. The sergeant still seemed to have reservations.

Rusty said, "I'd sooner you didn't say anything to the lieutenant."

"There ain't nothin' slow about Lieutenant Ames. He sees things for hisself."

"We've been afraid the army might try to take Andy and send him to a reservation, or maybe an orphanage . . . somethin' like that."

Bailey looked intently at the boy. "Long as this is what he really wants . . ."

Andy nodded. "I want to go home."

"Then I don't see where the army's got any business messin' around with him. And I don't think Lieutenant Ames would either."

The other soldier listened but never spoke. Rusty judged that he had come out of slavery, where no one had asked his opinion or even considered that he might have one. Whatever suited Sergeant Bailey would suit him too.

Pete Dawkins was not so compliant. "Damn anybody who'd send a white boy back to the Indians. Ain't you got no pride in you, Shannon?"

"You're a horse thief and a hangman. I don't see where you've got any call to talk to me about pride. Even your old daddy's ashamed of you."

"My old daddy might be wrong about a lot of things, but he was right about the Confederacy. Now we got Yankee soldiers overrunnin' the country, makin' white folks take orders from niggers. It's a hell of a world the Monahans and all you Union-lovin' scalywags have took us into."

Bailey knelt beside Pete, malice in his eyes. "I wonder, did Cotter get them ropes tight enough? I think I'll take another hitch on them."

Pete cursed. "You damned black crow, you're cuttin' off my blood."

"Be glad I ain't cuttin' off nothin' else. I am sore tempted."

Rusty had to walk by the old log house to get to the newer one where most of the family lived. Andy limped along beside him. Geneva stood in the open dog run. Rusty stopped in mid-stride, looking at her. All the old pain returned for a moment, all the burning inside. He touched his fingers to the brim of his hat. "Howdy, Geneva. You're lookin' real fine."

She really did, he thought. He was not just paying an empty compliment.

She said, "You brought in Pete Dawkins."

"The soldiers brought him in. Preacher and Andy and me, we just came with the soldiers."

"I hope they had to shoot him a little, the way he shot Evan."

"I'm afraid they didn't, but the army'll give him what he's got comin'."

"Rusty, I'd like you to see my baby."

"I was on my way up to the house." He did not really want to see the baby right now. It would remind him too much of old plans and dreams gone irretrievably astray. But he could not refuse her. "Just for a minute." He nodded for Andy to follow him.

Evan Gifford lay on a bed, his legs covered by a blanket. His arm was heavily bandaged. Geneva said, "Look who just came, Evan."

Gifford extended his good hand. "I heard you brought in Pete Dawkins."

Rusty accepted the handshake. "The soldiers did. I had nothin' to do with catchin' him."

"I was lookin' him square in the eye when he did this to me." Gifford lifted the wounded arm an inch. "Another second and I'd've shot him instead of him shootin' me.

But at least we gave him a good scrap, and we didn't let him get our horses."

Rusty remembered his earlier favorable judgment of Evan Gifford. Geneva had married a fighter.

Damn it, he thought, why can't I find something to hate about him?

Gifford asked, "Seen our baby yet?"

"Geneva was fixin' to show me."

The baby lay in a small handmade wooden crib. Geneva beamed as she lifted a corner of a blanket to reveal the tiny reddish face. "Ever see a prettier one in your life?"

"I can't say as I've seen that many."

Andy said nothing but observed the baby with curiosity.

Geneva said, "I think he's got Evan's face. Some of the family say he has my eyes. What do you think?"

"I'd have to study him awhile."

The baby's blue eyes were open but did not seem to be focused on anything in particular. Geneva kissed its tiny forehead. "It's about time for feedin'. I'd invite you to stay, Rusty, but it's not exactly a public event."

Rusty's face warmed. "No, I'd expect not." He tried not to allow himself the mental picture, but it came nevertheless. "Me and Andy will be goin' on."

He paused at the door for one more look at Geneva. She began unbuttoning her dress from the top. He turned quickly away.

Andy said, "Baby has red face. Like Comanche baby."

"I think that's the way they all look at first."

"Pretty woman. Why you don't have a woman?"

Josie stood in front of the new house, waiting. "You saw Geneva and the baby. I can tell by the look on your face."

She did not have to say what she was thinking; he could read it in her eyes. He said, "I never had any claim on her. She's married now, and to a good man. I'm happy about that."

He was not, and he knew Josie knew it.

She said, "You just haven't made up your mind to turn a-loose yet. But you will. And when you do, I'll be here."

"You deserve better than to be a substitute for somebody else."

"I'd settle for that, at first. But I think I could make a man forget he had ever wanted anybody besides me."

"I doubt I'd be that man."

"We'll just have to wait and see, won't we?"

Andy looked from one to the other. It was

obvious he had no idea what they were talking about.

The boy was the object of quiet curiosity at the family supper table. It would have been impolite to wear his hat in the house, so the long Comanche-style braids were in plain view. Rusty was not concerned about the Monahans' acceptance, but he was a little worried about Lieutenant Ames. He was haunted by what Jim Pickard had said about the army perhaps forcing the boy to a reservation or into an institution.

Ames put his fears to rest. "I have seen other white children taken from Indian captivity. He is hardly the first. I assume he is some kin of yours, Shannon?"

"By experience, not by blood. The Comanches took me when I was too little to remember much, but I was freed after a few days. Andy spent better than four years amongst them."

"So now you are trying to fit him back into white society."

"No sir. I'm takin' him back to rejoin the Comanches." He watched for what he thought was the inevitable adverse reaction. But Ames pondered in silence, his face devoid of expression that might indicate what was in his mind.

Rusty added, "His blood kin rejected him.

380

The Comanches are all the family he's got. I wish he'd stay with us, but if it can't be of his own accord maybe he'll be better off back where he came from."

"For now, perhaps. But what of the future? The sun is going down on the Indians' free times. They're being crowded off of their hunting grounds. They'll soon be so decimated by war and hunger that they can no longer remain independent. Assuming he is not killed in battle before then, what will become of him?"

"I've laid awake at night worryin' about that."

"But you are still taking him back?"

"I can't chain him up. If I don't take him he'll run away. If he's goin' anyhow, it's best I travel along and be sure he makes it."

"You may not get back. What assurance have you that the Indians will not kill you?"

Rusty glanced at the minister. "Preacher Webb has friends in high places."

"He's riding with you?"

"No. This is as far as he goes."

Webb said, "But my prayers will go with him."

James Monahan had held quiet through the meal, listening, hiding his thoughts behind half-closed eyes. "Prayers are all right, but sometimes an extra gun carries more weight. I'll go with you if you like, Rusty."

"If it comes to usin' guns, a dozen of us wouldn't be enough. No, it's best it be just me and Andy. When I've taken him far enough that I'm sure he can finish the trip alone, I'll turn back."

Josie raised a hand to her mouth. "But you'll be all alone out in Indian country."

"When I was a ranger I spent a lot of time in Indian country."

"At least you had a badge then."

"I never did. There weren't enough to go around. The best I ever had was a piece of paper. Badge or paper, neither one meant a thing to the Comanches. It still wouldn't."

Josie arose and quickly left the room, holding a handkerchief to her eyes as she stepped out onto the dog run. Clemmie pushed away from the table, intending to follow. Preacher Webb touched her hand, stopping her. "Clemmie, I think someone else should go and talk to her." He looked at Rusty.

Rusty remained seated for a moment, trying to decide what he could say. He still did not know as he walked out where she stood. "Josie . . ."

She looked away from him. "I didn't go to act like a baby. It usually takes a lot to make me cry."

"I know, but you're borrowin' trouble that may not ever happen. Chances are I'll never see an Indian. I'll take Andy across the river. From there he ought to have no trouble finishin' the trip alone. I should be back in three or four days."

"When do you plan to leave?"

"Andy's worn out. That leg is troublin' him. He needs a few days' rest before we start."

"A few days." She squeezed the handkerchief. "That's better than no days at-all."

"Josie, I don't want you takin' too much for granted. I like you, but anything past that . . ."

"Past that . . . who knows? After all, we do have a few days."

Clemmie and Preacher Webb walked out. Clemmie raised a lighted lantern to give her daughter a moment's anxious study. "Is everything all right out here?"

"It's all right, Mama. I didn't mean to break up everybody's supper."

"Most people eat more than is good for them anyway." Clemmie swung the lantern. "Come on, Warren, I want you to take a look at that new colt."

Rusty and Josie watched them walk past the shed and out to the barn. The lantern-light disappeared.

Josie asked, "When a preacher gets married, can he just do the marryin' himself, or has he got to find him another preacher?"

"I don't know. Guess I never thought about it."

"Been a Methodist minister by here a couple of times lately. I have a feelin' Mama and Preacher Webb will be needin' him. I reckon a sprinklin' preacher can tie the knot as tight as a deep-water preacher, don't you?"

"I suppose it's mainly up to the couple how strong the knot is."

"When I get married, that knot'll be so strong that wild horses couldn't pull it apart."

Rusty bedded down in the barn, along with Andy, Preacher Webb, and Lieutenant Ames. He was awakened in the night by Andy shaking his shoulder. Andy whispered, "Something wrong."

Rusty pushed up onto his elbow, peering into the darkness and seeing nothing. "What?"

"Don't know. Spirits, maybe."

"Spirits! More likely you heard an owl hoot."

He had noticed that owls made Andy nervous. Comanches were wary of them.

He heard horses running. The sound came from beyond the corrals. He flung his blanket aside and pushed to his feet. His first thought was an Indian raid.

Ames awakened. "What's the matter?"

Rusty hurried to the barn door to look outside. He saw nothing amiss, but he was fully alarmed.

He saw a dark figure lurch from the shed and fall to his knees, moaning. Rusty ran to him. Sergeant Bailey rasped, "Tell Lieutenant Ames. Them prisoners have got away!"

CHAPTER 17

Exploring with his fingers, Rusty found the point of a nail protruding through the post to which Pete Dawkins had been tied. Webb's lighted lantern revealed frayed fragments of rope indicating that Pete had rubbed his bonds against the nail until he had worried his way through them and freed his hands.

Sergeant Bailey's head was bloody. He told the lieutenant, "Private Cotter was on guard. Must be he went to sleep, or maybe Dawkins was just too sneaky for him. Busted him over the head with that shovel yonder. Then he busted me before I could get my rifle."

Ames gave vent to strong Yankee profanity. "I ought to've stood guard on them myself. Damned little sleep this shoulder has let me get anyway."

Bailey lamented, "Him and his partner, they got off with our guns."

Private Cotter would never stand court-martial for losing his prisoners. He was dead.

"Probably never knew what hit him," Rusty said.

Bailey rubbed his forehead and looked at the blood on his hand. "Thought he'd killed me too, like as not. He didn't know how hard my head is."

The lieutenant clenched a fist. "That's two of my soldiers he owes the army for."

The commotion had aroused James Monahan. He had hurried down from the new house, buttoning his britches. He found that the fugitives had run the extra horses out of the corral, but the animals had gone only a few yards and stopped. James easily drove them back into the pen.

He declared, "Pete owes this family too, more than he could pay in a hundred years. I'll get him, Lieutenant." He looked at Rusty. "You goin' with me or not?"

"I'll be ready in two minutes."

"It'll take me five. Preacher, how about you saddlin' my dun horse for me while I run back to the house and get my gun?"

The lieutenant protested, "It's a long time until daylight. You can't see the tracks."

"I know the first place he'll head for. If me and Rusty don't find him there, at least we'll have that much advantage when the sun comes up."

The lieutenant argued, "He's the army's prisoner. It's my place to recapture him."

Rusty said, "With all due respect, you're not strong enough to travel ten miles. We'll bring him back for you, either in the saddle or across it."

"I can't give you any legal authority . . ."

Rusty said, "I never officially got mustered out of the rangers. I've got papers that say I am one whether there's still a ranger force or not."

"You'd be laughed out of a civilian court, but a military court might accept it if I testify that I approved." He glanced at James. "How about you? Any history with the rangers?"

"No, I was hidin' from them most of the time."

While Rusty caught Alamo, Webb saddled James's horse. Sergeant Bailey saddled and mounted his own leggy black.

Rusty told him, "Pete fetched you a bad lick with that shovel. You've got no business ridin'."

"I don't ride on my head. You say you know where he's goin'. Let's be gettin' started."

Andy stood watching. "I go too?"

Rusty wondered about the instinct that had awakened the boy. Perhaps he had heard something but did not realize it. Or perhaps his time with the Comanches *had* given him some sort of sixth sense. "No, you stay here. Keep off of that leg as much as you can, and don't go anyplace 'til I come back."

Rusty and James did not have to compare notes. Both guessed Pete's first destination would be his father's farm. Even granted that the old man had disowned him and thrown him off the place, Pete would probably go there for fresh horses and, likely as not, to take any money his father might have. In time of trouble he had always run to Colonel Dawkins.

They put their horses into an easy lope for a while, then slowed to a trot. Sergeant Bailey was impatient to keep up the faster pace. "I ain't so bad hurt."

Rusty said, "We've got to think about the horses. We're liable to have to chase Pete a lot farther than his daddy's place."

James added, "He's bound to figure somebody is grabbin' at his shirttails. He'll be makin' all the tracks he can."

As they rode, James asked Rusty how things were at his farm down on the Colorado. Rusty told him they had managed a good harvest, but what they produced would be mainly for their own consumption. Barter trade was limited. There was no cash market at all.

James said, "Me and Evan spent a lot of the summer catchin' and brandin' wild cattle. Nobody paid much attention to them through the war, so they've multiplied. They're there for the takin'."

Rusty replied, "But they're not worth a continental. About all you can sell is hide and tallow. Even to do that, you have to be on the coast where the boats can load it up."

"That's now. By next year it'll be different. There's a cash market for cattle in Missouri, live and on the hoof. They'll pay in Yankee silver. Soon as the grass rises in the spring, I'll gather everything I can rustle up and drive them to Missouri."

"All that way afoot?"

James nodded. "Before the war lots of cattle were driven to Missouri and Illinois and down to New Orleans. I heard of a bunch that was walked all the way to New York City."

"That'd take time."

"Time we've got a-plenty of. Money we don't. You can't do much farmin' in the winter. You could be out puttin' your brand on unclaimed cattle same as me and Evan."

Rusty found the proposition interesting to contemplate. "It'd be somethin' to do."

James said, "In fact, I don't see no reason we couldn't throw our gathers into one good-sized bunch. By summer we'd be back from Missouri with our pockets jinglin' and the goose hangin' high. Who knows? I might even buy the Dawkins farm off of them Yankee tax collectors."

Rusty found himself warming to the idea, though he knew it was a long shot. "It's a far piece to Missouri. We'd better not be spendin' it 'til we get it in our pockets."

James grinned. "Half the fun is in thinkin' about what you're goin' to do with it. You can spend it a thousand times before you get it. When you have it, you can't spend it but once."

Scully kept looking over his shoulder into the darkness. "I tell you, I been hearin' somethin'."

"You hear your own cowardly heart beatin'," Pete declared. "Ain't nothin' behind us but a whippoorwill and an owl or two. We killed both of them nigger guards. Ain't nobody goin' to miss us 'til daylight."

"Then what are we pushin' these horses so hard for? I can feel mine givin' out under me already."

Pete said, "We'll get fresh ones from the old man. Then we'll head north up into the Nations. Won't nobody find us."

"There's lots of Indians up there. Some of them are apt to remember when we borrowed horses from them."

"Them Indians don't know one white man from another. We could tell them we're Ulysses S. Grant and Robert E. Lee. They wouldn't know the difference."

Scully argued, "As many times as we've run from Indians, I ain't none too keen about goin' up there amongst them."

"We'll stay where the peaceful ones are, the Cherokees and the Choctaws and such. We won't have no truck with the Comanches." Pete brightened as a new idea struck him. "Who knows? We might even set ourselves up as horse traders. Instead of borrowin' Indian horses out of the Nations and sellin' them in Texas, we could take Texas horses up into the Nations."

"Evenin' up the score?"

"Sure. We'd be the Indians' friends. And in return, they'd protect us if anybody came snoopin' around."

Scully was unconvinced. "Sounds good, but there's still many a mile between us and the Nations. How do you know your old man will give us anything? Last time, he was fixin' to shoot us both. If we'd stayed five more minutes, he would've."

"He's about done. You notice how he's shrunk up lately? Losin' Mama, losin' the war, has took the guts out of him. We won't *ask* for nothin'. We'll just take what we want. He can't do nothin' about it, the shape he's in."

"He ain't too weak to pull a trigger."

Pete shrugged. "But the will to do it ain't in him anymore."

Dawn was only a pink streak across the eastern sky when they rode into the Dawkins corrals. Pete's heart jumped as he heard a wooden gate strike against a post, and he brought up the army rifle he had taken from the black sergeant. He saw lantern light at the cow shed and realized one of the house servants was already doing the morning milking.

Pete's pulse slowed. "It's only old Jethro. Ought to be a couple of night horses in the pen yonder. Let's go get them."

Scully had spooked even worse than Pete. "You don't reckon he'd have a gun, do you?"

"Jethro wouldn't know which end the shot comes out of. Get ahold of yourself."

"I guess I'm nervous bein' this close to your old man. I can't help but remember how he was when we hanged them two Monahans. I never saw a man so cold and hard. He scared the hell out of me."

"Used to scare me too, but no more. Ain't nothin' left of him but a hollow husk. A good strong wind would blow him plumb away."

Two horses had stood in the corral overnight. The morning had become just light enough that Pete could see to rope them out, the smaller of the two for Scully, the strongest for himself.

Scully complained, "This one don't look like he'd go all the way to the Nations. Lucky if he gets across the county line."

"Stop belly-achin' and throw your saddle on him. If we come across a better one somewhere, we'll make a swap."

The lantern came bobbing along, its faint light dancing off the corral fence. A dark figure climbed up onto the second rail and held the lantern at arm's length.

"Who you-all? What you doin' there?"

"It's just me and Scully. We're tradin' horses."

"Marse Pete? Old Colonel ain't goin' to be pleased. You remember what he told you, that he'd shoot you if you was to ever come back."

"Well, I'm back just the same. You go on

up to the house and roust him out. Tell him I want all the vittles me and Scully can pack behind our saddles. And any cash money he's got in the house. We'll be there soon as we finish saddlin' up."

Jethro climbed down, muttering. "Old Colonel, he sure ain't goin' to be pleased." He went trotting off toward the big house, splashing milk from his bucket.

Pete snickered. "Right there is proof enough that the Yankees are crazy. Settin' the slaves free! Jethro would starve to death like an old pet dog if he didn't have somebody to feed him and tell him what to do. When Papa dies, or when he loses this place, what's goin' to become of people like Jethro?"

"I'm more worried about what's goin' to become of me and you. The army's got a long memory."

"For them nigger soldiers? I'll bet none of them could even sign their name to the company roster. They'll be forgotten about before we get to the Nations."

Scully's nervousness had been getting under Pete's skin. Even after Pete had freed himself from his bonds and had broken the first guard's head with a shovel, Scully had been whimpering that they would never get away, that they were sure to be hanged for what he had done.

"We were goin' to hang anyway," Pete had argued. "They can't do it to us but once."

The second soldier had come awake just in time for Pete to give him the same treatment. Pete then had cut Scully loose, gathered the soldiers' rifles, and saddled the first two horses he could catch. Daylight had shown both to bear the U.S. brand.

"Now we *are* in trouble," Scully had complained. "We've stolen army horses."

"The worst they can do is use a heavier rope."

Pete did not walk when he could ride. Though it was a short distance from the corrals to the big house, he mounted the fresh horse he had just taken. Scully followed along, leading his.

Caleb Dawkins met them at the door, standing in it to block their entry. He seemed smaller now than Pete had remembered him. He had lost weight, his clothes hanging loose. His shoulders had a tired slump as if he carried a heavy yoke. "I told you the last time, Pete, you are no longer welcome in this house."

"Jethro tell you what I want?"

"He told me. I have nothing here for you. Go, before I summon all the hands and have you forcibly thrown off of this place."

"You'd better not summon anybody you wouldn't want to see dead." Pete flourished the army rifle. "You're standin' in my way, old man. I'm comin' in."

He gave his father a push. The colonel stepped back, almost losing his balance. Pete felt exhilarated at his sense of new power. For most of his life, his father had only to give him a fierce look and Pete would shrink away. Colonel did not even have to say anything.

The old man's already dead and doesn't know it, he thought.

"I told Jethro to sack us up some grub. Where's it at?"

"I told him to forget it. If you came empty-handed, you'll leave the same way."

Frustration boiled into anger. "Damn you, old man, you owe me somethin'. I'm your son."

"A fact that a heavy heart has brought me to regret."

Pete jerked a thumb toward the kitchen door. "Scully, go in yonder and see what you can find. Hurry up." He turned back to his father. "You keep tellin' me how poor you are, but I believe you've still got money stashed away. I want it."

"All the money I had went to the cause. You know that."

"I just know you *told* me that, but I think you lied. Now, where've you got it?"

"It's a sorry state you've come to, Pete, that you'd rob your own father. I'm only glad your mother isn't here to see how low you've let yourself sink. You're on the run again, aren't you?"

"It's none of your concern if I am. You've already disowned me, so what difference does it make?"

"What did you do, steal some more horses?"

"Killed some nigger soldiers, is all."

"So now you've moved up to higher crimes. You've added murder to the list."

"It ain't murder, killin' a nigger. The country's overrun with them as it is."

"But if they were soldiers the Federals won't rest 'til they have a noose around your neck."

"There was thousands of soldiers killed in the war. What's three more, especially with them bein' black?" Pete took a threatening stance. "Now, where's that money at?"

Tears glistened in the colonel's dull eyes. "You'll find a metal box in the bottom of my desk yonder."

Pete took three quick strides and flung open the double doors in the lower part of the roll-top desk. He grabbed the box so eagerly that it slipped from his grasp and fell heavily to the floor. He lifted it to the desk top and nervously fumbled with the latch. He flipped the box open and plunged his hands into stacks of neatly banded currency. He yelled exuberantly. Then the yell broke off. His face fell.

"Confederate money!" He ripped the bands off several bundles before he turned in disbelief. "Confederate, every damned bit of it. But where's the real money?"

"That's it. That's all there is."

Pete let a handful of currency float to the floor. "You fool! You damned old fool! You were richer than Croesus, and you let it go to hell for a crazy notion."

"Not crazy. You wouldn't call it crazy if we had won."

Pete could not contain his rage. He drove his fist into his father's square chin. Colonel Dawkins staggered back, grasping at a chair. He missed it and fell heavily to the floor.

He made no effort to get up. He lay there, rubbing his hand across his bleeding mouth, then looking at it. In a voice so weak Pete barely heard it, he said, "I remember when you were eight, and you took diphtheria. You would have died, but your mother and I would not allow it." Bitterly he shook his head. "Better you had died an innocent boy than to become what you are."

Pete shouted, "Hurry up, Scully. We got to be movin'."

Scully came out of the kitchen with a cloth sack. "Didn't find much. Some bacon, some cold bread. Not even any coffee."

"It'll do. Let's go."

His father still lay on the floor, gasping as if he could not catch breath enough to fill his lungs. Pete barely yielded him a glance as he rushed out the door. He ran toward his tied horse, which took fright and pulled back hard against the reins. Pete had difficulty mounting him. Once in the saddle, he slapped the horse across the shoulders with the long reins. "Settle down, damn you!" For a moment it looked as if the animal would pitch.

"You want to run, you jughead?" Pete turned northward and drummed his heels against the horse's ribs. He had no spurs. "Then damn you, run!" He lashed the animal's shoulders again.

Scully had trouble keeping up. He struggled to tie the sack of food with his saddle strings while his own mount jumped a ditch and galloped after Pete's. "For God's sake, Pete . . ."

Pete let his horse run a mile or so before he slowed to an easier lope, then a long trot.

Scully caught up, complaining as usual. "You're goin' to kill these horses."

"Never let a horse think he's boss or he'll take advantage of you every time."

"How far back do you reckon the army is?"

"Wasn't nobody left but that lieutenant, and he took my bullet in his shoulder."

"But there's them Monahans, especially that James. And Rusty Shannon. They'd kill us on sight, give them half a chance."

Pete growled, "I wish you'd shut up. You tryin' to turn me into a coward too?" Scully's fears were beginning to get to him, though he hoped it did not show. Scully would probably go limp as a rag doll if he saw that Pete was weakening. What little strength the man had left, he was borrowing from Pete.

Pete kicked his horse back into a lope. "Since you're so damned scared, we'll pick up the pace."

After a time he began to sense his horse's stride becoming more labored. He knew he should slow down, but Scully's fear was infectious.

That next hill yonder, he thought. We'll stop and look back when we get to the top of it. If we don't see anybody, we'll rest the horses.

His horse never made it to the hill. He stepped in a badger hole and went down, slamming Pete to the ground. Pete arose on hands and knees, struggling for breath, coughing at the dust in his throat.

Scully was frightened. "You hurt, Pete?"

"I'm all right. Catch my horse. Don't let him get away."

"He ain't goin' noplace. He's crippled."

The animal limped heavily, favoring its right forefoot. Pete was dismayed. "Damned stupid horse!" He was angry enough to shoot the animal, but his rifle lay on the ground where the fall had spilled it. Legs wobbly, Pete walked over and picked up the weapon. He saw that the barrel was clogged with dirt. Firing it would be dangerous. It might explode in his hands.

Scully was long-faced. "What we goin' to do now? Your horse ain't fit to go on. If we try to ride this one double we'll break it down before we get to the river."

Pete quickly made up his mind. "We won't ride it double. Get down, Scully."

"Get down? What for?"

"Because I said so." He swung the rifle's muzzle toward his partner. "Get down."

Scully reluctantly complied. "What're you fixin' to do?"

Pete took the reins from Scully's hand and

swung into the saddle. "I'm takin' your horse."

"But what about me?"

"What *about* you? I'm sick of your bitchin' and complainin'. I ought to've left you behind a long time ago."

Scully's voice was near the breaking point. "What'll I do?"

"You'll walk like hell if you know what's good for you. Run, if you can. Or find you a hole somewhere and pull it in after you." He reined Scully's horse around and started north.

For a while he could hear Scully's voice, pleading, as Scully tried to run after him. He put the horse into a lope and soon outdistanced his partner. When he finally looked back he saw Scully sitting on the ground, a picture of despair.

Rusty did not know what to expect as he rode in to the Dawkins place. Several of the colonel's field hands were gathered in front of the big house. They seemed heavily burdened. Rusty nodded at James and the sergeant and rode up to the group. He expected hostility but saw no evidence of it. The men appeared saddened.

He said, "We're lookin' for Pete Dawkins. You-all seen him pass this way?"

One man took a step forward. Rusty had encountered him before, though he could not remember his name. The black man said, "He done come and gone. Him and that Scully. Caught fresh horses and left yonderway." He indicated the north.

"How long ago?"

The man looked at his companions and shrugged. "A right smart of a while. Ain't got no watch."

"Didn't say where he was headed?"

"Didn't say nothin' much to any of us. Might've said somethin' to the colonel. I wouldn't know."

"Maybe we'd better go talk to the colonel."

"I'm afraid you're too late. Ain't nobody goin' to talk to the colonel, not ever again. He's dead."

A cold chill ran through Rusty. "Pete killed him?" He found that hard to believe, even for Pete.

"No sir. But Pete knocked him down. Colonel never got up. Had him a heart seizure after Pete left. Wasn't nothin' I could do for him. He was gone before I could even finish sayin' the Lord's Prayer."

Rusty looked at James. In view of the long enmity, and the fact that Dawkins had hanged his father and brother, Rusty expected James to be glad. Instead, he seemed regretful.

James said, "I've thought of a hundred ways for the old devil to die and wished for every one of them. But this way never crossed my mind."

Sergeant Bailey had not spoken. Beyond the little conversation he might have overheard, he knew nothing about the violent history between the Dawkins family and the Monahans. He said, "We're settin' here. He's travelin'."

James's voice was bitter. "He'd *better* travel. Just one good shot at him, that's all I ask for. Just one good shot."

Rusty said, "We need to bring him in alive."

"We didn't promise that. You told the lieutenant we'd bring him back either in the saddle or tied across it. If I can get just one good shot, he'll be across it."

Rusty realized James had no intention of bringing Pete back alive. He looked for Bailey's reaction.

The sergeant said, "He's goin' to die anyway. Why not save the army some money?"

Rusty led the way out. The tracks were easy to follow, for Pete had made no apparent effort to hide them. They indicated that his and Scully's horses had run hard for the first mile or so, then slowed. The course was due north.

"Headin' for the Red River the quickest way they can," Rusty speculated.

James nodded. "Probably think they'll be safe when they get to the Nations. But they've stolen a way too many Indian horses. If any of them so-called friendlies recognize them, their lives won't be worth a Confederate dollar."

They came at length upon a crippled horse, standing with its head down. It turned away, trying to move on three legs.

Grimly James said, "Pete and Scully must be ridin' double. They're as good as dead now." He rode over for a closer look at the lame horse. He drew his pistol to shoot it but changed his mind. "I don't think its leg is broke. Just taken a bad sprain."

Rusty removed the saddle and bridle, dropping them to the ground so the horse could move unencumbered.

A little farther on, a man afoot spotted them about the same time they saw him. He began to run, stumbling, falling, getting up, and running again. James spurred ahead of Rusty and Bailey, his pistol in his hand.

"If that's Pete . . ."

Rusty soon saw that the fugitive was Scully.

James shouted, "Stop, Scully."

Scully darted to the left. James fired at the ground just past him. Scully darted back to the right. James fired again, the bullet kicking up dirt at Scully's feet. Scully dropped to his knees and began to cry.

"Don't shoot me! I never killed nobody!"

Rusty thrust the pistol into Scully's face. "Where's Pete?"

Scully had trouble controlling his voice. "He crippled his horse. He took mine and went on. Bound for the Nations."

James glanced at Rusty. "Just like we figured."

Rusty asked, "How far ahead is he?"

"I don't know. An hour. Maybe two."

"By the tracks, he's been pushin' hard."

"He don't care if he kills a horse. He just cares about gettin' away."

Rusty beckoned James and Bailey to one side. "What'll we do about Scully? Anybody want to stay and watch him?"

James said, "I vote we shoot him right here."

Bailey said, "The lieutenant would be right put out about that. Anyway, it's the other one we want the most."

Rusty turned to Scully. "We're goin' on

after Pete. You start walkin' back to the Dawkins place. We'll pick you up there."

James protested, "How do we know he won't keep walkin'?"

"Because he knows the army'll hunt him down and hang him like a sheep-killin' dog."

Scully cried, "I never killed nobody. The army's got no call to hang me."

"Then you wait for us at Dawkins's. Maybe Sergeant Bailey will testify for you."

Scully looked at Bailey and trembled. "You'll tell them it was Pete done it all? You'll tell them I didn't do nothin' to get hanged for?"

"I'll tell them what I know. I can't do no better than that."

Following Pete's trail was not a heavy challenge. Even the few times Rusty temporarily lost it, James or Sergeant Bailey quickly picked it up again. There was no mistaking Pete's intention. He was headed for the Red River as directly as the terrain would allow him to travel.

And there was no mistaking James's intention. He meant to kill Pete on sight. The fierce look in his eyes made a chill run down Rusty's back.

Rusty said, "There's no tellin' what we may run into if we have to follow him over to the other side." He had become acutely aware that they had left in too much of a hurry to be concerned about supplies. Hunger was beginning to gnaw at him. He suspected Bailey was running a fever, though the sergeant had not complained. But James had a determined look that said he would follow Pete across hell and out the far side if he had to.

Coming upon a freighter camp, they stopped only long enough to wolf down some cold bread and red beans and sample some weak coffee extended with parched grain. The boss freighter wore what was left of a Confederate uniform. He glared at the sergeant, but James's manner was grim enough to make him swallow whatever negative feelings he might have about black soldiers. His only comment was, "There's some places you won't want to go as long as he's with you."

James said, "To catch the man we're after, we'll go wherever we have to."

"If you catch him, I hope you ain't goin' to let that darky take him in. It's a damned poor white man who'd do that."

James's eyes narrowed dangerously. "When we catch him, he'll be *beggin'* us to let that darky take him in."

As they left the freighter camp, picking up the trail again, Rusty reminded James, "We promised the lieutenant we'd bring him in."

"*You* promised him. I didn't. If we bring him back alive there's too many ways he can cheat the hangman. Bring him in dead and there won't be no appeal, no bond, no parole."

"Even Pete Dawkins deserves his chance in court."

"You still talk like a ranger. There ain't no rangers anymore. You're just another civilian, same as me."

Rusty thought back on his former ranger commanders, August Burmeister and later Captain Whitfield. Badly as they might have hated a man like Pete Dawkins, they would have made every reasonable effort to bring him in for a jury's judgment rather than impose judgment of their own. "I guess I'm still a ranger at heart. If they're ever reorganized, I'll be the first in line to join up."

"Fine, but I'm not burdened with all that righteousness. If I get Pete in my sights, I'll kill him."

Rusty looked to Bailey for his opinion. Bailey said, "All I promised was that we'd bring him back. I didn't say what shape he'd be in."

They came at last to the river. The sign indicated that they were not far behind Pete. Horse droppings were still fresh. The rust-colored river was at low ebb, much of its water running unseen beneath the red sands. Only one narrow channel toward the center of the broad riverbed showed a current. The tracks were deep and bold.

Rusty took a deep breath, fighting back dread. He had crossed this river more than once, farther west. His experiences on the other side had invariably been unpleasant. This time, he felt, would be no different. "All right, let's be after him."

The horses' feet sank deeply into the wet sand and made a sucking sound as they lifted for each next step. The tracks almost instantly filled with water behind them. The three men had crossed only a quarter of the wide riverbed when James stopped.

"Somebody's comin' yonder."

On the north side of the river a rider came pushing his horse for all the speed he could summon. A dozen horsemen were in close pursuit. All seemed to be yelling.

James declared, "That's Pete, by God." He raised his rifle.

Bailey mused, "Looks like he's roused up half the Nations."

Pete plunged his horse into the shallow water. He hammered his boots against the animal's ribs and looked back over his shoulder. Rusty knew he had taken a rifle from Bailey, but he evidently no longer had it. He must have dropped it in his panicked flight.

From across the width of the river Pete's urgent voice rose almost into a scream. "Help me! For God's sake, help me!"

James muttered, "I'll help you. I'll shoot you right where you're at." He brought the rifle to his shoulder.

Rusty grabbed James's arm. "No. The Indians will think you're shootin' at them. There's way too many for us to tackle."

The Indians rode into the river after Pete, rapidly gaining on him. Pete's pleas made Rusty's skin go cold.

Midway across, the Indians overtook Pete and circled around him. Rusty heard one more high-pitched scream. Pete's horse broke free and splashed toward the three men on the south edge of the river. Pete was not on him.

James said, "They're liable to come for us next." He raised his rifle again but did not point it.

Three men might cut down some of the Indians but could not get them all. Rusty shivered, and not from cold.

The Indians turned back toward the north bank, still yelling in triumph. Behind them, half buried in the wet sand, lay a lifeless lump. The river ran redder as it moved around and past Pete Dawkins.

The three watched in silence as the Indians moved northward. Finally Bailey said, "We promised the lieutenant we'd bring him back."

James said, "I'm afraid there ain't enough left of him to *take* back."

Rusty rode out to intercept Pete's horse and lead it to the south bank. It belonged to the army. "We'll need it for Scully." He did not look again at whatever remained of Pete Dawkins.

CHAPTER 18

Lieutenant Ames walked fifty yards out to meet them as they rode up to the Monahan farm. He gave Scully only a quick glance. "I don't see Dawkins. Did he get away?"

Rusty said, "No, he didn't get away."

"You killed him, then?"

"*We* didn't. He ran into some old Indian acquaintances. They saved the army some time and money." He glanced toward James. "May have kept some other folks out of trouble too."

Ames gave Scully a second look. "At least you brought back this one."

"We'll want to talk to you about him, but we can do that later." Rusty looked beyond the officer, toward the two houses. "Everything been all right here while we were gone?"

"Fine. Your Comanche boy is a lot stronger. Evan Gifford was out of bed this morning, walking around. And it appears there is

414

to be a wedding in the family."

Rusty blinked. "A weddin'?" Alice was too young. And Josie? Surely not Josie.

"Clemmie and your minister Webb have decided to throw in their lot together."

Rusty smiled. "Been a while comin'."

James said, "Everybody's known it for a long time, everybody but *them*."

They unsaddled the horses and walked to the house. Andy stood just past the dog run, Josie a step behind him. Andy came down to meet Rusty halfway across the yard. He barely showed a limp.

"I am strong now, Rusty. I am ready to go."

Rusty wished he could think of a new argument against it, but they had already talked the subject to death without any weakening that he could see on Andy's part. Regretfully he said, "All right. Tomorrow, then."

Josie caught Rusty's hands. "Tomorrow?"

"I've argued myself hoarse, but a promise is a promise."

"I thought you were goin' to stay a few days."

"Pete Dawkins spoiled that. Maybe when I come back."

"*If* you come back."

"I will, I promise. I wouldn't want to miss

seein' Preacher and Clemmie get married."

"Maybe that'll give you some notions of your own."

It was time to change the subject. "I'm dry to my toes. Reckon there's some coffee in the kitchen?"

"If there isn't, I'll make some. Come on in the house."

Directly across the Red River lay the Indian reservations, but Rusty knew Andy's band was unlikely to be there, submitting themselves to military supervision and agency regulations. They would range free farther west on the Texas plains, wherever the buffalo grazed. Time had come for the autumn hunt to lay in meat for the long winter ahead.

Rusty and Andy were three days out from the Monahan farm. Andy had left his white-man clothing behind. He was back in his Comanche breechcloth as he had been when Rusty first saw him, bow and quiver slung over his shoulder. The two had taken their time, sparing the horses and watching for sign of hunting activity. They had begun encountering buffalo in scattered herds, but they saw no indications of slaughter. Though Indians typically utilized virtually all of a carcass, they left enough remnants on the killing and skinning ground to show they had been there.

Rusty said, "There ain't really that many Comanches when you spread them around over a country as big as this. And landmarks . . . ain't many of them either. Are you sure you can really find your people?"

"They have many camping grounds. I know them all. You bet I find them."

Andy's use of the language had improved in the days he had spent with the Monahans. Rusty attributed that to coaching by Josie and Alice, but Andy said old Vince Purdy had shown a strong interest in him too. He had taken the boy hunting and fishing and taught him a little about managing the garden.

"Good people," Rusty told him. "You'd find there's lots of fine folks like the Monahans if you'd give us a chance to show you."

He knew he had little chance of changing the boy's mind, but he had not given up trying. He would not give up until Andy rode off and left him. Rusty had already ridden farther than he had intended, hoping for something that might turn Andy around.

"You enjoyed yourself at the Monahans', didn't you?"

"Much. They make me remember more. I remember better now my mama, my daddy.

The Monahans much the same my mama and daddy."

"If your real folks could talk to you now, they'd say you belong with your own kind. They'd tell you to stay with us."

"They come to me in a dream, but they do not talk. My brother come in same dream and say I come back to Comanches. I hear my brother."

Andy pointed to buzzards circling far to the west. This was almost the time of year when they would begin drifting southward, but no chilly northers had prodded them yet with the first hint of winter. The buzzards were at such a distance that Rusty had not noticed them. Andy had a keener eye, or perhaps a more highly developed sensitivity to the subtle messages of nature.

"How'd you know they were there?" Rusty demanded. "I can barely see them even after you pointed them out to me."

"The spirits, I guess. Somehow I know."

"The spirits tellin' you anything else?"

"They say my people somewhere over there. They kill buffalo. They say it is time you turn back, or maybe my people kill *you*."

Rusty's backside tingled. Several times Andy had demonstrated that he possessed instincts beyond Rusty's understanding, an ability to sense presences he could not see.

"I can't just ride off and leave you by yourself."

"But it is what you said. We talked much about it."

"Talkin' about it ahead of time is one thing. But it's different when you get there and face havin' to do it. I'll always feel like I abandoned you."

"Abandoned?" Andy puzzled over the meaning of the word. "You keep promise, is all."

"Damned poor promise, the more I think about it." Rusty looked again toward the buzzards. "Maybe we ought to ride over there and have a look. It may not be a buffalo kill after all."

"I wish you turn back now."

"Just a little farther, Andy."

It was fully a mile to where the buzzards floated about. Two dark gray wolves skulked away as the horsemen approached. The wind carried an unmistakable smell of rotting flesh.

Scattered over a couple of hundred yards of ground were the leavings of a buffalo kill, heads, horns, intestines strung out by scavengers. Straight lines marked where travois had been used to haul the meat and hides. Rusty slapped at flies that buzzed around his face. "Let's get away from here."

They circled around upwind, away from the flies and the stench. "Looks like we've found your people. Or least where they've been."

"I find them easy now. Better you go."

Rusty felt a catch in his throat as he faced Andy. "This is a lot harder than I figured." He offered his hand. "If you ever decide you want to change, you know where I live."

Andy accepted his hand, then pointed southeastward where scrub timber lined a small creek. "You go to trees, hide 'til dark."

Rusty's eyes burned as he turned away and touched spurs gently to Alamo's hide. When he had first found Andy, he had no thought that he would ever become so attached to the boy. He had assumed that relatives would soon come and fetch Andy away, and that would be the end of it. Rusty was, after all, a bachelor lacking in experience helpful in raising a youngster beyond what he could remember of his own raising by Daddy Mike and Mother Dora. He tried not to look back, but he could not help it.

What he saw made his heart leap. Andy was racing toward him. Behind Andy, Comanche warriors were running their horses hard.

Andy was shouting at him, but the wind

tore the words away. The message was plain
enough: run for the timber. Rusty put
Alamo into a lope as Andy drew abreast of
him. He said, "Didn't your spirits tell you
about them?"

"Don't talk. Run."

"But they're your people. What're *you*
runnin' for?"

"For you. We get to trees, I turn back and
talk to them. Out here, they kill you first,
then they talk."

The timber was thin, for the creek was
narrow and barely running. Rusty slid
Alamo to a halt, jumped to the ground, and
grabbed his rifle.

Andy looked with disfavor at the weapon.
"You don't shoot. They kill you sure."

Rusty knew it would be futile to fight. He
might knock down two or three, but they
would have him in a minute. Still, he
wanted them to know he could. He wanted
each warrior to contemplate the possibility
that he might be one of the unlucky two or
three.

The Indians stopped short of the timber
and spread out in a ragged line. Andy said
again, "You don't shoot. I go talk."

"You better talk real good."

Rusty could feel the pulse pounding in his
neck. Dust choked him. He had to struggle

for breath as he watched Andy ride out toward the Indians, one hand held high. The line contracted as the warriors drew back together to receive him. It soon became obvious that most recognized him. They greeted him as one lost and returned from the dead.

Rusty began to breathe easier. But it was one thing for them to accept Andy. He was a blood brother. Rusty was a blood enemy.

The conference continued awhile, then Andy turned and rode back toward Rusty. His face was grim. Rusty's hopes sagged.

Andy regarded him a moment before he spoke. "I tell them what you do for me. They say they don't kill you yet. They want council first."

"What would you give for my chances?"

"Tonkawa Killer is very bad man. He wants to kill you now. Others say wait, talk to my brother. My brother will help."

"I take it your brother's not here, but Tonkawa Killer is."

"My brother hunts. Will be in camp to-night."

Rusty weighed his options and found them dismal. If he broke and ran he would be lucky to get two hundred yards. To fire into that bunch would amount to the same quick suicide.

"I'll go along, I guess."

"Give me rifle so they know you don't fight."

"The minute I turn loose of this rifle, I'm helpless."

"You helpless now." Andy reached out. Grudgingly Rusty handed him the weapon.

"You were right, Andy. I ought to've turned back yesterday. But I just couldn't."

"Not be scared. My brother fix."

Don't be scared. Easy to say for somebody who had never had to ride into a bunch of Comanche warriors with *kill* in their eyes. Rusty's skin crawled as if worms burrowed under it. The warriors quickly closed around him. He picked out one who appeared the most hostile and looked directly into his black and glittering eyes, trying to stare him down. It did not work.

Andy said, "That one is called Tonkawa Killer. Always he hates me. Calls me Texan boy. Wants me dead."

"Damned sure wants *me* dead. Look at him."

"When I break my leg, Tonkawa Killer there. Says it is good I die. Hit me with war club."

"He don't look happy to see you back."

"Afraid of my brother. He thinks I tell."

"You're goin' to, aren't you?"

"First I hear him talk. Then maybe I tell."

The Comanches conferred among themselves. Andy listened without comment. When the conference broke up, four of the warriors left the others and came to Rusty. They pointed northward and motioned for him to get on his horse.

Andy said, "The others go hunt some more. These take us to camp. Wait for my brother."

Rusty noted darkly that Tonkawa Killer was one of the four. "He looks like he might change his mind and kill both of us."

"Too afraid of my brother."

"Your brother must be a curly wolf."

Andy did not know the term. "No, his name means Steals the Ponies."

The warriors did not tie Rusty's hands. In their place, he thought, he might have done so. On the other hand, there would be no point in his trying to run. Where could he go? They would kill him in a minute.

He had been in enough Indian fights that the thought of another held no terrors, but never had he found himself trapped and helpless like this.

Only a damn fool . . . , he thought. Yet he knew he would take the same risk again if he felt it necessary for Andy.

The Indian camp was bustling with activity. Dogs barked at the incoming riders. Women were cutting buffalo meat into strips to be dried on racks hastily constructed of limbs and branches from trees along a nearby stream. Others cleaned the flesh from buffalo hides to be turned into robes and clothing and tepee coverings. The work stopped temporarily as women and children came to stare at the new arrivals. Tonkawa Killer shouted a few angry words. The crowd backed away but did not completely disperse.

Several women came and made a fuss over Andy. Everyone in camp seemed to know him. From their reactions, Rusty knew they had considered him forever lost. Only Tonkawa Killer appeared displeased at the boy's apparent resurrection from among his forefathers. If hate-filled looks could kill, Andy would have died a hundred times.

The women brought freshly cooked meat. Andy accepted it with pleasure. He motioned for Rusty to join him. The meat was not thoroughly cooked, but Rusty was too hungry to be choosy.

The first hunting party arrived awhile before sundown. Andy listened to the conversation, then told Rusty they had located another herd of buffalo, but it was too late in the day to begin a fresh kill. They would return in the morning for the slaughter.

"My brother is with others. He comes soon." Andy had a nervous eagerness about him. He walked to the edge of camp and stared off to the west. Rusty started to follow him but stopped when one of the warriors made a menacing gesture that told him to sit down. He sat.

There was no mistaking the arrival of Steals the Ponies. Apparently he had been told of Andy's return, for he raced ahead of the other hunters and galloped into camp without regard for the dust he raised or the roasting meat that it settled upon. He leaped to the ground. Andy ran to him, showing but little of his limp. They threw their arms around each other.

Rusty had long been told that Indian men were too stoic to cry. He saw that he had been misinformed. Steals the Ponies pushed Andy out to arm's length, tears in his eyes, and looked him over from head to foot as if he could not believe what he saw. Andy was telling him something in language Rusty could not understand. He pointed to his leg, showing where it had been broken.

Tonkawa Killer broke into the joyous reunion. He pointed his finger at Andy, his voice loud and accusative. Whatever he said, it aroused anger and denial from Andy and a heated argument from Steals the Ponies. Watching, Rusty thought the quarreling men were about to come to blows. Steals the Ponies pushed himself in front of Andy and took a protective stance.

Tonkawa Killer pointed again, said a few words more, then turned on his heel and stalked away. Steals the Ponies shouted something after him, but Tonkawa Killer made a show of ignoring it. Several warriors followed him, evidently taking his side in the argument.

Cold dread settled in the pit of Rusty's stomach.

Andy led his brother to where Rusty sat. Rusty stood up, trying to look as if he had no concern. Steals the Ponies stepped close and lifted Rusty's hat from his head. His eyes widened.

Rusty asked, "What's he lookin' at?"

"Your hair. It is red. My brother say red hair big medicine."

"Is that good or bad?"

"Good for me. You save me. Maybe not good for my brother."

"Tell him I don't mean him any harm. Tell him I want to be his friend." Rusty dropped his voice. "Tell him I want to get the hell away from here." He did not like the look of the conference Tonkawa Killer was having with his adherents.

Steals the Ponies and Andy went into another conversation while Rusty watched their faces and tried to decide whether it meant good news or not.

Andy turned. "My brother and me take you out of camp. We ride with you 'til you are safe from Tonkawa Killer."

"Tell your brother I am much obliged. I'm ready to start any time he is." Right now would not be too soon.

Steals the Ponies said something to one of the hunters. They brought up Rusty's and Andy's horses. Steals the Ponies made a motion for Rusty to mount. He did, quickly.

"Better get me my rifle, Andy."

Andy fetched it but handed it to Steals the Ponies. "Better my brother hold it. Give back when all is good."

Rusty felt naked and vulnerable without the rifle, but this was no time to bog down in details. "Sun'll be gone pretty soon. I want to put a lot of miles behind me while it's dark."

As they started to leave camp, Steals the Ponies turned to shout something at Tonkawa Killer. Whatever he said, it drew a response of raw malice.

Rusty said, "Looks to me like those two are ready to kill one another."

"Comanche never kill another Comanche."

"Never?"

"Never. But Tonkawa Killer says I lie, cause him big shame. Says I am not Comanche. He glad to kill me. Glad to kill you too. Only scared of my brother."

"Tell your brother I hope he has a long and happy life."

Rusty was relieved when he put the sight and smoky smell of the Indian camp behind him. He kept looking back, half expecting Tonkawa Killer to build his nerve and come in pursuit. He suspected Steals the Ponies had the same suspicion, for the Indian also kept watching their back trail.

They had ridden perhaps three miles, and the sun was at the horizon line, the shadows long and dark across the open buffalo prairie. Ahead lay the same narrow creek in which Rusty and Andy had taken refuge from the first set of hunters. The line of small timber looked black against the sun-gilded grass. Somehow Rusty felt that the creek was far enough from camp to be a safe haven. Beyond it, he should be all right.

Steals the Ponies reined up and spoke sharply to Andy. He handed Rusty's rifle to the boy, who passed it on to Rusty. Rusty saw alarm in Andy's eyes, though so far he had seen no reason for it.

Four Comanches rode up out of the creek bottom and stopped in a line. At one end, Tonkawa Killer brandished a lance.

Evidently they had circled around without allowing themselves to be seen. Rusty shivered. "Looks like he's not as afraid of your brother as you thought he was."

Steals the Ponies said something. Tensely, Andy translated. "My brother cannot shoot Tonkawa Killer. You can."

"There's three more besides him."

"They not fight. Come only to see."

Rusty threw the breech open. He felt a jolt as he saw that the chamber was empty. One of the Comanches had removed the cartridge. He fumbled in his pocket for another.

Tonkawa Killer made a loud shout and came charging. Rusty had trouble fishing out a cartridge while trying to watch the Comanche rushing at him. He saw the lance point bobbing, a dark scalp hanging from the shaft. He knew he was too slow.

He was aware of a swift movement beside him. Andy's bowstring sang as an arrow flew. It made a dull thump driving into Tonkawa Killer's chest.

The lance point dropped, digging into the ground. Tonkawa Killer was jerked half around, then toppled from his horse. The animal brushed by Rusty and ran on.

It happened so quickly that Rusty had time only to draw one sharp breath, then it was over. Tonkawa Killer lay threshing on the ground, fighting against death but rapidly losing. He shuddered and went still.

"My God, Andy."

The three Comanches at the creek seemed ready to charge, but Steals the Ponies rode forward and spoke sharply. The argument was over almost before it began. Two of the Indians dismounted and picked up the body while the third caught and returned Tonkawa Killer's horse. Casting hating glances at Andy and Rusty, they laid the lifeless warrior across the animal's back and led him toward camp.

Steals the Ponies watched them closely, his eyes grave. Andy's hands shook uncontrollably. He could not take his eyes from the small pool of blood where the downed warrior had lain. He had never killed a man. That he had done it now, and that the man he killed was Comanche, filled him with horror.

Steals the Ponies placed his hands on Andy's shoulders. "It is an awful thing you have done, little brother."

Andy wept. "He was about to kill Rusty."

"Now his brothers must try to kill you. You chose a Texan over your own. From now on, you will be an outcast."

"He took care of me. I could not let him die."

"It is easy to watch an enemy die. It takes a brave man to stand aside and allow it to happen to a friend. But sometimes it must be done."

"Rusty risked his life to bring me home."

"This is no longer your home. It never can be again."

"What can I do?"

"You were born white. We made you Comanche. Now you must be white again. By what name does your red-haired friend call you?"

"Andy. The name my mother and father gave me."

"You are Badger Boy no more. You must be Andy now, and for however long you may live."

Andy placed a hand against his heart. "I will always be Badger Boy. I will always be Comanche."

Steals the Ponies embraced him. "To me you will always be Badger Boy. But to the others . . . it will be as if you never lived. You must never return here."

Tears rolled down Andy's cheeks as he

clung to his Comanche brother.

Steals the Ponies said, "Go now, you and the red-hair. Go far while the night can hide you." He tore free of Andy. "Go. Forget."

"I will not forget."

"Then remember what is good in Comanche ways, but find your place in the white man's world." Steals the Ponies remounted his horse and rode off into the dusk. Shoulders sagging, Andy watched him until he disappeared.

Rusty's heartbeat gradually slowed to near normal. His mouth was dry as powder. He rode down to the creek and dismounted. He knelt and cupped his hands, sipping from them as the cold water trickled between his fingers.

Andy came down to join him, his face mirroring his anguish. "My brother says I must go with you now." His voice broke. "I go with you, or I die."

Rusty knew it was his fault. Reluctant to cut the tie with Andy, he had ridden too far into a hostile land. "I'm sorry."

Andy rubbed an arm across his eyes. It came away wet. "Too big to cry."

"Sometimes it's the best thing you can do." Rusty hugged the boy and let him cry himself out.

"My brother says I must be white now."

Again Andy placed his hand against his heart. "But here, always, part of me will be Comanche."

And you'll never be sure just who you really are, Rusty thought darkly. He knew, for he had been there.

The boy pulled up onto his horse and reined it into the creek. "Soon be dark. We go long way in dark."

Rusty's throat was tight as he moved to catch up. More to himself than to Andy, he said, "A long way. But you have the longest road to travel."

ABOUT THE AUTHOR

Elmer Kelton, of San Angelo, Texas, is the most honored of all Western writers. The author of more than forty books, he is a six-time winner of the Spur Award, has earned four Western Heritage Awards from the National Cowboy Hall of Fame, and was named the greatest Western author of all time by the Western Writers of America in 1995. His most recent novels from Forge Books are *The Buckskin Line* and *The Smiling Country.*

The employees of Thorndike Press hope you have enjoyed this Large Print book. All our Thorndike and Wheeler Large Print titles are designed for easy reading, and all our books are made to last. Other Thorndike Press Large Print books are available at your library, through selected bookstores, or directly from us.

For information about titles, please call:

(800) 223-1244

or visit our Web site at:

www.gale.com/thorndike
www.gale.com/wheeler

To share your comments, please write:

Publisher
Thorndike Press
295 Kennedy Memorial Drive
Waterville, ME 04901